P9-BYJ-122

PRAISE FOR
TAMING A WILD SCOT

"Get ready for a rich, exciting new voice in Scottish historical romance! Rowan Keats captures all the passion and heart of the Highlands as she expertly weaves a wonderful tale of passion, intrigue, and love that you won't want to put down. I'm already looking forward to the next book in what is sure to be a must-read series."

—Monica McCarty, *New York Times*
Bestselling Author of *The Hunter*

TAMING A WILD SCOT

A CLAIMED BY THE HIGHLANDER NOVEL

ROWAN KEATS

A SIGNET ECLIPSE BOOK

SIGNET ECLIPSE
Published by the Penguin Group
Penguin Group (USA) LLC, 375 Hudson Street,
New York, New York 10014

USA | Canada | UK | Ireland | Australia | New Zealand | India | South Africa | China
penguin.com
A Penguin Random House Company

First published by Signet Eclipse, an imprint of New American Library,
a division of Penguin Group (USA) LLC

First Printing, November 2013

Copyright © Rowan Keats, 2013
Penguin supports copyright. Copyright fuels creativity, encourages diverse voices,
promotes free speech, and creates a vibrant culture. Thank you for buying an
authorized edition of this book and for complying with copyright laws by not
reproducing, scanning, or distributing any part of it in any form without permission. You are supporting writers and allowing Penguin to continue to publish
books for every reader.

SIGNET ECLIPSE and logo are trademarks of Penguin Group(USA) LLC.

ISBN 978-0-451-41607-0

Printed in the United States of America
10 9 8 7 6 5 4 3 2 1

PUBLISHER'S NOTE
This is a work of fiction. Names, characters, places, and incidents either are the
product of the author's imagination or are used fictitiously, and any resemblance
to actual persons, living or dead, business establishments, events, or locales is
entirely coincidental.

If you purchased this book without a cover you should be aware that this book
is stolen property. It was reported as "unsold and destroyed" to the publisher
and neither the author nor the publisher has received any payment for this
"stripped book."

ACKNOWLEDGMENTS

Seeing this book in print is a dream come true for me. I grew up reading medieval romances, especially those of Kathleen Woodiwiss, Iris Johansen, and Julie Garwood, and hoped one day I'd tell my own romantic tales of days gone by. I'd like to extend my deepest thanks to my editor, Kerry Donovan, for giving me the opportunity to bring this story and these characters to life.

I'd also like to thank my family—in particular my daughter, Taylor—for the buckets of love and support. I couldn't have done it without you. Really.

Chapter 1

Lochurkie Castle
Aberdeenshire, Scotland
November 1285

The foul-smelling guard trundled off to bed, taking the last torch in the windowless dungeon with him. Darkness poured into the room, swallowing every feeble mote of light. Losing sight of the desperate claw marks left in the dirt wall by her predecessors should have been a blessing. Instead, a mild sense of panic rose in Ana's chest. The narrow space around her closed in, and the air grew thick and difficult to breathe.

Dear God. She did not want to die in this dark hole, completely forgotten.

Yet that ending was a certainty.

Barely able to move in the confines of the primitive oubliette, she laid her forehead on the damp dirt that encircled her body, resting her tired neck muscles. Two days without water and food had weakened her. Her legs trembled with fatigue, her tongue was as dry as old leather, and her heart beat a quick, shallow pace in her chest. Some of her grief could be attributed to her location—the agonizing ache in her knees and the gritty taste of dirt in her mouth, for example—but mostly, her malaises were due to the lack of water.

Her jailers didn't expect her to live much past the third day—indeed, they'd bet on it. Some unlucky souls endured the oubliette for as long as five, but Ana was slim of build. Her belly had long since ceased to cramp with hunger and now rolled with a vague sense of nausea. The urge to pee hadn't nagged her in hours. She could feel the skin on her face thinning, the bones of her cheeks and jaws becoming more prominent. As a healer, she knew the signs of approaching death. It wouldn't be much longer.

Had she been in better health before the trial, perhaps she would have lasted another day, but tending to the earl of Lochurkie for eighteen straight hours before his death had taken a toll.

She grimaced.

Calling it a trial gave the proceeding far more legitimacy than it deserved. Anyone who'd ever had a pail of milk go sour or culled a poor harvest from a field had brought witness against her. Every wound she had healed over the past year, every life she had saved, had been forgotten. *A purveyor of evil magic*, her accusers had cried. *In league with the banshees*, some said. *Witch*.

Of course, the most damning evidence had come at the hands of the earl's sister, Isabail. The woman's concise description of how her brother had fallen ill shortly after consuming a tisane brewed by Ana had sealed her fate. The whisper in the room after that was *poison*. An assessment Ana agreed with—but she was not the poisoner.

She fisted her hands. Killing someone was the very opposite of her calling.

Exhausted by even that wee movement, she sagged against the wall, her bruised and swollen knees absorbing her weight. Protesting her innocence had gotten her nowhere. She'd been sentenced to death by pit or gallows. No one had sided with her, not even those few she considered her friends. She was going to die alone in this godforsaken hole.

Tears stung her eyes, but she willed them away.

Losing body fluids would only bring the end on faster.

Oddly, even though the end was inevitable and excruciating pain shot through her body at every turn, she wanted to postpone her last moment as long as possible. Despite everything that had happened to her, she desperately wanted to live. Even for a few minutes longer.

When she died, this thin branch of the Bisset bloodline would die, too.

And with it would go the campfire dream.

Her mother—a healer like herself—had met her Maker almost ten years past, and her father—a traveling merchant—had dropped dead at the helm of his caravan wagon last winter. But for as long as Ana could remember, their evening ritual had included a detailing of the home they'd someday possess. A real home, not a bedroll in the back of a wagon. A thatch-roofed house nestled in a deep glen, next to a winding burn . . . with a fieldstone hearth and a large garden bursting with fresh herbs.

Ana closed her eyes. A home might only ever be a dream, but she could've planted a garden.

A rattle of heavy iron chain and a low groan echoed through the cavern.

The only other occupant of the dungeon was a large, badly beaten man chained to the far wall of the room above. The guards had called him MacCurran, but no one in Lochurkie carried that name. He was a stranger. A stranger who was receiving regular food and water.

She tried not to resent that, but failed.

Beatings could be endured; a lack of water could not.

Another sound broke the silence of the night—a muffled grunt. It was accompanied by the slide of a leather boot on the dirt floor.

Ana opened her eyes and peered up at the mouth of the hole. Sure enough, the flickering gleam of a torch brightened the roof above her head. Someone was visiting MacCurran. At this hour? After the guard had gone to bed? A very odd occurrence.

"Hallo?" she called out. Her mouth was so dry all she managed was a croak, so she licked her lips and tried again. "Hallo?"

A terse exchange of whispers took place somewhere out of sight, then nothing.

No one responded to her call.

Chain links clinked, then fell to the packed dirt floor with a thump. More scuffled footsteps and another moan from the prisoner, this one louder. The glow of the torchlight dimmed, moving slowly but steadily away. The visitors were leaving. The thick pitch of midnight would soon clog her throat again.

A prideless plea spilled from Ana's lips, driven by raw desperation.

"Please, don't go."

The circle of light on the ceiling continued to slip away.

"Please."

The torchlight paused. Another harsh exchange of murmurs took place, ending with a short, final order. Then the circle of light grew larger. And larger and brighter still. They were coming back. Her bottom lip aquiver with gratitude, she shielded her eyes from the glare and waited to see a human face.

A hooded figure leaned over the mouth of the oubliette. A man, judging by the imposing height and broad shoulders. His face was hidden in shadow, the color of his brat lost in the murk. He stood over her for a moment, as if considering what to do, then threw down a rope.

"Tie it about your waist."

It was a voice that brooked no refusal. Smooth and smoky like whisky, but edged with steel.

She stared at the dangling rope. Escaping her fate had not been her aim—all she had hoped for was a glimpse of another person and a brief dialogue before death claimed her. But this man was offering her freedom. A chance at a future. *Life.*

Even as weak as she was, how could she not leap at it?

She grasped the rough braid of hemp and quickly pulled the rope around her waist. Tying the knot was more of a challenge—her fingers were stiff and uncooperative, and her unbound hair kept getting in the way. But after a few stumbling tries and a grunt of disapproval from her savior, she managed to get the rope knotted.

" 'Tis done."

He didn't answer, just set the torch in a bracket on the wall and began tugging her up through the hole with surprising gentleness. Sadly, his care did little to ease the journey. As her legs stretched out and blood flowed freely once more, every inch of her skin burst into flame and a thousand tiny knives sliced into her flesh. A scream rose up her throat, but she contained it with a fierce clamp of her teeth on her bottom lip.

When she neared the top, he grabbed her arm and lifted her over the edge.

Lying facedown on the dirt floor, Ana experienced a wicked bout of nausea. Desperate not to vomit, she flung out a hand, grabbed his sleeve, and used his solid body to sit up. As weak as she was, she likely wouldn't have achieved her objective had her savior not put his strength behind her.

"Gently now," he said. With a firm hand at her back,

he bit the cork stopper from his oilskin pouch and put the bag to her lips. He allowed a trickle of water to flow into her mouth. The cold, wet taste was heaven, and she swallowed eagerly.

The trickle wasn't enough. Her dry, cracked lips clamored for more. But he was right to curb the flow—if she drank too quickly, it would make her ill. The slow pace of drips entering her mouth was still a heavenly reprieve. Closing her eyes, she savored each one. Her tongue felt less like a batt of cotton with each glorious drop.

She was still desperately thirsty when he put the stopper back in the bag, but she said nothing. How could she begrudge his help in any way?

"To your feet now." His hands slid under her arms and, in one effortless movement, he hauled her upright. Sharp pain stabbed the soles of her feet, and she whimpered. She held her own for a moment, thighs trembling, and then her knees buckled.

"The pain will ease the more you move," he said as she collapsed against his warm, steadfast chest.

"Niall!"

Her savior tossed a glance over his shoulder. "Aye?"

"We're ready. The kitchen gillies will rise soon to start the baking. Let's have at it."

He turned to her once more, his long, straight nose the only feature she could properly see. The rest of his face was obscured by the hood, leaving only a vague suggestion of grim lips and a square chin. "Not one sound further, or all this will be for naught."

Fear that she would fail him swamped her. Her aching body howled for rest and food. But she nodded.

He looped her arm around his neck, tucked her close to his side, and set off. The torch was left behind, a lone beacon in the darkness.

Ana stumbled alongside him, barely able to place one foot in front of the other. Were it not for his support, she'd not have made it three paces. His arm was strong and warm, and he lifted her with every step he took, even up the slime-coated stone stairs. The sharp pains in her legs obscured the occasional tug on her hair as they moved. They made surprisingly good time to the postern gate of Lochurkie Castle.

Half a dozen men stood waiting at the gate, two of them supporting the beaten prisoner MacCurran, whose head hung limply. All of them wore dark lèines and the same style of brat. In the inky bleakness of predawn, she could not make out the colors.

They exited the gate, closing the heavy wooden portal quietly behind them. Ducking low, they scurried through the long, dry grass of the open field to the edge of the forest.

There, they halted.

Her savior leaned her against a sapling elm. He took off his oilskin and handed it to her, along with a small chunk of bread. "This is where we must part ways."

Ana's grip on the narrow tree trunk tightened. His reluctance to take her farther was understandable—she was a burden. She looked back at the castle. Torches were lit now in several places, and it wouldn't be long before their escape was discovered. Once the guards gave chase, eluding capture would be nigh on impossible, but these brief moments of freedom and the hope that stirred in her chest were more than she'd had an hour ago.

"I am deeply grateful to you for bringing me this far."

He looked away, silent for a moment. "Just stay to the trees and keep moving." His men turned to leave, but he hesitated. Unsheathing the dirk at his belt, he offered it to her, hilt first. "In case you've a need."

She took the weapon, the stag-antler grip fitting surprisingly well in her hand. Polished steel gleamed in the moonlight. Did he mean for her to slay an attacker? Or herself if things looked too grim? She couldn't be sure.

"Godspeed, lass."

And then he was gone, his large shape swallowed by the dark gloom of the woods.

Ana stared at the spot where he'd disappeared, unable to move. Where was she to go? How was she to survive? She could not outrun a cadre of healthy male guards. Only moments ago, she would have met her dismal fate with nothing more than a bittersweet sadness; now she was overwhelmed with fear and dread.

A shout echoed through the night from the direction of the castle. The guards were alerted. She slipped the oilskin about her neck and tucked the bread into her sark. Things were about to get infinitely more difficult.

Run.

She pushed herself upright, ignoring the pains that shot up her legs. Her chances were slim, to be sure. But survival was possible, with a little luck. No one knew these woods better than she. She'd combed them many times, looking for ramsons, blackthorn bark, rowan berries, and other herbs. She knew which path led to the burn, and she knew the burn was her best bet if she wanted to outsmart the hounds.

She took a trembling step forward, leaving the support of the tree behind.

Her knees wobbled alarmingly and her heart beat with the fury of a hummingbird's wings, but she made it to the next tree before she collapsed. The rough bark scraped skin from her palms and her breath hissed between clenched teeth. *Pain means you're alive, Ana.* How many times had her mother said that? More than she could recall.

Alive was good. Alive was worth preserving.

She stumbled over moss-covered roots to another tree, and then another. It was a challenge to spy the trunks in the dark, and she made her way as much by feel as by sight. The pain in her legs receded, whether due to her regular movements or her mulish determination to ignore it, she didn't know. All that registered in her thoughts was the sound of baying hounds. The hunt was on.

She'd be a fool to hope that the guards would follow the trail of her mysterious benefactor and his men. They were convinced she had murdered their lord. Woman or not, she could expect no leniency. She glanced at the trio of dead birch trees to her left, recognizing them. The path to the burn lay some hundred paces ahead, and the burn itself another fifty beyond that. She was moving too slowly. Making better time was critical. She had to leave the security of the trees behind and take the travel-worn path.

Was she strong enough?

Perhaps not, but the dogs were gaining on her.

With the image of her flesh torn asunder by snapping teeth gruesomely clear in her thoughts, she shoved away from the tree and ran for the path. The pound of her feet on the leaf-covered loam seemed excessively loud, but dwelling on that served no purpose. The burn was her goal. She could afford to think of nothing else. Until she was wading in the water and her scent was swept away by the current, she had no hope of survival.

Not far behind her, someone shouted. The huntsman had spotted her trail.

A moment later, the dogs had turned in her direction, their baying even louder.

Her heart thumped madly against her ribs and her breath wheezed through parched lips, but Ana did not stop. At the fork in the path, she veered left, clutching a hand to her chest as if that could prevent it from bursting. Her legs felt as if they did not belong to her, and a sapping weariness was creeping up her body. Her tongue thickened to a crusty lump, and the appeal of stopping to take a sip from the oilskin pouch grew near unbearable.

But she kept running.

The burn was only thirty paces away. If her breathing weren't so labored, she'd be able to hear its merry trickle by now.

A fallen branch lay in her path, but she lacked the strength to leap it, so she went around. It was time she could not afford to lose. The barking was so close now it blocked out the hammer of her heartbeat. Surely a frenzied hound would sink its teeth into her leg at any moment.

Spotting the dip in the terrain that marked the meandering route of the burn, Ana dove through a hazelnut thicket and splashed into the flow. Icy water poured into her boots and drenched her woolen skirts. The uneven bed of the burn made every step perilous, but she plowed on—through a gossamer spiderweb, over a slippery, algae-coated boulder, under a leaning fir tree. Her skirts dragged at her legs, exhausting her to the point of numbness, but she kept going.

Her boot slipped on a rock, her ankle twisted painfully, and she stumbled in the water, nearly going down. Only an instinctive jerk to the right saved her. But it came at a price—her elbow was jabbed by a broken tree branch, the sharp wood piercing her skin and robbing her of what little breath she had. Her hand went numb and she nearly dropped the knife.

The temptation to give up and fall to her knees might have won out at that moment, save for one thing—just above the gnarled fingers of the late-autumn trees, the sky was brightening. No longer black, but a deep shade of indigo. The sun was fighting its way to the horizon, desperate to see another day, and she could do no less.

Ana swept her long hair out of her face. She clutched her injured elbow, pressed the wound with her fingers to stop the bleeding, and continued her dash through the burn. Her breaths came in gusty gulps, each one burning in her throat.

Sometime after she entered the water—an eternity, it seemed—the hounds abruptly ceased their cry. The odd yelp and howl still rose into the night, but the constant voice of a pack on a clear scent died off.

Experience told Ana that the longer she remained in the burn and took care not to touch land or shrub, the better her chances were of escape. But she couldn't stay in the water forever—it slowed her down, and a good scent hound could pick up the trail again farther downstream, especially if it caught a whiff of the blood she'd left behind on the stick. At some point, she'd need to leave the burn and make her way cross-land.

Near the waterfall, perhaps. There was a rugged trail leading down the cliff to the river.

Goal in mind, she found a new reserve of strength. Her back straightened, her knees firmed, and she splashed forward over a bed of smooth round stones. If she made it to the river, she'd be safe. Unlike most people, she knew how to swim. If she shed her long skirts and dove in, the water would carry her to freedom. She could do this.

Unfortunately, her heart proved uncooperative. As

she picked up her pace, it skipped a few beats, and then began to flutter against her ribs in a wholly unsatisfying and frightening manner. A weakness stole through her limbs, making them feel twice as heavy as they'd felt only moments before. Her head swam, her breaths shortened, and a sudden dread that she would die consumed her.

Ana stopped running.

She stood in the icy stream, her arms wrapped around her body, shivering, trying to catch her breath, trying not to faint. Closing her eyes, she forced her breaths through her nose, rather than her mouth, and struggled to contain the frantic beats of her heart.

Be still, crazed heart. I will not die here. Not so close to safety.

Long moments passed like that, just breathing and shivering. Finally, to her immense relief, the pace of her heart abruptly slowed, returning to its heavy but more natural pound. She opened her eyes, ready to resume her flight.

The scowling face of a helmed Lochurkie guard stared back at her. He grabbed her uninjured elbow, his thick fingers digging into her flesh. "Got ya, ya bleedin' wench."

Ana reacted instinctively. The only thought spinning through her head was the fleeting promise of freedom. She slashed at the guard with the hunting knife.

The blade cut through his cotun sleeve and the flesh of his arm with almost equal ease. Blood gushed, the guard howled, and her mouth soured. She, who'd taken a solemn oath to heal and preserve life, had willingly and consciously harmed another being. But what alternative was there? He was so much larger and stronger than she. And didn't she deserve to live? Ana swallowed tightly and fought for her freedom. Yanking her elbow free, she shoved the guard away and ran in the direction of the cliff.

The river was so close.

Just a few hundred feet and she could slide down the path.

A large bramble whipped her face as she passed, but she paid no mind to the deep scratches it left behind. Her gaze was locked on the lone gray-barked Scots fir directly ahead. It stood at the top of the path.

The guard shouted to his cohorts and gave chase. Heavy footsteps and angry assurances of retribution followed her through the brush. Her pace was much slower than his, her strength still feeble in comparison. She prayed that she would reach the edge before he caught her.

And she very nearly did.

She was but a step away from the rough dirt path leading down the cliff when a meaty hand latched onto her long, loose hair and yanked her backward. Completely exhausted by her bid for escape, she had no hope of maintaining her balance. She fell heavily, striking the ground with her hip and then her head. Her head hit something hard—a rock or a tree root—and a dizzying blur of black spots crowded her vision. The guard sprang at her, and she barely had the wits to roll to one side.

But she did roll.

Right off the edge.

She grabbed for one of the roots of the fir tree as she slid—and missed. The guard's hand was still tangled in her hair, but his grip was not sufficient to hold her weight. Strands began to break and tear free, and suddenly Ana was falling.

Her last image was of the scowling guard clutching a handful of red hair.

Then darkness swallowed her.

Chapter 2

Barony of Duthes
Scottish Highlands
January 1286

Standing under the shadowed awning of the baker's stall, Niall MacCurran surveyed the walled manor house, from the highest stone parapet to the lowly wooden drawbridge. Six archers and nine men-at-arms paced the ramparts. Two square towers rose into the gray sky on either side of the barmekin gate, each housing at least two dozen soldiers. A pair of chain mail–clad men guarded the open portcullis—each armed with a sharp poleax.

"That's not a manor," murmured Niall's half brother, Aiden. "It's a bloody fortress."

"Aye."

"With steep braes on three sides and a dry moat on the fourth, we'll not be scaling the walls."

"Agreed," Niall said, his breath fogging the air in front of his face.

"Bloody waste of time, this was."

Niall's gaze slid across the village square to the woman perusing the offerings of the vegetable vendor. Like other female marketgoers, she wore an uninspiring brown gown topped by a white apron and a linen brèid. That display of matronly modesty and the loose fit of her coarse woolen clothing did surprisingly little to shield her from the attentions of a pack of eager young lads—they passed her by with many a second glance and a few bold grins. Perhaps they were as intrigued as he was by the lock of dark red hair that had escaped her head covering.

"Not if Baron Duthes is our thief," he said.

Hair the color of fine Burgundy wine was uncommon. He could recall seeing similarly hued tresses only once before—in the flickering torchlight of a dank prison.

"He was nowhere near Dunstoras the night the necklace was stolen," Aiden said grimly. "According to our few remaining friends at court, he was in Edinburgh."

Niall tugged his gaze away from the red-haired woman. His brother was examining the baker's pasties with halfhearted interest. The guise of a simple farmer suited Aiden well, his muscular body lending veracity to his claim of a life of physical labor. Two purple smudges under his eyes were all that remained of the torture he had endured at the hands of the earl of Lochurkie. "The queen's necklace is here, I promise you."

"Your informant only caught a glimpse of the necklace." His brother selected a meat tart and tossed the baker a coin. "It may not be the one we seek."

"How many heart-shaped rubies can there be?"

Aiden shrugged. "To prove it, you'll need to get inside the manor."

"I'll get in."

"The guards at the gate challenge every unfamiliar face. I see no way past them."

Niall's attention returned to the woman picking through the turnips and cabbages at the vegetable stall. A few snowflakes drifted down from the January sky, but not enough to hinder his view. She was accompanied by a tabard-draped guard who was carrying her purchases. "Where there's a will, there's a way."

His brother cast a sharp look over his shoulder. "Do you know that woman?"

"Aye," Niall said. She had fuller lips, rosier cheeks, and an unfamiliar pink scar on her lovely brow, but he trusted his memory of that dark night in November. "'Tis the lass I rescued from Lochurkie."

"The murderess?"

In the weeks following Aiden's escape from prison, they'd heard several rumors about the redheaded woman, including that one. "Aye."

"Did you not say she was knocking on Death's door?"

A familiar knot twisted in Niall's gut. Leaving the lass behind had cost him many a sleepless night imagining her dismal fate. The hopeless look in her eyes as he bid her adieu had haunted him for days. "Aye."

Aiden bestowed the meat tart upon a scrawny young lad who was eyeing his bounty with desperate longing. "Then how did she escape the castle guards?"

How indeed? Had her frail appearance that night been a ruse? If so, it had been a good one. But he couldn't deny the uncanny coincidence of finding her *here*, in the same village that held Queen Yolande's stolen necklace, more than sixty miles from Lochurkie. "It matters not. She has access to the manor."

His brother dusted pastry crumbs from his hands. "Think you can sway her to our cause?"

Niall was not known for his silver tongue. He did well enough with the ladies when it suited him, but he much preferred guarding the hidden passages beneath Dunstoras over the endless small talk required to coax a smile from the fairer sex. Still, everything he valued rested on proving his brother had not stolen the necklace—Aiden's honor, *his* honor, and the future of the entire MacCurran clan. "I'll do whate'er is necessary."

"I don't doubt your commitment," Aiden replied, "but time rides a fleet horse. The king intends to bestow Dunstoras upon a new lord when he next holds court. At best, we have a fortnight. If you fail—"

"I will not fail."

"You cannot be certain of that."

"I will not fail," Niall repeated firmly.

Aiden sighed. "Were it only me, your word would be enough. But I cannot hang the fate of our clan upon your promise of success—no matter how ardently spoken. The challenge before you is too difficult. I must return to Lochurkie."

"Are you mad? Was one stay in their dungeon not enough for you?"

His brother rubbed his bare chin. "The risk is not as great as you suggest. None will recognize me with my beard gone."

"'Tis a fool's errand, Aiden. Your memories of those days are scattered. You cannot even be certain there *was* a man in a black wolf cloak."

"My wits were not as addled as you think," Aiden insisted. "I saw him twice. Once at Dunstoras on the night the necklace was stolen, and a second time in the dungeons of Lochurkie."

"Dunstoras was a madhouse after the murders. People crying and shouting, soldiers dashing for their swords. No one knew who to blame. The alarm was raised at every shadow."

"I saw him before the murders, not after. In the passageway to the kitchens. Had I known then what he was about . . ." Aiden gripped the hilt of his dirk with a white-knuckled fist. "And, dear brother, let us not forget the way the night ended. The earl's men located the missing necklace—in *my* rooms. How do you explain that, if not for the man in black?"

"I can't," admitted Niall with a sigh. "But returning to Lochurkie is still a fool's errand."

"Perhaps. But I owe it to the memory of my kith and kin to see our honor restored—any way I can."

Niall's lips tightened. "They were my kin, too."

"Of course they were. I did not mean to imply otherwise. But I'm the chief. The responsibility for claiming vengeance lies with me."

Aye, Aiden was the chief. But it was Niall who captained the Curaidhnean Dubh—the Black Warriors, the handpicked group of men tasked with keeping Dunstoras safe. If anyone was to blame for their current circumstances, it was he. Not only had he allowed a murdering thief to enter Dunstoras, he'd failed to bring the cur to justice. He'd let down his clan . . . what little clan remained. "You cannot go alone."

"Don't fash yourself. Leod and Duncan have agreed to accompany me."

With Dunstoras fortress seized by the king and most of their remaining kin in hiding, there were few warriors to accompany him. And even fewer healthy ones. "Leod cannot travel with his injured leg," Niall said. "Take Graeme instead."

A wry smile twisted his brother's lips. "Offering me the finest sword in your band of merry men? I should be wounded by that aspersion. Have you completely lost faith in my ability to protect myself?"

"There's a price on your head. Every man you encounter on the way to Lochurkie will be seeking to claim it."

"None of them are likely to be my equal with a blade." Aiden placed a hand on Niall's shoulder. "I'm not a half-wit, though. Since you offered, I'll happily take Graeme."

Niall nodded, reassured. Then he glanced back at

the vegetable stall. The red-haired beauty was holding a copper coin in one hand and two fat neeps in the other, haggling with the vendor. "And whilst you gad about the highlands, I'll go after the necklace."

"If you find it, be sure you split a gut for wee Hugh."

Niall's thoughts spun back in time. Hugh, their cousin Wulf's young lad, had been poisoned alongside his mother and the king's courier the night the necklace disappeared. Bright as a new penny, quick to laugh, and adoring of his "uncle" Niall. Niall had dug several graves that day, but none more difficult than that one. "Rest assured. I'll avenge him."

"Good." His brother squeezed his shoulder. "Send a messenger the instant you learn anything."

Niall pulled his woolen brat over his head. "Count on it."

Ana paid the vegetable vendor and handed the two turnips to her guard, satisfied with her bargain. A bland broth should be well tolerated by the baron's wife, Elayne, providing her with some much needed sustenance. Neither ginger nor mint had soothed the woman's belly. Even heavy with child, she was thin as a willow switch.

"Take these back to the manor and have Cook begin chopping them immediately," she said to her young guard. "I'll be but a moment behind you. I must purchase some cardamom."

"Aye, Goodhealer Ana."

As the lad scurried off, she turned toward the spice

merchant's stall—only to draw up short, confronted by a solid wall of male flesh wrapped in a thick winter brat. Unusually tall and broad of shoulder, he loomed over her, most of his face hidden by the multicolored wool pulled low over his head. Most of his face, that is, save for a long, straight nose.

Ana stiffened.

She knew that nose—or at least she thought she did—and it was not a nose she'd ever imagined seeing again. The owner knew an unfortunate detail of her past. Heart skittering, she peered into the depths of his hood. "Are we acquainted, sir?"

A low, lazy chuckle rose from his chest. "I should say so, lass." He shoved the hood back, and Ana's breath caught. The strong lines of his face were a perfect match for his nose—hard and masculine and beautiful. But not beautiful in an elegant way. Nay, with that mocking smile and overlong dark hair, the only word that sprang to mind was *dangerous*. And he swiftly proved her right. As she stood there, enthralled, he cupped her chin in a pair of large hands and pressed a heart-stopping kiss to her lips. A tingling promise of delight.

And then it was over.

She stared into the face of her rescuer at Lochurkie, shocked by the wave of soft heat that poured through her. Despite their mutually entwined history, this man was a stranger. Apart from the nose, only his deep voice was familiar—

The tension in her shoulders eased.

Perhaps his appeal wasn't so surprising after all. Had not those low, rumbling tones coaxed her back from the brink of death? Inspired her to move in spite of excruciating pain? Rekindled her will to survive? Aye, they had. They had also made every nightmare she had endured since her ordeal more bearable. She might well be in love with that voice.

"'Tis I, your husband, Robbie, returned at long last from Aberdeen," he announced, loud enough for all to hear. "Rumors of my demise on the docks were greatly exaggerated, I fear."

She blinked. *Robbie? Her husband?*

An instinctive denial bubbled to her lips, but she bit it back. All around her, villagers had stopped to listen, enthralled by an impromptu reunion. She tightened her brat around her shoulders. Attention—especially aimed at her life before arriving in the village—was the last thing she needed. If the constable caught word she was wanted in Lochurkie for murder, all would be lost. Besides, she owed this man a huge debt—how could she deny him, even if he demanded a terrible price?

She forced a smile. "Robbie. Dear Lord, I thought you were gone for good."

"Nay, wife, never for good," he said, dark amusement in his eyes. "Even a battle waged against insurmountable odds couldn't keep me from your side." He slid the sleeve of his dark green lèine up, revealing a thick scar, which ran from elbow to shoulder on his right arm. "I'd have benefited from your tender ministrations, though, sweetling."

The scar was old, but the injury was real. He had very nearly lost that arm.

Ana met his gaze.

He shrugged off her sympathy and glanced around at their avid audience. "Let's away home, lass. We've a need for a proper homecoming."

She hesitated. This was not an opportune time to be waylaid. The turnip broth required her supervision. Cook had a habit of oversalting his soups, a heavy hand that could cause a myriad of problems for the babe. And without the cardamom, Lady Elayne might be unable to keep the soup in her belly, making the entire trip to the market pointless.

Noting her reluctance, "Robbie" tossed a heavy arm over her shoulders and tucked her close against his body. "Lead on, my love."

Trapped—by both his arm and the debt she owed him—Ana escorted her *husband* away from the west wall of the fortified manor house and down the lane toward the tiny heather-thatched bothy she occupied at the edge of the village. The bothy was offered in soccage to the village midwife. The previous tenant, Auld Mairi, had died at Christmas, leaving Ana as the primary healer—a role she'd much rather have avoided.

She unlatched the wooden door and beckoned him inside the one-room abode.

Ducking under the lintel log, he entered. The shutters were closed against the winter chill and, without a lit candle, the room was dim. Still, he perused the space at length, from the narrow cot nestled against the far wall to the solid maple table she used for crafting her medicines, ending with a nod. "This will do."

Never one to mince her words, Ana asked, "Do for what?"

"My purpose is not yours to know." He closed the door, took a flint from the pouch at his belt, and bent to light the kindling stacked in the fire pit. A flame burst into life with surprising speed. "All that's needed is for you to accept me publicly as your husband and allow me to accompany you to the manor whene'er you go."

"And if I choose not to do so?"

Standing, he favored her with a grave stare. "Then I'll be forced to share my knowledge of your past with the constable."

"Two can dance that jig, goodman." She crossed her arms over her chest. "Play me false and I'll share the whole of your activities that night. You freed another prisoner, in addition to me."

He smiled—a crooked smile that stirred something deep in Ana's belly. "No one will believe your story. I've patents in my possession that name me brother of a laird. If called upon, he'll stand for me, and your word will be discounted."

The confident set of his shoulders and the easy way he met her eyes told her he spoke the truth. Ana's heart sank. Duthes was a lovely village and she had hoped to settle here. Plant the garden she had vowed to seed, make some friends, maybe even set up a stall on market day to sell her tisanes and unguents. But it was not to be. As with every place she went, her welcome had all too quickly worn thin.

She scanned the small room, already planning what she would pack.

The gray woolen blanket folded at the end of the bed, the sturdy boots the shoemaker had traded for a remedy for his gout, the herbs drying in sheaves on the wall. When her gaze lit upon the shabby leather satchel hanging by the door, she bit her lip. Her healer's pouch. How could she have forgotten Lady Elayne, even for a moment? The young baroness was deathly ill. Leaving wasn't possible. Not yet.

"If you're thinking to run, think again."

Although that had indeed been the bend of her thoughts, Ana denied it. "I'm not so quick to renege on my debts as you might think. I owe you my life, so I'll aid you." But only for a time—until Elayne and the babe were in good health. Then she'd be gone, no matter what threat he made against her person.

"There's a good lass." He unpinned his brat and tossed it onto the cot, then peered into the iron cauldron hanging over the banked coals in the fire pit. "Have you naught to eat? A bowl of pottage, perhaps?"

She bristled at his condescending *good lass*. "I have a name. If you hope to convince the villagers that you are indeed my husband, it might be wise to learn it."

His gaze lifted. He studied her for a long moment, his blue eyes hard, his expression unreadable. "Take care, Ana. I'm not a man you should cross."

A spot of annoyance bloomed in her chest, just under her breastbone. So full of anger and threats, this man. It was all too easy to forget that he'd saved her life. But as discomfited as she was by his reappearance, she owed him more than she would ever be able to repay. Only a mean-spirited hag would begrudge him a meal.

And he *had* learned her name.

"I've some bannock and a round of cheese," she offered, unable to soften her tone into anything resembling gracious. At his nod, she brushed by him to reach the small wooden chest next to the bed. The brief rub of his sturdy arm against hers sparked a memory of him lifting her up the dungeon steps. Strange. She could barely remember the agonizing pain in her legs, but her recollection of the warm strength of his body remained as vivid as if it had happened yesterday.

The chest opened with a creak of damp wood. In addition to the bread and cheese, it held her store of kale, beans, and onions. She broke off a sizable piece of cheese and handed it and the bread to her guest.

He grunted his thanks. "Whisky?"

"I've naught but water. If you seek more potent brew, you'd best visit the alehouse." Alcohol interfered with her ability to heal, so she did not consume it. People looked askance when she declined ale, but she could not risk the outcome of her patients.

"Water from the village pond?" he asked, frowning.

"Nay, from the baron's well. He's been kind enough to let me draw from it."

"Water it is, then." As she did not possess a stool or

a chair, he claimed her narrow cot, his large size caus-
ing the rickety frame to squeak in protest. Then he bit
into his meal with hearty eagerness. She studied him
out of the corner of her eye as she repacked the chest.
His lèine had ridden up over his knees, displaying a
fine pair of brawny legs decorated with a scattering of
hair. A man familiar with hard labor, it would seem.

Ana fetched him a cup of water from the pail by the
door, trying not to let her imagination stray to how
they would pass the night. Who would get the bed? It
was too narrow to accommodate both of them—thank
heaven—but she didn't relish spending the night on
the cold, hard floor. Especially as she only had one
blanket.

"You took a great risk, claiming to be my dead husband. How did you know that I had presented myself
as a widow?"

He pointed to her linen brèid. "You cover your hair
like a wedded woman, but require a guard to accompany you to the marketplace. It seemed safe to assume
there was no husband."

A keen eye—she'd give him that. "How long do you
intend to stay?"

"As long as it takes."

She frowned. "That's not an answer."

He shrugged. "It's all I can offer."

"Might I know your true identity, at least?"

"As much as I'd enjoy hearing my name drop from
your sweet lips, lass, it's best we keep this ruse as simple as possible. If you knew my true name, you might

stumble over it a time or two and I can't have that. Here, in this village, I'm just Robbie."

Heat bloomed in Ana's cheeks. Pleasure at his compliment battled with a quiver of disquiet in her belly. Sharing her bothy with her handsome rescuer might be possible if their arrangement remained impersonal and based on threats, but if he insisted on making such intimate and provocative comments . . .

She spun away from the sight of him lounging on her cot and buried her trembling hands in the folds of her skirt. "You forget that I already know your given name. Someone hailed you as Niall that night."

"And you recall so, three months later? How curious."

A second wave of heat attacked her cheeks. Not curious at all, really. Over that time, her imagination had built her mysterious savior into a paragon of grace and valor. But the real man did not compare favorably. Too rude, too demanding, too . . . alarming. "Can we agree upon a false history, then? How long have we been wed? Where did we live before venturing to Duthes? Where are your kin?"

"All will be defined in good time."

She snatched her healer's pouch from the peg and began stuffing it with herbs. Lemon balm, while not as effective as cardamom, would soothe Lady Elayne's belly. "I am not a skilled dissembler. I cannot conjure credible lies with ease."

"Then don't lie."

"How can I not? The villagers here believe me to be

the widow of a traveling merchant, because that is what I told them. I've never said aught to them about my husband working on the docks in Aberdeen. Now you expect me to—"

"Cease, woman."

Taking a deep breath, she turned.

He had tossed aside the remaining bread and regained his feet. Holding her gaze firmly with his, he crossed the room. "Leave the story-weaving to me. If you find yourself alone, explain that you were too ashamed to admit your husband lost his caravan to a turn of the dice." Unsmiling, he brushed a callused thumb over her cheek. "The color that fills your cheeks as you prevaricate will convince them it's the truth."

The rough caress sent a thrill of excitement from her cheek to her belly. It had been a long time since she had felt the tug of desire. But this was no eager young swain courting her attention—he was a blackguard on a nefarious mission. A rogue of the worst kind. Encouraging his boldness would be unwise. She took a step back.

"Perhaps," she said flatly.

He did not take the broad hint in her voice. Instead, his fingers grazed the scar on her brow. "How did you come by this injury? When last I saw you, it did not exist."

With her heart racing and her breath difficult to catch, Ana took a second step back, forcing him to drop his hand. Why did her body continue to respond to him, when his rudeness knew no bounds? "I fell."

He frowned. "That night? Or some time later?"

"Does it matter?"

"Answer the question."

Although tempted to refuse, Ana decided not to bait the bear. Who knew what he was capable of? "That night. While escaping a castle guard."

A grimace flitted over his face. "Filthy wretch."

She studied him with curiosity. Was that a hint of chivalrous anger in his eyes? Or was her fertile imagination seeing something that was not there? "I survived. That alone is a miracle, I'd say."

"Indeed." His expression cooled. "Why were you tossed in the oubliette? What crime did you commit?"

"Should you not have asked that question *before* you freed me?"

He said nothing, just continued to stare at her with an unforgiving look.

Ana relented. "I was accused of murdering the earl of Lochurkie."

"A very serious charge."

"Aye."

His eyebrows lifted. "The man had six stone on you. How would a waif like you bring down John Grant?"

"Poison."

His gaze slid to the sheaves of dried herbs on the wall. "Are you recounting the truth? Did you really kill the earl?"

Ana had no desire to be tainted by even the slightest suggestion that she would take a life. "No, I did not. But someone did."

"With poison."

"Aye."

A dark look stole over his face. "What were the manifestations of this poison?"

"Wide eyes, delirium, rapid heartbeat, raspy breathing, and convulsions."

He pinned her gaze. "Can you name the cause?"

"Dwale, or some infusion that included it, most likely. It's a well-known poison, and there are curatives. Had I been permitted to continue tending the earl, he might not have died. Instead, because I had recently paid a visit to the apothecary, I was dragged to the dungeon at the first rumblings of poison." No need to mention the accusations of witchcraft.

"I've heard that dwale is an easy way to poison a group of people—all who sample a specific dish, for example."

The bitter cast of his words gave her pause. An example? Or a piece of personal history? "Perhaps," she said softly. "'Tis rumored that King Duncan used it to poison an army of invading Danes. Ground to a fine powder, it will dissolve well in ale or whisky . . . or even children's mead."

He said nothing, but the muscles of his jaw tightened.

"I've tried many a time to reason out Lord Lochurkie's murderer," she said. "Only three people tended him in those last hours before he took grave—myself, his sister, Isabail, and his personal attendant, Daniel—and I cannot believe any of us were eager to see his end. He was a good man."

Her companion snorted. "A good man? Come now. Does one good man brutally torture another?"

Ah, yes. The other prisoner he'd given aid to that night. *MacCurran.* "I cannot speak to why he would have tormented your friend, but I can tell you that the John Grant I came to know would never have done such a thing without righteous cause."

"Then your judgment is sorely lacking," he snapped. "My friend did nothing to earn such abuse. He was dragged to Lochurkie's dungeon, accused of a crime he did not commit, and beaten near to death when he would not confess."

Ana stiffened. "Perhaps there was some misunderstanding."

"The events were deliberate, I assure you."

"How can you know that? Grant is dead. He cannot speak to his deeds."

He favored her with a hard stare. "Because my friend is alive to tell the tale. No thanks to Lochurkie."

"But—"

"Enough," he said, throwing up his hands. "Defend the man further at risk to your life."

She bit her lip. After a year spent in Lochurkie, tending the lord and his family on numerous occasions, she was confident in her assessment of John Grant. But pursuing that hare would be unwise. All foolish daydreams aside, her rescuer was clearly a dangerous man.

Ana's hand slid to the stag-antler knife she kept on her belt. *His* knife, given to her in kindness. Her fingers tightened on the hilt. Which only proved that even a blackguard could be generous on occasion.

"No doubt my faith was misplaced," she said, her tone conciliatory.

His gaze fell to her hand, then returned to her face. His lips twisted with icy amusement. "Hold fast to your weapon if it eases you, lass, but know that nothing, not even a blade honed to a razor's edge, will stop me from attaining my goal."

Her cheeks burned with embarrassment, but she left her hand where it was. "Is it not possible for you to gain whatever it is you seek without abiding here with me? I vow to assist you in any way that I can."

"No."

There was not an ounce of give in the man, and the cruel edge that had infused his voice since the talk of poison made her decidedly uneasy. She was gathering herself for a passionate protest, in spite of her resolve not to raise his ire, when a sharp rap sounded upon her door.

"Goodhealer Ana! Open the door in the name of the constable of Duthes."

Chapter 3

Niall's hand instinctively reached for his sword—a sword that for once was *not* strapped to his side. Common villeins did not carry weapons of war and, to support their disguises, both he and Aiden had left their long blades back at camp. He shot Ana a look as he stepped forward to open the door. Had he misjudged her fear of the law? Had she somehow signaled her distress as they left the market?

She shook her head.

Her face was pale, her eyes dark with concern. She was as surprised by this visit as he was. Sucking in a deep breath and envisioning the various ways he might fight his way to safety with only a simple dirk, he tugged open the door. A tall, bearded man garbed in a belted red tunic stood before him, flanked by a pair of guards with black leather hoods.

"Constable?"

The other man frowned. "We are not acquainted, sirrah. Who might you be?"

Niall met his stare calmly. *Damn.* He'd neglected to

learn Ana's family name. The constable was unlikely to buy into the ruse if he couldn't recite his own name.

Ana hugged his arm, pressing her soft body into his side. "Good day to you, Constable Hurley. Allow me to introduce my husband, Robbie Bisset, recently returned from Aberdeen."

The constable's gaze flickered to Ana's face, then back to Niall's. "I was unaware that your husband was hale and hearty, Goodhealer. Did you not inform us that he had passed away?"

She nodded, a pretty pink flush rising in her cheeks. "A tale I'm greatly relieved to say was false. Robbie was badly injured on the docks, but he survived. And now he's come back to me."

"How fortuitous," the constable said, still studying Niall.

"Indeed," she agreed. "Is there a cause for your visit today, Constable?"

"Aye. The baroness has taken a turn for the worse. She's asking for you."

Ana darted for the table, grabbed up her leather pouch, and gestured to the street. "Let's away to the manor then."

Niall gently but firmly took possession of Ana's satchel. She wouldn't stray far from the tools of her trade. Staking his claim with a hand to the small of her back, he addressed Hurley. "I'm certain you have pressing matters of the estate to attend, Constable. Please do not delay on our account. Nothing would please me more than to accompany my dear wife to the manor."

Hurley glanced at Ana, then nodded. "As you wish."

Cutting the encounter short, Niall guided Ana past the constable. "Good day to you, Mr. Hurley."

They left the somewhat bemused constable behind and headed down the gravel lane. A cart pulled by a sleepy-eyed ox stood in front of the bothy next door, and a pair of burly peasants were unloading sacks under the supervision of a plump, bald fellow wearing a wax-splattered apron—the town candle maker, it would seem. Ana waved a greeting to her neighbor as they passed.

Although the sun had reached the highest point in the sky, the wintery air felt no warmer than it had when Niall had rolled out of his pallet at dawn. Leaving his brat back at Ana's bothy had been unwise—the cold wind cut through his lèine with ease. He envied the rosy cheeks of the young children playing hoops in the street.

"Are you warm enough?" he asked Ana, as they wove through the shoppers and vendors hawking their wares in the market square.

She glanced up at him. "Would you offer me your lèine if I were not?"

"Nay, but I might purchase a thicker brat for you from the wool merchant."

A frowned creased her brow. "That would only stir the gossips. Few can spare the coin to purchase such an item on a whim. You would know that, if you were truly my husband."

"If I were truly your husband," he said, "allowing you to take chill would shame me."

She shrugged. "Better a pinch of shame than an empty stomach."

"Only a woman would think such."

They crossed the wooden drawbridge to the manor gate. The two guards, clearly familiar with Ana's face, nodded crisply to her and ushered them under the portcullis. Once inside, Niall noted a half dozen men-at-arms scattered about the yard, each wearing hauberks of costly ring mail. The inner close of the manor was a tiny patch of trampled earth that somehow managed to include a stable, a kitchen, and a chapel. Two more soldiers defended the solid oak door to the main house, but not a single soul was practicing his craft in the lists. Slaggards.

Skirting the covered well in the center of the courtyard, they advanced to the door.

Again Ana was recognized, and again they passed without challenge.

Inside the great hall, remnants of the midday meal were being cleared away. The trestle tables were being wiped and dismantled. Hounds were sniffing the rushes in search of crumbs and bones. Two young pages were headed back to the kitchen with a large cauldron, and a laundry maid was gathering the soiled linens from the high table. All were busy and none took note of their passage across the room, save for the pinch-faced steward who spared them a brief glance as he hunted through the keys on his belt.

Niall was struck anew by his good fortune in finding Ana—and by the whole sorry mess of coincidences that accompanied that good fortune. As they climbed the candlelit stone stairs to the second level, he squeezed her arm. "There are to be no deaths whilst I'm in Duthes. I will not have it."

She frowned. "Am I to be a miracle worker, then? Prevent all falls, all injuries in the lists, all accidents with the plow?"

His fingers tightened. "No *suspicious* deaths."

"You mean no poisonings."

Indeed, that was exactly what he meant, but he chose not to leave her any open doors for mischief. "I mean you must be a paragon. Hold yourself to the highest standards of healing."

Mounting the last step, she freed her arm with a sharp tug. "I would do so whether you bid me or not."

The indignant blaze in her eyes brought her too-serious face to life, and Niall found himself entranced. "Excellent."

Ana gathered her skirts with a huffed breath and marched down the corridor to an alcove-set iron-studded door. It was opened swiftly to her knock, and a dark-eyed young maiden beckoned her into the room. "Welcome, Goodhealer. The baroness is asking for you."

Glancing inside the chamber and spying the drawn curtains around the bed, Niall paused. As much as he'd relish an opportunity to search Baron Duthes's private quarters, this was not the time. "Here's your satchel, sweetling. I'll leave you alone to do your good work."

She tossed him an arch look. "You don't intend to wait for me?"

He shook his head. "You could be a considerable time and I must see the carpenters about an urgent matter. We've a pressing need for a larger, sturdier bed."

The handmaiden withdrew with a faint smile and the whisper of her linen hem over the rushes. Ana blushed madly. "I think the priority must be finding work, husband. Perhaps you should see the reeve instead."

"Perhaps I'll do both," he said agreeably, enjoying her reaction.

Still a delightful shade of pink, Ana closed the chamber door in his face.

Amusement fading, he peered down the corridor in both directions. He had been tasked with finding a stolen treasure. If his informant could be trusted, the exquisite ruby necklace King Alexander had commissioned as a wedding gift for his new bride was hidden somewhere in this manor. Under lock and key, for certain. But in what room? A fortified manor this size would have upward of two dozen chambers; it would take a full fortnight to search all of them. A fortnight he didn't have.

He'd have to focus on the obvious places first. The baron's coffers, for example, which were almost certainly in the lower levels of the manor house.

Leaping the stairs two at a time, Niall arrived back at the main floor in a trice. He glanced quickly into the great hall to make certain no one was watching, then slipped down the stairs to the cellars. Here the corridor was wider and the candles farther apart. Grain sacks and barrels of pickled beets and onions lined the walls. If the trail of floury footprints was any indication, the passageway led to the kitchens.

With the midday meal complete, comings and goings should be minimal.

Several doors lined the corridor, each with iron hinges and door pulls. Storage rooms, no doubt housing Duthes's dwindling supply of winter food. The room he sought lay midway down the corridor, a seemingly narrow chamber tucked tightly between two other doors.

He crossed the hall and lifted the lock dangling from the latch.

Solid iron, with nary a hint of rust.

Without a key, the only option was brute force. Niall unsheathed his knife, aimed the steel butt of the blade, and smashed it down on the lock with all his might. Other than an uncomfortably loud rattle, he got nothing for his efforts. The lock held firm.

He hit it twice more, wincing at the noise. Still no success.

As he paused to consider other options, the rap of booted feet echoed on the stone stairs behind him. He did a quick count of the footsteps. At least three men, some of whom were wearing ring mail, judging by the clinking.

He was about to be discovered.

Ana drew back the bed curtains and quickly assessed the woman reclining against the pillows. Elayne lacked the sturdy build of her younger sisters, and the wasting sickness that had troubled her for the past eight months had left her painfully thin. Today, with her skin pale and her light brown hair darkened with sweat, the young baroness looked as if she might expire on her next breath.

"Did something happen to cause this?" Ana asked Elayne's handmaiden, Bébinn.

"Nay. She's been feeling poorly all day and has been lying abed, retching as she so often does." Bébinn pointed to the bucket at the foot of the bed. "But this last time I found blood in her sputum."

Ana glanced in the bucket. Thin traces of crimson laced the contents, suggesting Elayne's throat was raw from constant disgorging. A quick healing spell could have taken care of that, but not with Bébinn in the room. The handmaiden was as pious as a bishop. Any suggestion of heathen rites and the girl would run for the friar.

Ana laid a hand on the baroness's forehead. Cool and damp. No fever. "Did you eat today?" she asked.

Lady Elayne shook her head. "Nothing appeals."

"Not even bits of bread?"

"The mere thought of food has me begging for the

pail." She closed her eyes. "Just leave me be. Let me die in peace."

Her weariness was understandable. Eight months of constant nausea, driven to retching by the mere scent of food, had taken a heavy toll. Most women suffered her condition for half that time, and most were stronger when illness beset them. Elayne, from all accounts, had been pale and listless before quickening, and nurturing the bairn within her was drawing on reserves the girl simply didn't have.

"If you die, you'll take the bairn with you," Ana said crisply. "You'd never forgive me if I allowed that." Sliding her arm beneath the young woman's shoulders, she encouraged Elayne to sit up. "You need to take a wee walk, then try some bread soaked in clarified butter. I have Cook making you some broth, as well, but we'll proceed slowly."

"I'm too tired to walk."

"We won't go far," Ana said, helping the girl shift her feet to the floor. "Digestion is aided by movement. To have a hope of keeping food in your belly, you must take short walks, drink sweet wine, and eat frequent small portions. Lean on me, Your Ladyship. I'll help you take a turn about the chamber."

Elayne looped her arm around Ana's neck and pushed to her feet, cradling her rounded belly. Her entire body trembled, but with support, she was able to walk several steps toward the hearth. "Bébinn assures me nothing will work, that this illness is my cross to bear for being a daughter of Eve."

With a harsh scrape of wooden legs on stone, the handmaiden moved one of the high-backed chairs by the fire to allow them to pass. "Those are not my words," she contested. "Brother Colban spake them. He says the amount a woman suffers bringing a child into the world is commensurate with her sins."

Ana wanted to ask how a proper young woman of ten and six, who'd regularly attended mass and confessed her sins, could possibly have accumulated eight months' worth of sin, but she dared not. The friar had not given Ana his blessing yet. In his mind, she was a stranger and still unproven. Had Auld Mairi's journeywoman not run off and wed a man from a neighboring town, he'd never have taken Ana's oath to practice healing.

"Even if He intends for you to endure this illness the whole of your term," she said gently to Elayne, "you mustn't forget that the Lord Almighty helps those who help themselves. If you've the means to ease the nausea, you should use it."

"I'm not convinced such means exist."

"Take each day as it comes," Ana said. "Claim every bite swallowed as a victory."

Sensing the baroness's legs were about to give out, she lowered Elayne onto the chair closest to the fire. The girl's hands were cold and clammy. Ana beckoned to Bébinn, who quickly stepped forward and covered Elayne's knees with a soft woolen blanket.

The young woman's symptoms suggested a weakness in her blood. Ana had seen a similar frailty in lasses who'd newly begun their menses, and also in women with child, but never so severe. "Did you sample the black pudding I had Cook send up yestereve?"

Elayne grimaced. "Nay, the smell was unbearable."

Finding the heat of the fire excessive, Ana loosened the ties on her sark. She mentally ran through the list of foods she knew had served other weak-blooded women well. Lentils, which could be baked in a lightly spiced dish. Clams, but those were few and far between in these parts. Grains. "If you succeed in keeping the vegetable broth in your belly, we'll try some oats with honey and cream."

"Oats and vegetables are for cattle."

"And for childbearing women." She didn't bother to mention that most villagers ate oats and vegetables—and little else—on a daily basis. The baroness lived a very different life from her husband's tenants. "How are the bairn's movements?"

Smoothing her hands over her belly, Elayne smiled for the first time. "Strong and sure. He's a brawny lad, constantly kicking."

"Good." Ana bent to tuck the blanket around the baroness's back. As she leaned forward, one of her pendants—a silver rod entwined with a bronze snake—slipped free of her sark and swung into view.

Bébinn gasped. "Lord save us." Stepping back, she crossed herself.

Grabbing the swinging pendant, Ana straightened. Her stomach sank at the young woman's wide-eyed expression. Holding the token up so the handmaiden could clearly see it, she said, "There's naught to fear, Bébinn. 'Tis an ancient Greek symbol of healing called the Rod of Asclepius, gifted to me by my mother."

"Satan takes the form of a snake."

"Satan takes whatever form he feels will gain him power," Ana responded firmly. "Not all serpents are evil. Do you recall the tale of Moses and the copper snake?"

The handmaiden frowned.

Pressing her advantage, Ana added, "When poisonous snakes attacked the Israelites, the Lord bade Moses to craft a bronze snake and place it upon a pole. Any who had been bitten and then gazed upon that serpent would live." She paused to let the crux of the story sink in. "This snake is bronze, too. 'Tis a sign of healing, not Satan."

Bébinn's features softened.

Ana reached inside her sark for the second pendant she wore—a pewter cross. "It rests around my neck next to the most sacred of symbols." She pressed the warm pewter to her chilled lips, then held it up, too. "The Holy Rood."

A flicker of relief passed over the handmaiden's face.

"Each and every day, I thank God Almighty for blessing me with the ability to heal."

Bébinn smiled. "Indeed."

Ana turned to Elayne. The baroness's expression reflected only mild curiosity. Ana tucked the two pendants inside the neckline of her sark and tightened the ties. "I'll return anon. I've some lemon balm to add to the broth. Bébinn will tend you while I am visiting the cook."

Nodding respectfully to both women, Ana left the room. Once she was in the corridor with the chamber door shut solidly behind her, she sagged against the wall. The rough stones caught at the wool fabric of her dress, pulling threads, but her heart was beating too fast to straighten. The fate that awaited her if Bébinn shared what she had seen with the friar would not be pleasant. He would label her a witch, forsooth. Drowning and burning at the stake were the two most common deaths for witches—both of which, she knew, were horrid ways to die.

She shook off old memories and pushed away from the wall. Bébinn had been successfully distracted this time, but counting on luck to save the day was beyond foolish. She had to take more care and ensure the woman never had cause to look at her strangely again.

Else she might end up like her mother.

Smoothing her skirts with damp palms, Ana strode to the stairs.

Niall adjusted his grip on his knife.

If he waited in the shadows at the base of the stairs and caught them by surprise, he could vanquish the entire group of men. But the discovery of dead soldiers in the cellars would cause an unacceptable stir. This moment called for a strategic retreat.

He reached for the nearest door and tugged. It rattled but didn't budge—a lock hung from that latch, too. The buttery, perhaps? It made sense that the baron's expensive casks of French wine and aged whisky be kept under key. He glanced at the door across the corridor. It was locked, too. Duthes's steward was a very untrusting man.

The boot steps were nearing the bottom of the stairs.

He blew out the candle above his head to darken the corridor and dove for another door. This one swung open, revealing stack upon serpentine stack of colorful cloth bolts. Spindles of various sizes wrapped with wool and thread filled every nook and cranny. He squeezed inside only seconds before four burly soldiers descended into view. Thankfully, the hinges didn't groan as he closed the door behind him. With the door marginally ajar, he watched the men march forward.

No laughing or joking among this lot. The leader was a mountain of a man with a swarthy complexion. All were grim-faced, stiff-shouldered warriors alert and ready for treachery. Hands on the hilts of their blades, they peered into every nook as they passed. The baron might not have a large army, but he hired skilled men.

Although Niall was confident the soldiers hadn't seen him, his heart pounded as they drew closer. His hand tightened on the wooden handle of his knife, the twisted-rope pattern offering him a sure grip. If they discovered him, he'd take the leader first, then the slim-faced one with the cold eyes. A deep stab into the collar, a quick slash across the throat. After that, his strategy would largely depend on how the others reacted.

Wasted planning, as it turned out—the soldiers halted one door before reaching him. A large iron key was produced, the latch unlocked, and the door swung wide on groaning hinges. Niall could no longer see the men, but he could hear them rattling about inside what was likely not the buttery at all, but the armory.

"Allez-y, allez-y. Vite, vite."

Niall grimaced. Normans.

Not unexpected, of course. Trained soldiers—especially those with coin enough for armor and steel weapons—were in short supply in the Eastern Highlands. Many a lord hired mercenaries from the continent. Still, you couldn't pay for passion, and these laggards would never defend Scotland the way a Highlander would.

Though perhaps that wasn't a pressing concern for Baron Duthes. With the Norse raiders subdued and the English king reluctant to foster bad blood with his dead sister's former husband, the only turmoil that darkened Scotland's doors these days was the petty bickering between powerful families.

"Ramassez les epées de pratique."

They were gathering practice swords for a session in the lists. Wood scraped along the floor, something heavy hit the wall, and a heavy metal object crashed to the ground. *"Cochon!"*

It wasn't clear who or what the soldier was cursing as a pig, but the other men laughed.

"Tu es chanceux qu'il n'a pas coupé ta bite."

As the men continued their hunt for practice swords, more rattles and bangs emanated from the armory. Seizing his opportunity, Niall stepped into the corridor. The open door to the armory effectively hid him from the soldiers' view, but just to be safe he grabbed a dusty sack of cornmeal from a nearby pile and tossed the hundred-pound weight across his shoulders. He was dressed as a common laborer; he might as well play the part. With his eyes appropriately downcast and his legs making strong, sure strides, he headed for the kitchen.

He was just about to round the corner and disappear, when one of the soldiers spoke.

"Allo, ma petite poule. Where do you go in such a great hurry?"

Niall paused. Apparently, one of the soldiers had stopped a woman at the bottom of the stairs. He had no cause to believe it was Ana, save for an odd tingle on the back of his neck. It was probably one of the seamstresses. Or a weaver lass.

"What I do is none of your concern. Let me pass."

Or perhaps not. The tart tones of Ana's peeved voice rippled down his spine. Niall slipped the sack of cornmeal to the ground and turned. Sure enough, his wife stood at the far end of the corridor, her hands on her hips, impeded by the outstretched arm of the huge sergeant.

Niall frowned. But before he could take a step, Ana's gaze lifted to meet his.

The message in her eyes was clear and certain: *Do not interfere.*

His lips tightened. Was she mad? Did she really believe he would stand back and allow a mongrel to waylay his wife in a dark corridor? Even a false wife?

Eyes on the big brute, he moved forward.

"Why so grave, my lovely?" The Norman put his hand on Ana's face, and icy fury sped through Niall's veins like spring runoff. Almost without thought, his knife was in his hand. "Are Scottish men so lacking in bed that they cannot put a smile upon your face?"

"Perhaps you should pose that question to my husband."

The soldier grinned and patted the hilt of his sword. "I would be happy to."

She pointed over his shoulder. "Excellent. He's right behind you."

Niall skidded to a halt less than three feet from his target. Every muscle in his body was pumped with rage, but thanks to Ana, he'd lost the edge of surprise. He could still cripple this filthy hedge-rat—teach him a lesson he'd never forget—but not quietly. And there was the rub. As the sergeant spun around, Niall slid his dirk into the sheath at his belt.

The soldier's eyes widened with disbelief. "This is your wife?"

"Aye." The piece of shite had no notion how close he'd come to losing an arm. The only thing saving him even now was that he was no longer touching Ana. Niall offered his hand to his wife. Their wedded state was only a ruse, but he must play it like the truth. And if she were truly his, he'd *never* allow another man to touch her. "Come, sweetling. I've yet to visit with the carpenter."

Her eyes narrowed, but she put her hand in his. "I've nothing to say to the carpenter."

He tugged her gently toward him and whispered in her ear, "Then I'll not hear any complaints about the bed squeaking each time we use it."

As he'd hoped, sparks replaced the fear in her eyes and her pale cheeks warmed to pink.

He shifted his gaze to the French soldier. "I trust we'll meet again," he said softly.

The other man's eyes met his without wavering. "No doubt."

Niall escorted Ana to the kitchen, but it took long moments for his blood to cool. He blamed it on his pride—backing away from a fight, even for good reason, galled him to no end. But it may have had more to do with the way Ana's fingers were tightly entwined with his.

Aiden scooped up his accoutrements and stepped around the mountain that was Ivarr to tie his bags to the saddle of his horse. With a bit of hard riding, they could make Braemar by nightfall and cross the River Dee at first light.

"Two days, laird," Ivarr argued. "Give us two days to find the necklace. Then we'll all journey to Lochurkie together."

With a sharp tug, Aiden cinched his saddle tight. "We've wasted far too much time on this cursed hunt as it is. I can't give up two days more."

"But you're the chief. You ought not to journey with such puny protection."

Aiden spun around. "'Tis precisely because I am the chief that I must go. It's my responsibility to see Dunstoras returned to MacCurran hands, and I'll not sit on my arse praying for success when I can be honoring the memories of our lost kin."

Ivarr's lips thinned. "We are not sitting on our arses."

"The results are much the same," Aiden said. "We are no closer to knowing who stole the necklace, and the king is about to give Dunstoras over to a new lord."

Graeme looked up from his packing. "Not for lack of effort."

Aiden slipped the bridle over his horse's head. Perhaps not, but the ground they'd covered in search of answers these past two months ultimately meant nothing. His father had spent forty long, hard years building the reputation and wealth of the MacCurran clan—helping Walter Comyn free the king from English tyranny during his minority, fighting alongside the king at Largs, and even accompanying Princess Margaret to Norway for her wedding. Now, under Aiden's leadership, the one possession his father prized above all else—Dunstoras—was about to be lost. "True enough," he said. "But that effort has not sired results. It's time to take a riskier stand."

"Traveling in a small party is an invitation to brigands and rogues," Ivarr said.

"Niall insists on remaining here to find the necklace," Aiden said with a shrug. "We've no choice but to divide our efforts."

"I do not speak idly," the big warrior cautioned. "Cormac and I found a small band of thieves in the hills northwest of here, preying on hapless travelers."

Seated on a log by the fire, Leod trimmed a thin shaving of aspen from the robin he was whittling. "Thieves tend to be rather wary of attacking armed men."

"We're hardly hapless travelers," said Aiden. "But to be safe, we'll circle them wide on our trek up the glen."

"What do you truly hope to find in Lochurkie, laird?"

"Answers."

"And how do you intend to get them?" Using the sharp tip of his dirk, Leod cut two tiny nostrils on the beak of his bird. "The earl is dead."

"He wasn't the only one who knew the identity of the man in black. There were others."

"Perhaps," Leod said gently. "But I think it may be your pride driving your need to return, not your wits."

There was a degree of truth to that, and it stung. "Lady Isabail, the earl's sister, knows more than she has admitted. As chatelaine, she is responsible for all who bed under her roof. She chooses a place for them at mealtimes, plies them with ale and wine, and finds a pallet for them to lay their heads on at night. She *must* know the identity of the man in black."

"And if you discover your man in black is merely a specter conjured by your imagination? Will you still be satisfied with your answer?"

"Aye." But the man in black was real; Aiden had no doubt of that. The cloaked cretin had cost him his home, his family, and his reputation. One way or another, he intended to track him down and make him pay.

"Uncle Aiden?"

Aiden spun around. Jamie, Wulf's eldest son, stood behind him, looking a little like a beaten pup. "You're to stay in camp and mind your elders," he told the boy. "I'll be back as soon as I can."

"Why can't I come along?"

"It isn't safe, lad. Your da would kill me if I put you in harm's way."

Aiden hoisted himself into the saddle and waited patiently for his reluctant partners to mount. Across the clearing, Leod held up the finished robin for all to see, then tossed it to Aiden. "I hope your little bird sings you a sweet song, laird. And I wish you a safe journey."

Aiden nodded.

Moments later, he rode out of the camp, accompanied by Duncan and Graeme.

Chapter 4

As the hush of the forest closed around Niall, a familiar calm spread through his body. In the distance, a woodpecker hammered at some bug-ridden timber, and to his left, a gray jay stood guard on the branch of a towering elm. Beyond that, there was nothing but trees and snow-dusted earth for as far as the eye could see. And that pleased him.

Niall stepped off the path and headed into the thick of the trees.

Most travelers kept to the beaten trail, but Niall had been born under the boughs, not in the comforts of a home. A bastard never officially claimed by his lord father and born to a woman shunned by the village good folk for plying her chosen trade, he'd learned his way about the forest at a young age, living off the land and camping under the stars for most of his early life. As a Black Warrior, those skills had proven useful. Keeping the secrets of Dunstoras meant staying out of sight, even from their kin.

Fallen leaves crunched underfoot and his boots

lifted the light dusting of snow from the ground, leaving a noticeable track. When he got a little closer to the camp, he'd take more care. Right now, making good time was more important.

Ever wary, he scanned the woods around him as he marched. But he relied on more than sight alone. Smells and sounds, especially in the crisp air of winter, added valuable details to his study. The pungent scent of badger guided him around, rather than over, a large mound of dirt that clearly hid a sett. The distinctive clicking of capercaillie had him avoiding an open stand—and the thunderous noise of the large birds taking startled flight.

Niall noted the disturbed leaves on the ground long before he reached the half-fallen tree that told him to turn left. Peering surreptitiously into the tree branches ahead, he was able to spot the vague outlines of several figures hiding in the shadows. An ambush in the making. *Bloody hell.* Of all the days he had to be without his sword, why this one?

Restrained by circumstance several times already, Niall was not about to turn from another fight. There had been too few opportunities to release the rage he'd felt since the deaths of Hugh and the others. And if he were honest, he'd admit the frustration at not being able to skewer Ana's soldier still knotted his gut. He had accompanied her back to Lady Elayne's chamber after her visit with the cook, but failed to meet up with the wretch on his way out of the manor.

Keeping his gaze level and the set of his shoulders

easy and carefree, he marched steadily forward. He counted five men in the trees. Judging by their positions, they intended to ambush him when he reached the rotting yew stump about fifty paces ahead.

Which suited him just fine. He could use the stump to his advantage.

As for his opponents . . . Soldiers didn't climb trees. These men were likely outlaws, men living outside clan rule, thieving for their supper. Perhaps they'd been unable to pay their tithe, or perhaps they'd been chased off by the village priest for their adherence to the old pagan ways. How or why they ended up in the woods was unimportant. What mattered was how desperate they were. A man with nothing to lose fought like a demon.

Whistling a jaunty tune, he glanced into the branches.

They didn't appear to be overly lean or gaunt. Rather sturdily built, in truth.

Unsheathing his dirk, he marched up to the stump and halted. As anticipated, five grim-faced wretches quickly surrounded him, thumping to the frosty ground with their weapons at the ready. They made no demand for his gold, no call to put down his weapon. They simply attacked.

And Niall responded instinctively.

He pivoted to face a great bear of a man roaring toward him, ax swinging. Swiftly stepping inside the arc of the axman's blade, he thrust his dirk into the crease of his neck. Blood sprayed and the fellow crumpled.

Niall tugged his dirk free and ducked left, putting the stump between him and the second axman. Just in time. The double-edged blade whizzed by his ear and crunched into the wood.

A squat, bearded fellow attacked from the right, slashing.

Niall grabbed the hapless fellow's arm and yanked him forward. Momentum made simple work of plunging his dirk into the man's barrel chest. He shoved the faltering body into the path of his oncoming attackers and leapt atop the stump. Taking advantage of a momentary hesitation on the part of his foes, he vaulted to the ground behind the second axman and finished him with a swift jab between the ribs.

The remaining two outlaws were wiser than he gave them credit for—seeing three of their number slain in as many minutes, they spun on their heels and ran into the trees.

Niall did not give chase. Defending himself was one thing; slaying men as they fled, quite another. He lowered his arm and surveyed the scene around him. Three fallen men—a waste of life by any measure. Not that they'd given him any choice. Their intent had been murder, not thievery.

He frowned.

Brigands were opportunists. Ambushing a traveler along a trodden path made perfect sense. But here, amid the thick wood, in an ill-frequented part of the forest? What could they hope to gain?

Unless they were purposely accosting those entering or leaving the Black Warrior camp.

How likely was that? His men were very skilled. They had perfected the art of slipping silently through the woods and they'd have noticed were they being followed. And surely even a half-witted thief was savvy enough to seek out a fat merchant en route to the village rather than attacking a trained soldier.

Which suggested two things: Someone had told the outlaws which landmarks the Black Warriors used to find their way to camp . . . and someone had offered them a hefty prize in exchange for their services.

Niall wiped his blood-spattered face with a sleeve.

How unpleasant.

As inconceivable as the notion might be, it seemed there was a traitor among the Black Warriors.

By the time Ana coaxed several spoonfuls of turnip broth down Lady Elayne's throat and escorted her back to bed, the late-afternoon shadows had overtaken all but the thinnest shards of daylight in the courtyard. A dusting of snow lay on the slate roof of the manor house, reminding her that she'd need to gather some fresh kindling on her way home. She closed the shutters and fastened them against the pull of a brisk northern breeze.

"Any queasiness in your belly, Your Ladyship?"

"Nay." Elayne's response was little more than a murmur.

Ana turned. As she suspected, the young woman lay against the pillows, her eyelids drooping. Her skin no longer glistened with clammy sweat and her cheeks held a faint touch of pink. "I'll leave you to rest, then, but have Bébinn send for me if there's a need."

"Uh-hmm."

Ana approached the bed. The handmaiden had departed a few moments ago to answer a summons from Baron Duthes, and with the baroness now drifting into sleep, Ana could heal without fear of discovery. Ever so gently, she shook Elayne's arm.

The girl did not stir.

Discovery was always a grave concern. Her talent for healing was no ordinary skill. Ana rubbed her hands together, drawing energy from deep inside her core as she did so. Immediately, she felt a telltale bloom of warmth in her gut. She wasn't entirely certain where her gift came from, save that her mother had been similarly blessed, as had her mother before her. And it truly was a blessing—when called upon, her healing powers were capable of great marvels. But as beneficial as those marvels were, they invariably begot fear and loathing, even among those who were saved from certain death—in part because of the telltale stigmata. As the gift flowed into her chest and down her arms, an intricate red pattern not unlike the finely wrought stitching on Lady Elayne's linen nightrail rose upon her hands. Swirls and arcs that in no way could be labeled normal.

Ana glanced at the chamber door. It was firmly shut.

Delicately, she touched her hot fingers to Elayne's neck.

This time, the girl stirred. But not enough to wake. Ana closed her eyes, imagined the raw flesh lining the baroness's throat, and sent waves of heat through her hands to the injured area. As the healing commenced, the waves returned in full force—this time as cold, dark humors that numbed Ana's arms and made her bones ache. It was a fair trade of pain for pain. *Nothing came for free*, her mother would have said.

Elayne's injury was minor, so the pain was minor, as well. Once the aches had passed, all Ana felt was a light sense of fatigue, and in a thrice, the healing was done.

She pulled back.

Elayne slept on undisturbed. A light smile graced her lips.

Taking a moment to warm her chilled arms in front of the fire, Ana stirred the coals in the hearth and tossed a fresh log on the fire. By the time golden flames were licking up the bark, the lacy pattern on her hands had faded away. She picked up her leather satchel, gave Elayne one last check, and then headed for home.

Although preparations for the eventide meal had not yet begun, the great hall was surprisingly busy. Baron Duthes and his huntsmen were discussing the challenges of the afternoon hunt as they warmed their hands by the hearth, the steward and his poulterers were collecting the half dozen black grouse the hunters had brought home, and Bébinn stood off to one side chatting with her husband, Garnait, one of the baron's men-at-arms. As Ana descended the stairs, Bébinn looked up.

Their eyes met briefly; then the handmaiden's gaze dropped to the floor. She whispered something to Garnait, who threw a frown in Ana's direction.

Ana's stomach knotted.

It would seem she hadn't been as convincing with her tale of Moses as she'd hoped. If the handmaiden had already shared what she'd seen with her husband, how long would it be before she was spilling her vitriol in the friar's ear?

"Goodhealer Ana?"

She spun around. A young page with a long streak of soot on the front of his blue serge tunic stood behind her. "Aye?"

"Baron Duthes begs a moment of your time."

She lifted her gaze over his shoulder. The potbellied baron had left his men and now sat in a huge carved armchair that faced out into the great hall. 'Twas the seat upon which he heard petitions and meted out judgments each Thursday. Given the fat pair of birds hanging on his squire's string, his mood should have been light. Instead, his lips were set in a thin line.

"Of course," she said, swallowing hard. Gripping her satchel with tight fingers, she followed the wee lad across the hall.

As she neared, the baron favored her with a serious stare. He waved her toward the stool. "Sit, sit."

Ana sat. Offering her a seat was a good sign, wasn't it? "Can I be of some assistance, Baron?"

"I require clarification," he said grimly. "Bébinn has given me her accounting of the day's events. Now I would have yours."

Ana's heart knocked against her ribs. *Dear Lord.* Had the handmaiden already accused her of engaging in heathen rites? Was she being asked to explain the pendant? "Sir?"

"Why is my wife expelling blood?"

Relief poured through her body in a heady rush. He was merely concerned about Elayne. "Although frightening to see, sir, the blood in the baroness's sputum was not of significant amount. An irritation of the throat, that is all. She ate well this eve, and I expect no blood tomorrow, even should she be unable to hold her meal."

Fingering the jeweled silver collar of his station, he absorbed her words. "Bébinn believes the baroness's health to be dire."

"Does she?" Ana did not give the handmaiden the honor of her gaze. "I was unaware that she was trained as a healer. Perhaps you would prefer Bébinn tend your wife and not I?"

The baron glared. "Mistress, you overstep your bounds. Bébinn is my wife's cousin, where you are but a stranger. I have every reason to take her word over yours. Were it not for the attestations of Auld Mairi's two apprentices and the safe delivery of my piper's bairn at Yule, I would never let you near the baroness."

Ana bit her lip. Curse her quick tongue. "Please forgive my insolence. I only seek to keep the baroness in the best of health. She is not well—I do not deny that. Her inability to hold food in her belly and her weak blood threaten both her and the babe. But I know what I am about, and with my aid and God's will, sir, they will both enjoy the summer weather when it arrives."

His frown did not ease. "Each time you visit, she eats well. The moment you leave, she's spewing the contents of her belly."

"Because the usual fare does not suit her. She must eat very bland food."

"And how are we to meet her needs without you present?"

Ana chose her words carefully. "I have given Bébinn a list of appropriate aliments." At this juncture it would be unwise to tell him the handmaiden refused to spend any time in the kitchen coaching the cook.

"That is insufficient. Collect your things. You will move into the manor."

And have Bébinn reporting on her every action? *Nay.* "I've other villagers under my care, Baron. And my husband returned from Aberdeen today."

"So Constable Hurley informed me. How fortuitous."

"Indeed," she said, feeling another blush rise into her cheeks. Why did even the mildest thought of her faux husband warm her to the tips of her toes? She stood. "Sir, I feel I serve you and your tenants best by remaining in my bothy. But I'll endeavor to visit the baroness more frequently—perhaps before each meal."

Arms folded stiffly across his chest, his heavy brow lowered, he studied her.

It took every ounce of willpower Ana possessed not to look away.

Finally, he nodded. "You may remain in your bothy for now. But my wife and son are very dear to me, Goodhealer. Should you fail to keep them hale and hearty, my wrath will know no bounds. Do I make myself clear?"

His message was very difficult to misconstrue.

"Aye. Very clear."

He waved her off. "Go."

With her satchel clutched to her chest, Ana beat a quick path to the door.

A thousand paces from the camp, Niall heard a familiar sharp whistle. He'd been spotted by one of his men, but there was no sign of anyone in the trees around him. He responded with a light whistle of his own, and an instant later, a hooded figure limped out from behind a gray tree trunk.

Leod.

"So?" the other man asked, a broad grin splitting his thin face. "Were you successful? Did ya sweet-talk the lass into lifting her skirts?"

Niall scowled. "Aiden talks too much."

"That would be a no, then."

Niall slowed as Leod came abreast of him. Gouged in the calf by a wild boar tusk a sennight ago, the warrior could not yet keep apace. "My goal was to get inside the manor, you cur, not inside the lass."

Leod laughed. "Lord, she must be ugly."

An image of Ana rose to mind, the same one he'd held in his thoughts for months—the sight of her perfect oval face, large blue eyes, and glorious dark red hair cascading down her back as she clung to a sapling in the pale light of a waning moon. She'd been far too thin then, but still incredibly beautiful. The desire to see that hair unbound again—to weave his fingers through it—scorched a molten path through his veins. "Nay."

"We spend months in the woods, far from the pretty young milkmaids in Dunstoras, and all you deign to share is *nay*? Surely you can do better than that?"

Sharing had never been Niall's wont. "Nay."

"Wretch." Leod hobbled quietly alongside for few moments, then pointed to Niall's face. "You might want to visit the burn afore entering the camp."

"Why?"

"That blood's not likely to please young Jamie."

Niall halted abruptly. "Aiden left Jamie behind?"

Leod snorted. "Aye. He wasn't about to take the lad to Lochurkie now, was he?"

Gods be damned. It had been Aiden who'd insisted on bringing Jamie to Duthes. The lad had always been the timid sort, but since the deaths of his mother and younger brother, he'd become fearful of his own shadow. The disappearance of his da had not helped matters. Wulf had stormed out of the castle the night of the murders, grief-stricken and howling for vengeance, never to be seen again. They'd combed the woods for days afterward and found no trace.

"Leaving him with me was not the better option," Niall said.

"But you be his kin."

"Only in blood," Niall said, marching toward the stately elm that marked his camp. "He knows me not. A bastard cousin is rarely invited to sup with the family. The lad's knees shake when I but look at him."

"Mayhap, but the laird has named him your page."

"I don't need a page."

They ducked under a low sweep of pine bough and entered the clearing where the Black Warriors had set up camp.

Ivarr was seated on a fallen log, sharpening his sword, and Cormac was stirring a pot over the fire. Niall spotted his young cousin right off—over by the horses, a curry brush in hand. Golden-haired like his mum, a sturdy form like his da. The lad was watching him, but the moment he realized Niall's gaze had found him, he shrank behind Niall's massive black destrier.

"Jamie," Niall called.

The lad peered from under the horse's neck, half-hidden by the long mane.

He waved the boy over.

Jamie tossed the brush into a bucket and slowly crossed the clearing to stand before Niall. His eyes held bleak shadows—far bleaker than a lad of ten and two ought to know—and they widened as he spied the smears of blood on Niall's face and clothing.

"Fear not," Niall said. "None of it is mine."

"D-did you kill a man?"

Niall nodded. "A thief who tried to skewer me."

The lad turned green and his bottom lip began to quiver. Not a moment later, he emptied his spleen all over Niall's boots—an odorous brown coating of what appeared to be soup. His gaze flew up to meet Niall's. Tears filled his eyes.

Niall searched for the appropriate response and came up dry. Good thing he hadn't mentioned he'd actually slain three men, not one.

With a low keen of despair, the lad wrapped his arms around his belly and ran off.

Leod did a rather poor job of stifling a laugh. "That went well."

Niall used a piece of kindling to tap the muck off his boots. Communicating with Hugh had been effortless. He'd been a babbling brook of tales, willing to share even the smallest of adventures. Every encounter with Jamie, on the other hand, was a disaster. He never knew what to say to the boy.

Ivarr and Cormac joined him, both smirking.

"I think it's an improvement on your usual scent," Cormac said, sniffing the air. Attired entirely in green and brown, his pale ashwood bow slung over his back, he looked every bit the woodsman.

"And those boots were in sad want of a good polish," Ivarr added. As usual, the big warrior had pinned his multihued woolen brat across his chest and under his right arm to allow freer movement of his sword arm.

"Do not make sport at the lad's expense," Niall

chided quietly. "Best we ignore what happened and allow him to recoup his pride."

The smiles faded, and they nodded agreeably. Ivarr pointed to the blood spatters on Niall's clothing. "So? Care to share the tale?"

"Ambushed by thieves," Niall said, shrugging. He studied the faces of his men as he spoke. Cormac, lean and blue-eyed. Ivarr, square-jawed and quick to smile. Leod, thin and a tad pale. It was a bitter struggle to imagine any of them betraying him. They'd been brothers-in-arms for more than ten years. Defended one another in battle. Bound one another's wounds. Shared food and whisky and a private thought or two. "Five scurrilous rats intent on stealing my purse."

Ivarr's brows soared. "And you killed only one?"

"Three."

A wry smile rose to Cormac's lips. "Wretch. Here we are, playing nursemaid to the lad, and you're off having a grand old time."

"Shall we take to the woods and rout out the vermin?" asked Leod. "Cormac and Ivarr found evidence of a camp to the northwest."

Niall nodded. "Approach them, but do not slay them. Watching the trails as closely as they do, they're sure to have marked the comings and goings of all. I would learn what strangers have passed through the village in recent months. One of them surely brought the necklace."

A deep frown furrowed Cormac's brow. "You want us to *spare* them?"

"Information is more valuable than a dead body."

"And we accept the word of thieves and murderers now, do we?"

Niall's gaze collided with the archer's. "I'll bend an ear to any who can deliver me vengeance. Thieves, murderers, traitors—it matters not. I care nothing but for the information they supply."

"And if they lie? We'll be chasing our bloody tails."

"Thieves are loyal only to coin. Offer them a purse."

A growl rose in Cormac's chest, and his hands fisted at his sides. "Give them the very thing they sought to gain by attacking you? Nay, I'll not do it."

The archer had always been fierce and full of anger. But was his insistence on slaying these thieves motivated by more than a need to defend a fellow warrior? A desire to cover his tracks, perhaps? "You'll do as I say."

The words were delivered quietly, but with the bite of steel. Niall did not stomach revolt, even from long-time friends.

Cormac dropped his gaze to his boots, his long dark hair swinging forward to hide his face. "Aye." His humble mien lasted no more than a heartbeat, though. He lifted his gaze to Niall's, a wry grin on his face. "But I'll not enjoy it."

"Fair enough."

"We've a pot of bawd bree on the fire," Ivarr said into the silence that followed. "If you care to sup."

Niall shook his head. "I'll be laying my pallet in the village for a time."

"With the lass?" Leod asked.

"Aye."

"Bloody hell," Cormac grumbled. "Our lot is becoming sorrier by the moment. You get the battles *and* the lasses."

"'Tis not so merry a tune as you would sing," Niall said. Now would be the time to share what he'd learned of Ana's crime, to tell them about the poison. But he did not. "She has red hair."

"And a fiery disposition to go along with it?" Ivarr asked, grinning.

"Aye."

"Freckles?"

Niall shook his head. "Nary a one."

"At least, none that you've yet seen," Cormac added slyly.

The others laughed. Niall got lost in the vision of Ana lying naked in his arms. He'd happily spend a few hours exploring her skin for evidence of a freckle. Not that she was likely to let him look. He'd be lucky to see her hair unbound. "I've located the baron's coffers, but the lock on the door will not be easy to breach."

Ivarr grimaced. "Only a miserly man has need of a lock."

"Would a hammer and chisel do the deed?" Leod asked.

"Only if I had a mind to rouse half the manor with my efforts," Niall responded. "The chamber is in an oft-used passageway. I'd prefer a saddler's needle and a hoof pick."

"Why those?"

"Properly inserted into the keyhole, they can release the lock catch."

Leod blinked. "Truly?"

"Truly." It had been many years since he'd picked a lock, but with a little luck and bit of time, he could open it.

"Dare I ask how you acquired such a nefarious skill?"

The years before his father claimed him were not ones he cared to talk about. Most other warriors came from well-to-do families. They knew nothing of the desperation inspired by going days without food. "Not all of us were raised on milk and honey."

Niall crossed the camp to the lean-to where their gear was stored. Digging through his horse tack, he located the tools he needed. A square of soft leather wrapped around them prevented rattling.

"Is it a simple task?" Ivarr asked. "Releasing the latch?"

Niall shrugged. "It requires patience and a deft hand."

"Pardon me for saying such, but if speed is of the essence, should we not consider robbing the steward?"

His query met with silence.

"He carries the key to every lock at his belt," Ivarr reminded them.

"He's also a prominent figure whose absence would be swiftly noticed," Cormac pointed out. "We'd not have much time before the alarm was raised. . . ."

The faces of all were grim. No one was eager to attack an innocent man, but stealing the key was an option that must be considered.

Niall stuffed the lock-picking tools, his two spare lèines, and a black brat into a burlap bag.

"We cannot be certain the necklace is in the baron's coffers," he said. "If we rob the steward, we'll lose our chance to search the rest of the keep. For now, we stay the course."

He added a few more items to his bag, then heaved it over his shoulder and turned to face his men. "If I fail to return in two days' time, consider me lost."

"And the necklace?" Leod asked.

There was no need to exhort them not to give up. They'd each sworn a lifelong vow to protect Dunstoras and its laird. "Do what you must."

The warriors nodded.

Niall studied each of their faces again. He could not see a traitor in any of them, but the knot in his gut said he wasn't wrong. He'd need to be especially wary until he sorted the faithful from the wrathful. Leaving Jamie in the camp was risky, but he had to believe the real threat was to the necklace, not the lad. There was no place for the boy in the village.

"Leod, take a water pouch and go in search of young Jamie." To the two other men, he said, "Question the thieves. I'll return anon."

Then he headed home to his wife.

Chapter 5

As Ana passed through the torchlit courtyard, she glanced at the kirk.

The arched oak door was open, and the flickering light of numerous votive candles brightened the gloomy interior. A man stood before the stone altar, his head bowed respectfully. She could not see his tonsure, but the flowing black cappa and crisp white undertunic identified him just the same: Brother Colban.

She halted.

Here might be a chance to recoup the day's losses. If she spent an hour on her knees in the kirk, visibly proving her sanctity to the friar, would he not be more likely to discount any rumors of her heathen affiliations? Surely, he would.

Of course, an evening prayer would delay her return to the bothy.

Ana's cheeks warmed. After her encounter with Niall in the cellars and the teasing comments about the bed, that was probably a good thing. His attempt to defend her had softened her opinion of him most alarmingly. If she weren't more careful, she might come to think of him as her valiant savior again. That would never do. Not while they shared an abode.

She covered her hair with her brat and stepped over the raised threshold of the narrow kirk.

The leather soles of her shoes tapped lightly on the slabs of granite that formed the floor. Ana drew the sign of the cross on her body as she approached the altar. She waited for the friar to note her presence, but after a long moment her impatience got the best of her.

"Brother Colban?"

He genuflected, then turned. Long of face, with pale blue eyes and a chin sharp as a pike, the friar could quell the blithest of souls with a simple look. Three lines creased the fleshy ridge above his prominent nose, so deep they appeared to be carved there. No similar creases flanked his mouth, though. Ana could not ever recall seeing the man smile. "Aye?"

"I've a desire to pray this eve. Will you take my confession?"

He wore his piety like stiff armor, his nod spare. "Of course."

Although Ana still gave ritual thanks to the heathen gods for her gift, she had accepted the Christian God as the one true god. The Church demanded she forsake all other gods in favor of the Lord Almighty, but there was no room in the Christian world for her healing magic, and she could not—nay, *would* not—forsake that. So, she begged the Lord's forgiveness for her actions. Silently. In private.

She slipped to her knees before the friar. The granite floor bit into her flesh through the wool of her skirts, but she paid it no heed. This was the easy part. Her knees would be throbbing by the time she was done.

Brother Colban placed his hand atop her head, and she bowed.

"Have you despaired of His mercy since your last confession?"

"Nay."

"Have you used the Lord's name in vain?"

"Twice," she replied.

"Have you committed adultery?"

"Nay."

"Have you kept holy the Sabbath Day?"

"I have."

"Have you coveted thy neighbor's goods?"

"Aye. Just today, I coveted the food on the baroness's table."

"Have you lied?"

"Six times."

"Have you been lazy or idle?"

"Nay."

"Had impure thoughts?"

Ana hesitated. Not until today. And only for a man the rest of the village saw as her husband. Did that count? She glanced up. "Is it impure to have lascivious thoughts about one's husband?"

The friar stared at her. His pale blue eyes seemed to bore right into her soul. "Not if you were bound before God."

Ana swallowed. *Mercy*. Why hadn't she simply admitted her sin? Instead, by asking a foolish question, she'd cornered herself into a lie. *Please forgive me, Father.* "Then nay."

He continued to stare at her for a lengthy moment, then said, "Have you any other sins you wish to confess?"

Ana bowed her head again. "Nay."

"Do you have true sorrow for your sins?"

"Aye." No doubt about that—she was writhing with shame inside. Offending God upset her greatly, especially here in His house. What an unworthy wretch she was.

"May Our Lord Jesus Christ, Son of the Almighty God, through His most gracious mercy absolve you. By His authority, I hereby absolve you of your sins so that you might stand pure of heart before the tribunal of Our Lord, and so that you might have eternal life. In the name of the Father . . ." She saw the dim shadow of his blessing on the granite floor. "And of the Son . . ." A second blessing. "And of the Holy Spirit . . ." And a third. "Amen."

"Amen."

"You may now do penance—recite two dozen Lord's Prayers."

He stepped away, leaving her on her knees before the linen-draped altar and its jeweled golden rood. She clasped her hands together and bowed her head. There she remained, praying to the Lord God, until her knees ached with more ferocity than her guilt. An hour. Perhaps longer.

Then she rose to her feet with a wince.

"Be aware, Goodhealer . . ."

Ana turned to face the friar, who now sat at a small pine table with a quill in hand, inscribing records on a thick sheaf of parchment.

". . . that absolution is only granted for sins that are confessed."

"Of course, Brother Colban." What else was she to say?

He laid the quill on his desk and stood. The heavy white silk of his vestments rippled in the candlelight. "I sense great turmoil within you, Goodhealer. I am not convinced that said turmoil has been stirred by evil, but it does concern me. Dark thoughts are an invitation to the devil."

Ana suddenly found it difficult to draw air. Her throat was tight and dry. "I—"

"Daily prayer is a necessity."

"I pray each and every morn, Brother Colban," she assured him hoarsely.

His hard blue eyes bored into her. "You think the devil is so easily dissuaded? Nay. Once he has claimed a corner of your soul, he'll move heaven and earth to claim it all. You must pray here in the kirk, where I can direct your words to God. And you must bend the knee for Vespers as well as Lauds. Sext, too, if necessary. Banish the dark taint before it consumes you."

Pray *three* times a day? "My time is not my own, I fear. The baron has asked me to tend his wife at every meal."

"If you will not pray, then the end is already written." He raised the wooden crucifix dangling from his belt to his lips. "May God have mercy on your soul."

"I will most assuredly pray," Ana said quietly. The blackfriar could either be her downfall or her most powerful ally. It was up to her to determine which he would be. "But forgive me, Brother Colban, I cannot always supplicate when the kirk bell tolls."

"Your everlasting life is at risk, Goodhealer. Prove your worthiness."

There was no leniency in the man's expression. None at all. Did he not understand the demands on her time? "People fall ill when they do, and bairns meet the world at the hours of the Lord's choosing, not my own."

Her response earned her a narrowed stare. "God will forgive the delay."

But a dying villager or a breech babe would not. "I'll do what I can."

"That is insufficient," he said sharply. "Pray or be damned."

Ana felt the promise of his blessing slipping away. Yet, to have a hope of making Duthes her home—of growing the garden she'd vowed to plant—she needed it. "Then I will pray."

He smiled coldly. "Excellent. May God go with you, Goodhealer."

"And with you, Brother Colban."

Ana genuflected, then scurried from the kirk. What was she to do now? How could she live up to her promise to pray three times a day? If she missed even one prayer, Brother Colban would pounce upon her failing with self-righteous glee. He would accuse her of heathen leanings, of opening her heart and soul to Satan, and from there it was a short leap to allegations of witchcraft.

Although leaving Duthes was the last thing she wanted, it might be wise to prepare.

The hearth in the bothy was stone cold when Niall returned from the forest. He peered into the iron cauldron and wrinkled his nose at the congealed contents. Refusing the bawd bree had been an error. There was nary a scrap of meat to be seen in Ana's pottage—'twas naught but barley and beans. A man could not live on such meager fare. Apparently, the tales Wulf had told him of the fine eating a man enjoyed in the care of a wife were just that—tales. Crouching, he crumbled some dried peat into the pit beneath the cauldron, stacked some kindling, and lit the fire once more.

The peat was just beginning to catch flame when a thump came from the woodpile at the rear of the hut. Niall surged to his feet. Had the Norman sergeant returned to cause Ana more grief? If so, the cur would regret his decision. He slipped quietly out the door and rounded the corner in a flash, his dirk at the ready. A dark shape was shoving something between the split logs.

Swift as a northern wildcat, Niall attacked. He

rammed the intruder up against the woodpile using the full weight of his body and laid the sharp edge of his blade at the wretch's throat. "Explain yourself or die."

Even as the challenge left his tongue, however, he was rethinking his strategy—a soft gasp had escaped his captive's lips and a series of gentle, feminine curves met his press, not the vigorously taut muscles of a soldier. *Ana.*

He eased the dirk away from the tender flesh of her neck, but did not give anything else. The delicate scent of lavender filled his nostrils, sending a sweet rush of need to his loins—much as it had when he kissed her in the market. But as he considered her actions, his pleasure was swiftly dashed. She was hiding something. *From him.*

"What are you doing?" he demanded hoarsely.

"I—"

"No lies. I want the truth."

To which she said nothing.

He reached around her and yanked the item she'd been stuffing in the woodpile from her hands. A twill bag. Keeping her pinned against the wood with one knee between her legs, he tugged on the drawstring to open the sack and rummaged inside. Clothes. A comb. Several jars of unguent. A small iron box containing personal effects, which included a man's ring, carefully wrapped in a square of velvet. The vixen had lied to him. She was leaving.

"Dearest wife," he drawled, replacing the lid on the

box with a metallic snap. "Surely you weren't planning to run. You gave me your word."

"I am not running," she replied tightly. "I am simply preparing."

"A woolly word cannot disguise the truth of your actions."

She squirmed against him, and Niall suffered a fierce jolt of desire. Dear God, why *this* woman? Aye, she was beautiful, but she was also deceitful. Plotting behind his back. Ruining his well-laid plans. Worse, the wench might well have had a hand in the deaths of his clansmen—in the death of wee Hugh.

"I'll not explain myself," she said hotly. "I do what I must."

"As do I." He released her, and when she spun to face him, he tossed her the bag. Her linen brèid had slipped down, pooling around her neck and revealing a shimmering swathe of hair. Although the color he so admired was not discernible in the moonlight, Niall's fingers itched to touch the silken strands. But he held on to his sanity. "And you'll not enjoy the outcome."

She frowned. "What might that be?"

He didn't answer. Gripping her elbow, he tugged her back toward the door. She resisted, digging her heels into the dirt, but it was a futile rebellion. His strength easily exceeded hers. When the battle of wills grew tiresome, he threw an arm about her waist, lifted her feet off the ground, and carried her into the bothy.

"You have no right to abuse me so," she snarled, as

he put her down and shut the door. "You are *not* my husband."

He smiled coolly. "Feel free to make a complaint to the constable."

Her lips thinned.

Sadly, the pinch of her lips only made him want to kiss them into submission. But that would prove him a fool. The first kiss had nearly brought him to his knees in the market. His head had spun with the sheer intensity of his desire and he'd come dangerously close to spoiling his mission by tumbling her right there and then. But nothing could stand in the way of retrieving the necklace.

Nothing.

Scooping up the burlap pouch he'd brought with him from the camp, Niall dug inside for a length of hemp rope. "Hold out your hands."

"Your pardon?" She stared at the rope with dawning horror. "You can't mean to—"

"I surely do." He snatched the twill bag and tossed it on the bed. Then he gathered both her hands in one of his. "Your word is shite. Only a madman would trust you now."

"You will *not* tie me." She jerked to one side, trying to break free.

He held her easily. He looped the rope around her wrists and cinched it tight with one quick movement. But not too tight. No need to bruise her delicate skin. Then he drew her to the bed and tied the loose end to the post.

"Sit."

She glared at him, refusing to obey.

Shaking his head at her obstinance, he gave her a light shove.

She toppled onto the heather-filled mattress with a gurgle of purple-faced rage. "You filthy, wretched whoreson."

Surprisingly, those words still had the power to cut him. The wound was not deep, but it stung just the same. "Insult my mother if it eases you, but 'twill not change your fate."

"Only a sorry excuse for a man would tie a woman down."

He arched a brow. "Only a sorry excuse for a woman would renounce her word."

Shame accomplished what force could not. Her gaze fell and her furious color abated. With her bottom lip nipped between her teeth and conviction furrowing her brow, she wriggled to a sitting position on the edge of the bed. The awkward movements gave him an excellent, if temporary, view of her ankles. Slim and pale, much like her wrists. He found himself disappointed when the layers of her skirts hid them once more.

"How will I prepare supper if I'm bound to the bed?"

He shrugged. "The soup heats as we speak."

"I cannot hold a bowl."

"Then I'll hold it for you."

Color returned to her cheeks. "You mean to feed me like a wee bairn?"

The answer to that was obvious, so he turned to stir the soup. A savory scent rose from the cauldron as the fat melted and thick gravy formed around the vegetables. Perhaps the meal would be bearable after all.

"I was *not* leaving."

"Not the now," he agreed. "Later, when all were abed."

"Nay," she protested. "I would not abandon the baroness. Not unless I had no choice."

"And what circumstance would drive you to that end, pray tell? A stranger masquerading as your husband? A blackguard threatening to expose your past? A fiend strapping you to the bed?"

"A madman bent on setting fire to my soul."

A quick glance confirmed she was serious. "The priest?"

"Aye."

"Why would he wish such a fate on you?"

"He thinks I pray to the heathen gods."

Niall had encountered several zealous clerics in his time—robed devotees who railed against his Pict heritage and scorned his heathen rituals. It was easy enough to imagine a blackfriar harrying a healer for any successes that were not directly linked to Christian prayer. *Too* easy, in truth. The vixen was a skilled liar. 'Twas far more likely she'd crafted the tale to stir his sympathy and evoke her release.

Using Ana's only clay bowl, he scooped up some bubbling soup. He fished a hazelwood spoon from the pouch at his belt, then crossed the room and sank to a crouch at her knee. Raising the broth-brimmed spoon to her lips, he bid her, "Eat."

Her chin lifted with foolish pride, and she tightened her lips, refusing his offering.

Niall shook his head. "Are you not the one who said, *Better a pinch of shame than an empty stomach*?"

"I'll not eat while I'm bound like cattle in my own home."

"Then you'll go hungry," he said, rising to full height. The savory smell of the food stirred a growl from his belly, and without further ado, he proceeded to empty the bowl in front of her. Despite the sorry lack of meat and an overabundance of onions, which he detested, it was a fine stew.

She watched him consume every bite, even licked her lips as he spooned the last of the broth into his mouth. But when he held out the bowl and arched a questioning brow at her, she turned her head. Stubborn lass. She'd endure the night on an empty stomach.

Niall swung the cauldron away from the flames burning in the pit and blew out the candle. The firelight cast a subtle golden glow around the room, drawing unnecessary attention to the feminine slopes of Ana's body. He frowned. He needed no encouragement to imagine her curves beneath his hands—those thoughts already hounded him incessantly. As he approached the bed, she launched from her perch like a wild bird on a jess, yanking at her tether.

"Tie me if you will, beat me if you must, but I'll ne'er submit willingly."

He grabbed her hands. Stroking her lightly with his thumbs, he calmed her like he would a new hawk—with quiet words and a gentle touch. "Cease. You injure yourself for naught. I'm not a man to force himself upon a reluctant maid."

She ceased her struggles, but her eyes remained wary.

"If you submit," he said, "I assure you, it *will* be willingly."

With a snort of disbelief, she slid to the packed dirt floor next to the bedpost.

He untied his belt and tugged his lèine over his head. Ana averted her gaze from his body as he dropped to the mattress and removed his boots. A single threadbare blanket lay folded on the bed. Niall tossed it and his heavy winter cloak over Ana's shoulders, then reclined on the heather mattress. Having slept in the open forest on many a frigid winter night, he was content with the heat of a contained fire and a roof over his head. A blanket was a luxury.

Clad only in his braes, his hands pillowing his head, he stared up at the thatched roof. What had he done to offend the gods? Something dire, to be sure. To send him a woman of rare beauty and courage, who stirred his blood and his imagination as few women had done before, and then give her a duplicitous soul, that was cruel punishment.

He'd had his fill of untrustworthy women.

But that didn't make it any easier to lie there. Not with her soft, warm body lying mere inches from his fingers. Not with her gentle breaths sighing in his ear. Not with her sweet fragrance filling his nose. Cruel punishment indeed.

Niall forced his eyes to close.

Sleep might not come easy, but it *would* come.

When the cadence of Niall's breathing fell into a deep, regular pattern, Ana began to work on the knot of the rope in earnest. If the wretch thought she would sit here all night, cowering under the blanket like a chastened child, he was sadly mistaken.

Unfortunately, the knot lay neatly between her wrists, making it impossible to reach with her fingers. So, she tackled the rope with her teeth. But even that wasn't easy—whatever else she might disparage about him, Niall could tie a fine knot. The blasted rope refused to loosen.

Ana resisted a growl of frustration and kept at it.

Even if it took her hours, she was determined to get free.

As luck would have it, it did not take her hours. Although the movement sorely abraded her wrists, she gradually twisted her hands, opening the knot to her teeth. Finally able to gain purchase, she chewed at the rope until one end was free. After that, it took only minutes to untie her leash.

She was just about to spring to her feet and make her escape when a large, heavily muscled arm encircled her waist, hoisted her onto the bed, and shackled her. Not to the bed this time, to his body. Ana struggled, but her labors were in vain. There was not an ounce of give in his hold.

"Let me go."

"Nay."

She clawed at his bare arm. "I will not rest until I am free."

"Then you will greet the day with bleary eyes."

"As will you," she promised hotly. "I will happily see you sleepless as I work to get free."

"You'll not enjoy my company should you rob me of rest, lass."

"I care not. Your company is already unbearable."

With a heavy sigh, Niall tucked her tightly against him, threw a leg over hers, and leaned into her. Just like that, she was effectively pinned. His body pressed her into the mattress, his weight like warm steel.

"Sleep," he murmured into her hair.

Ana stared at the fire in the pit, barely able to breathe. Not because his weight was excessive—he'd put just enough of his body over hers to stop her from moving—but because she could feel every inch of him along her back and legs. And the glimpse she'd gotten of him as he settled for the night had scorched a permanent portrait in her thoughts: dark blue symbols tattooed across his left shoulder, a rippled belly, and narrow hips. Every muscle was exquisitely carved from silk and stone, every limb a perfect blend of power and grace. She'd never seen a man so braw.

Did he truly believe she could slumber in his arms? Impossible.

She couldn't deny the comfort provided by the heat of his body, however. An hour spent on the inhospitable dirt floor had chilled her rump and feet to the point of numbness. But as she lay cocooned in his embrace, the cold bite of winter fled with the swiftness of a humiliated foe—her icy flesh thawed and her shivers ceased. She had the strangest urge to press herself deeper into his arms—to take full advantage of the protection he was offering—but she dared not move. His breaths, now softly fluttering the hairs behind her left ear, had slowed again. Moving would surely rouse him, and Ana much preferred the sleeping giant to the bitter knight.

At the moment, his only interest was rest. If he woke fully and grew conscious of the feminine curves pressed into his groin, he might change his mind about forcing an unwilling maid. With any luck, his grasp on her would ease during the night, and she'd be free before such awareness took hold.

All she had to do was remain awake until her opportunity arose.

Given her fierce determination to be free, that should pose no problem.

Niall woke to the sound of a barely discernible whimper.

It was still dark in the hut, and his right arm felt as if a thousand pins were poking his flesh. Ana lay in his arms, her sweet form fitted perfectly to his, but her sleep was not restful. A shudder rocked her body, and she murmured something unintelligible. Something that sounded like a protest.

He frowned.

Was she reliving the night he'd abandoned her in the forest? The night she'd been chased by a Lochurkie guard and injured her head? That scar would forever serve as a reminder of how he'd failed her.

"Nay," Ana murmured, jerking.

He gathered her closer, ignoring the uncomfortable heaviness of his arm and the voice in his head that called her *enemy*. "Hush, lass. You're safe. The wretch is long gone."

She collapsed against his chest with a sigh, and Niall felt a moment's satisfaction. But then she gripped his forearm, her nails digging deeply, and she cried quite distinctly, "Mother! Oh, gods, nay! *Nay!*"

The last word extended into a low keen of despair and Niall felt her pain vibrate though his body. Unfamiliar with the ways of comforting a woman, he simply continued to hold her tight, all the while gently rubbing her back and kissing the top of her head.

Eventually, the nightmare faded. The stiffness left her limbs and her breathing evened.

Niall held her until he was certain she had regained a peaceful slumber, and then he eased from her side and rolled off the bed. *Hellfire*. He'd known it would be a mistake to touch her, but he hadn't guessed just how serious it would be. Holding her in his arms had felt unbelievably *right*, like a gaping hole in his gut had been filled.

Flexing his hand to revive it, he studied the woman on the mattress, trying with all his might to harden his heart. She was *not* the bonnie, courageous lass he insisted on seeing. Everything pointed to her involvement in the devastation of his clan—her presence in Duthes, her knowledge of poisons, her survival against unbelievable odds—so why did he continue to desire her with all the fury of a Highland tempest?

It made no sense.

He was generally impervious to the wiles of women.

But from the moment he first laid eyes on her, something about Ana had stirred him. Rescuing her had not been his intent, but once he looked down upon her beautiful, bone-thin face, he'd been unable to turn away. And afterward, as they ran for the forest, her quiet determination to press on in spite of pain and weariness and trembling illness had impressed him to no end. He knew big, strapping men who would have dropped under such conditions.

He turned away.

Damn, he was doing it again. Her waiflike appearance in the dungeon had likely been a ruse, which meant she was hale and hearty that night, not infirm. Putting another peat brick on the fire, he summoned his memories of Lochurkie. Truth be told, though, if her frailty had been a ruse, it'd been a bloody good one. Hauling her up the dungeon steps had demanded little effort—she'd weighed no more than a goose down pillow.

But he couldn't deny she'd been plotting to run this eve.

If she succeeded in leaving, his ability to enter the manor uncontested would vanish along with her—an unacceptable circumstance. Yet, come morning, he'd have no choice but to set her free. She couldn't tend to her patients with a rope about her wrists. How then would he keep her in the village? Reveal his interest in the necklace and allege a willingness to share the prize?

Nay. The fewer people who knew his intentions, the better. He knew too little of Ana's roots to trust her with even that much. Who knew what affiliations she had? She might well be in league with the brigands in the woods. He needed something less revealing. A possession, perhaps, that she couldn't bear to part with.

He glanced over his shoulder.

Her twill sack lay crumpled in a heap at the end of the bed.

What about the items in her metal box? Given the care with which it was wrapped, wasn't it likely the ring held a personal appeal to her? Even if it held no sentimental value, a gold ring set with a sapphire would surely be her most worthy possession. Would it be enough to hold her?

Only the morning would tell.

He glanced up through the chimney hole in the roof. Stars winked from a sky black as coal. The moment of truth was still several hours away—which meant he should return to the bed, or prepare to spend the remainder of the night on the floor. One option held infinitely more charm than the other, but he grabbed his burlap satchel to use as a pillow and settled himself on the floor next to the bed.

Resistance always strengthened the steel.

Chapter 6

"What name does the friar go by?"

Ana groggily opened her eyes. Niall was staring at her from the other side of the fire pit. The handsome wretch was now fully attired and devouring another piece of her precious round of cheese. Exhausted by a less than restful night, she yawned and stretched, surprised to find her hands free. Had he left her free all night? Had she slept through her best chance of escape? "What does it matter?" she grumbled as she sat up.

He tossed her the rest of the cheese. "I intend to speak with him."

"About what?"

"Among other things, his inappropriate comments to my wife."

She blinked at him. *Take a holy man to task for inappropriate comments? Is he mad?* "You'll only raise his ire."

"Worry not. How shall I address him?"

"Brother Colban." Ana nibbled on the piquant yellow cheese. Would he leave her alone while he visited with the friar? Would she get an opportunity to free herself? She got her answer a moment later, when Niall crossed the room to collect his cloak from the bed.

"I'll be gone a wee while. I expect you to still be in Duthes when I return."

"What you expect and what actually occurs may be two very different things."

He pinned her gaze with his. "Leave and you'll forfeit this."

He held something up in his hand, and she saw the glint of gold.

Spying her father's heavy gold band in his hand was a punch to her gut. Foolish girl. Why had she dug the box from beneath the bothy wall? It had been safely hidden there. Why hadn't she left it alone until the day she ran? *Because it was all she had left to remember her da.* Leaving it behind was impossible to contemplate. Somehow, Niall had guessed that.

Still, he couldn't know precisely what it meant to her. He couldn't know what memories were attached to it. Nor did she ever want him to learn.

"Losing the ring would be a blow," she acknowledged, smiling ruefully. "It's the only item of any value ever traded to me for my services."

His eyes narrowed. "From whom did you get it?"

"A wealthy merchant in Aberdeen. He offered the ring to me in exchange for saving his life. Poor sot fell under the wheel of a fully loaded wagon." Ana crossed her fingers and hid them behind her skirts. She was a terrible liar. Her only salvation was that this story closely mimicked the truth. Her father had indeed been injured by a wagon in Aberdeen, and she had indeed healed him. But that wasn't the day he gave her the ring.

Niall stared at her.

It took every bit of courage Ana possessed not to squirm under his intense gaze. Could he see the lie blazing in her eyes? Could he sense the fearful beat of her heart?

Apparently not. He tucked the ring into the pouch at his belt and said, "If you care to get it back, you'll remain faithful until I complete my task."

"Is your *task* likely to draw the attention of the constable?"

"Not if it's well done."

She frowned. "That's hardly reassuring."

"Just go about your business. Leave the worriment to me."

How Ana wished she could do just that—hand off her cares and forget about them. Were she an ordinary maid with uncomplicated troubles, it might be possible. But her burdens were not the sort to share. Life had already taught her that cruel lesson.

"Today, my business includes an open door after the Terce bell rings. The village poor are invited to seek my services at no charge the third Tuesday of every month."

He arched a brow. "A requirement of your tenancy?"

"My way of giving thanks for all I have."

His expression remained hard and difficult to read, yet Ana sensed her response surprised him. "Will you be visiting the baroness today?"

She slid off the bed, brushing out the wrinkles in her dress and adjusting her brat. Normally, she did not sleep in her clothes—she had too few gowns to be so careless—but changing into a night rail last eve had been fraught with peril. Not the least of which was a lack of privacy. "Aye, as soon as I've made myself presentable."

"You look lovely."

A quick glance confirmed he was serious. Rather intensely so. She lifted a hand to her hair. The tresses were as tangled as she feared. "I think your eyesight is failing you."

Retrieving her sack from the table against the far wall, Ana dug for her comb. She removed the brèid now pooled around her neck and unwound the leather thong at the end of her thick braid. Her hair was a nuisance, too straight to be attractive and too full to be easily tamed. Tugging the comb ruthlessly through the loosened braid, she made quick work of subduing the knotted strands. When she was done, her hair gleamed in the firelight like a sheet of fine silk.

She swiftly wove a fresh braid, retied the thong, and scooped up the brèid, prepared to cover her head once more.

"Wait," Niall said hoarsely.

Ana turned.

He no longer stood a safe distance away—only an

arm's length separated them. She knew not how to interpret the look on his face, but it made her heart beat faster. The first word that came to her mind was *hunger*. As one moment passed in silence, and then another, Ana sensed it was not the inches that kept them apart, but the sheer strength of Niall's will.

Her gaze, unbidden, dropped to his lips. They were the finest she'd ever seen on a man—firm and wide, with just a dash of sinful curve in the upper one. *Would he kiss her again? And if he did, how should she respond?*

The first kiss had been a simple press of flesh. Definitely intriguing, but the full impact had been lost to the shock of the moment—the curious crowd, his dramatic claim, her choking fear. By the time her wits settled, it was over.

She lifted her gaze, hoping the primitive burn of desire in his eyes had faded.

It had not. If anything, her study of his lips had fueled it to a white-hot blaze.

Ana swallowed thickly. An odd feeling of melting from the inside besieged her. Her belly grew warm, and her chest insisted on drawing inadequate, shallow breaths. Conveniently forgetting the bevy of heart-rending mistakes she'd made in the past, her body was urging her to make one more.

And it was all too tempting to yield.

Fortunately, Niall's willpower exceeded her own. He did not kiss her. With a sight more composure than she would have guessed, he reached out and pulled a small piece of bark from her hair.

She watched the wood chip float to the ground. This outcome was better. *Absolutely.* There was no room in her life for a man, handsome as the devil or not. She gave him a wide berth as she set sail toward the door. Grabbing her healer's pouch, she gave him the barest of nods. "I'll return anon."

"Ana."

Her pulse skittered at the husky timbre of his voice. An unfair weapon, that. She paused, hand on the door latch. Slowly, she swiveled to face him. "Aye?"

All suggestion of barely contained passion had been wiped from his expression. His eyes were once again polished, flat stones. "Wait for me at the manor. I'll accompany you home."

"That's a needless courtesy," she said, shaking her head. "I travel hither and yon every day without an escort."

"You were a widow then. Now you're a wife."

Although principle demanded she remind him that their marriage was a ruse, Ana erred on the side of caution. The danger had passed. Why poke a slumbering badger? There would be plenty of time to test his temper when next they blew out the candle.

She nodded. "I'll wait."

Then she turned tail and ran.

Morning prayers were over when Niall reached the village square, but the last stragglers had yet to depart the chapel. He lingered outside for a few moments, but the wait swiftly grew tiresome. Spying a pair of hands working in the nearby stables and knowing the quickest way into their good regards was to ease their lot, he picked up a shovel and mucked out a stall. Once the smiles broke out and the joking began, he carefully guided the conversation to the weeks following Lochurkie's death.

Unfortunately, his efforts were wasted. The lads could not recall any visitors to the manor prior to the Yule festivities, save for a caravan of traveling merchants.

The sun crept higher in the sky, and Niall glanced toward the kirk. No one had come or gone from the small stone building in some time. The friar was finally alone. He hung up his shovel, nodded his farewells to the stable hands, and stepped inside.

The thin-faced friar was seated at a small pine desk close to the door, a quill in hand and a sheaf of parchment on the table before him. As the village record keeper, he was responsible for noting all events of consequence including marriages, births, and deaths. Head down, seemingly engrossed in his task, the holy man failed to acknowledge Niall's arrival.

After the long wait outside, Niall's patience had run thin. He nudged the leg of the table with his boot, rattling the ink pot.

"Brother Colban, is it?"

About to apply ink to parchment, the priest paused. He waited for the table to cease wobbling, then scripted a word with strong sure strokes. When his ink ran dry, he looked up. "I am." His cool gaze ran from Niall's unshaven face to his scuffed boots, a frown rising to his brow. "And you are?"

Niall offered a grimy hand. "Robbie Bisset, husband of Ana Bisset."

"Ah, that explains the unfamiliar face." The friar hesitated briefly, then met him palm to palm. "Welcome to Duthes, goodman. How can I assist you?"

"I've come to discuss my wife."

"Oh?"

"She says she was here last eve, praying in the kirk."

The friar stared at him for a long moment. "Do you have cause to doubt her?"

Niall snorted. "I've been absent from her bed nigh on eight months, and whilst I was gone, she received word I was dead. The better question might be: Do I have reason to trust her?"

"You fear she may have found another in your absence?"

Niall straightened his shoulders and drew in a full chest of air. "Aye. Though it best not be true."

Even in the face of Niall's bristling might, the friar did not sit back. A confidence born of his important position held him steady. No one would dare attack the village friar. "I cannot speak for the entirety of her time, but I *can* attest to her presence in the kirk last night. She prayed here for some time."

"She also swears you demanded she bend the knee every spare moment."

"I did."

Niall shook his head. "I'm a great believer in the

sanctity of prayer, Brother Colban, but I cannot permit that."

A heavy frown settled on the friar's brow. "Her soul is at risk, goodman."

"That may be so," Niall said. "But a man must be the master of his own house. Whilst my wife is here praying, there's no food on the table, no mending of my clothes, no chores done about the bothy."

"Surely you would make a small sacrifice to save her soul?"

"Nay. Not the now. My house is in shambles. Ana has been without the guidance of a husband for too long, and she's inappropriately willful. I must curb her wayward spirit or face the rest of my days with a brazen chit." Not all of that was a lie. *Willful* was scarcely a strong enough word to describe Ana. "The Lord values a submissive wife, does he not?"

Friar Colban nodded. "Indeed, he does. *Wives, submit to your husbands, as is fitting in the Lord.*"

"Well, then—"

The wide beam of sunlight cast through the open door flickered, and a sweaty, soot-covered lad ran into the chapel. "*Fire!* There's a fire in the kitchens, Friar!"

So unexpected was the interruption, that the friar simply stood there for a moment, stunned.

Niall stepped into the breach. Dunstoras had once been gutted by fire. It had occurred long before Niall's birth, but sooty reminders of the devastation remained on the granite stones to this day—and nine lives had been lost. If Duthes Manor was to escape a similar fate, every hand and every bucket would be needed. "Ring the bell backward," he ordered the holy man.

The friar jumped up from his stool and raced for the bell tower steps.

To the young lad, Niall said, "Off to the garrison with you. Round up every able body."

The boy left the kirk at a run, and Niall followed, dashing for the well. In the courtyard, fat plumes of dark gray smoke oozed from the rectangular kitchen entrance, but as yet no flames were visible.

"Find every bucket you can, lads!" he yelled to the gawking stable hands. "Hurry now."

As he reached the well, the kirk bell began to toll out the chimes—in reverse order—sounding the alarm. Niall grabbed the wooden handle and swiftly cranked the bucket up from the depths of the well. He poured the water into a pail held by one of the stable boys and immediately dropped the well bucket back down the hole. The first lad ran off toward the kitchen, replaced by another. As more men arrived to help, Niall said crisply, "Form a line. Pass the buckets from one man to another."

Again and again he pulled up a full load of water and poured it into a waiting pail. He favored speed over accuracy and ignored the water that sloshed over his clothes and boots. Before long, his lèine was soaked clear through. His shoulders ached with the strain, but he did not allow throbbing muscles to slow him down— too many lives were at stake.

The trail of buckets doubled up, snaking toward the kitchen door, as more villeins and guards joined the effort. Full buckets went down one side, empty buckets returned up the other. Niall had no time to check on their success. Exhaustion crept upon him. Another man took over the dumping of the bucket into the pails, which eased his efforts considerably, but even so, his shoulders began to tremble. Blisters rose on his hands, filled with fluid, and tore open on the wooden handle of the crank.

Niall gritted his teeth, pushed the pain to the back of his thoughts, and pressed on.

He cranked up another bucket, the weight of which seemed to equal that of a full-grown man. Just before it reached the top of the well, his hands slipped on the crank, and the bucket plummeted. Fingers numb, it took all his concentration to squeeze the handle and halt the bucket's drop, but he succeeded.

Another man—the wheelwright or the blacksmith, judging by his large arms—nudged him aside and took over the crank. "Fine job," he said gruffly. "Away with you now."

Niall stepped back.

Finally able to think beyond how quickly he could draw the next bucket, he glanced at the kitchen. The smoke rising into the sky had thinned to a thin, pale ribbon.

"Let me see those hands."

He spun around. Ana stood next to him, a dark streak of soot smudged across her cheek and a faint gray tint to her normally white brèid. She was paler than he'd ever seen her. He frowned. "Are you ill?"

"Nay."

"Where were you when the fire broke out?"

She opened her leather satchel and dug inside for a small earthenware pot stopped with melted wax. "Inside."

"Where inside?"

"Does it matter?"

He grabbed her chin and angled her face toward the sun, checking for any hint of injury. Beyond the soot, thankfully, he saw nothing. He released her. "Aye, it matters. Answer me."

"I was consulting with the cook."

"In the *kitchen*?"

"Of course, in the kitchen." Using her knife, she pried the wax from the pot. Then she took one of his hands in her much smaller palm, unfolded his fist, and slathered unguent on his red, raw blisters. Her hands trembled as she worked. "Where else does one meet with the cook?"

The image of her running blindly through a smoke-filled corridor, chased by fire and choking on hot fumes, flayed his thoughts. He'd imagined her safe in the upper chambers with the baroness all this time, not fleeing for her life. "You are a healer, not a scullion. What in God's eternal glory possessed you to enter the kitchen?"

She shrugged. "I am tasked with ensuring the baroness eats well."

"The cook should attend you, not the other way around. Do not go into the kitchen again."

"The cook owes me no service," she responded with a frown. "He's a busy man and, frankly, all credit for my safety rightfully belongs to him. He hustled me out the instant he realized there was a problem."

At least there was one person with proper sense. "What happened?"

"One of the kitchen hands dropped a pot of oil near the ovens and it caught flame. Don't worry. The lad is fine," she said, applying the same thick paste to his other hand. "He was wearing shoes. Only his ankles were burned and not too severely. The half-wit who threw water on the flaming oil is a mite worse off."

A very prosaic description of events. Were it not for the quaver in her voice, he might have believed her completely unaffected. But she'd been frightened. And he didn't like that. "Are you certain you're well?"

"Aye. Just a wee disquieted." She massaged the unguent into his flesh. "Fires can have dire consequences."

"That they can."

Niall tugged his hands free. His pulse ought to have slowed by now—instead, every touch of her fingers set it aleap again. "How far did the fire reach?"

"'Twas contained to the lower level, but the smoke is everywhere. The baron's men are in the cellars now, assessing the damage."

A rivulet of sweat trickled down Niall's brow, and he wiped it with his sleeve. *Damn.* Even if the scorching were minimal, repairs would take some time. It might be days before he could safely make an attempt to open the lock. Days he could ill afford to lose.

"I must see the steward. I'll volunteer to help."

"You've done enough *helping* for today," she said. "Those hands need care."

Niall glanced at his palms. They hurt, but no more than if he'd fought a lengthy battle with his sword and targe in hand. "Save your charity for those who need it. The wounds are trifling."

Heaving a sigh, Ana thrust the pot of unguent at his midriff. "Apply it frequently. You'll thank me in the morn when you spread your hands." Then she turned to walk away.

Niall reached for her arm, but stopped himself just short of touching her sleeve. The unguent would sully her linens. "Where do you go?"

Pausing, she pointed to the leafless rowan tree behind the chapel. On the stone bench beneath its gnarled branches sat four soot-covered kitchen workers, each favoring an injured limb. "There are other, more grateful, souls in distress."

Niall's gaze slid to the open kirk door, where Brother Colban stood welcoming the faithful for midmorning prayers. The friar would have a full house today. A near disaster was a powerful reminder to get one's affairs in order. Had he convinced the holy man to leave Ana alone? It was impossible to know for certain, with their discussion cut short.

"Fetch me when you're done," he said to Ana. "I'll be in the cellars."

"I can make my own way home," she responded.

Unwilling to address her back, he stalked around to

look her in the eye. "Did I not make myself clear? My wife does not walk alone while I am able to escort her."

"Why bother with such niceties? Once you are gone—"

Niall bristled. His mind refused to contemplate life after he acquired the necklace. "I decide the rules of the game, not you. Fetch me, or you'll face my wrath."

"You, goodman, are a tyrant."

He feathered his thumb over the flushed crest of her cheek. "And you, goodwife, are a wayward lass in want of a firm hand."

A storm gathered in her blue eyes. "You would dare to strike me?"

"Nay," he said softly. "I mean this sort of firm hand." And then he kissed her.

Ana wasn't prepared for a kiss. This morning, aye. Now? In the middle of the manor courtyard, with both of them smelling thickly of smoke? Nay.

Especially as it wasn't an ordinary kiss.

Ordinary kisses were meaningless—she knew them as a man's paltry offering to a woman he was determined to bed. Pleasurable, but lamentably short-lived. All too swiftly, an eager swain lost interest in a woman's lips and migrated his attention to another part of her body. Niall's kiss was different. It was a full-on siege of her senses that focused completely on her mouth. He kissed her as if nothing else in the world mattered beyond this one moment, this one heartbeat, this one connection of their lips.

It began softly, like a brush of velvet over her skin, and every inch of her body instantly came alive. He touched nothing but her lips, but the ripples went everywhere, in a thousand different directions, each one a promise of untold physical delight. Seeking more of the same, she tilted her head up. And just like that, nothing about the kiss was gentle. His claim became fierce and his tongue boldly swept across her lips in an undeniable demand for surrender.

But even as her lips bruised under the relentless pressure, desire—hot and aching—flooded her veins. Restless need and tingling urges besieged her womanly parts. Her breasts grew full and achy. Knees weak, she sagged against his steadfast chest, her hands clutching the front of his damp lèine. She opened her mouth and welcomed him in.

He responded with a low, barely audible groan and a slight stiffening of his body—almost as if he were fighting a primitive urge to toss her over his shoulder and abscond with her. But if that was his desire, he did not act on it.

With surprising tenderness, he broke off the kiss.

They leaned, forehead to forehead, for a moment. Neither of them was breathing easy.

Lips throbbing, face scalding, Ana took a step back and glanced around to see if anyone in the courtyard had made note of their highly inappropriate embrace. She met several amused faces, but none of them belonged to the friar, thank heaven. The holy man had disappeared inside the kirk.

Her gaze returned to Niall, whose face was now a study in inscrutability. How could he look so cool and calm, when she was shattered into pieces?

"Fetch me when you're done," he said.

Then he walked away.

Ana watched him duck under the blackened lintel of the kitchen entrance and disappear. Her lips were eagerly anticipating the moment when her tasks were complete and she could seek him out again. But deep in her belly, a tight knot of anxiety fought with her desire.

Playacting as wife was one thing; succumbing to the ruse, quite another.

Wedded bliss was not for her. Her parents' lives had been destroyed by the healing gift. Her mother had met a cruel end, that was certain. But her father's suffering hadn't ended there—haunted by his memories and fearful that his daughter would meet a similar fate, he had never stopped running, never found peace. He had died a broken man. A devout Christian from a proud family, he should be interred on holy ground. Instead, he was buried along the side of a mountain road in an unmarked grave. Ana's eyes stung, and she rubbed them.

There could be no future with Niall, other than heartbreak. She had to remember that.

Such was the curse of the healing gift. *Nothing came for free.*

Chapter 7

A piece of parchment was nailed to the pillory post in the center of the town square.

Aiden squinted at the fluttering edges, trying to make out the words inked on the weathered notice, but at this distance his eyesight failed him. Did the notice concern him and his escape? Offer a reward for his capture? Three months after the deed, it hardly seemed likely, but he wasn't willing to venture any closer to find out. The pillory was currently empty, and he intended to see it remained that way.

"There she is," whispered Duncan.

Aiden glanced left. Sure enough, a small entourage had passed through the castle gate and turned in their direction—a pair of women accompanied by a gilt-spurred knight and two armed guards. The younger of the two women wore a dark blue cloak. A deep, sable-trimmed hood hid her silvery-blond hair, but Aiden knew her just the same: Isabail Grant, the former earl's sister.

Playing the role of lady of the manor to the hilt, she

nodded graciously to the villagers as she passed, even addressing a few by name. Pale skinned and delicate as a snowflake, she resembled her brother in only the smallest of ways—the ease with which she wore the mantle of nobility and the natural elegance she displayed in every step.

He frowned.

Had he another option, he'd never ensnare a woman in his intrigues. Unfortunately, Isabail was his only connection to the man in black. She would have personally greeted every guest who slept under her brother's roof and ensured their comfort was well met. She *had* to know who her brother had kept company with those days.

"Engaging her will not be easy," Graeme said.

Aiden nodded. "For now, we simply follow. Wait for the right opportunity."

"How long can we afford to bide our time?"

"Two days, three at the most," Aiden responded. "Naming the thief will not be enough to convince the king of my innocence. I'll need proof that the man in the wolf cloak stole the necklace."

"What proof can we present?"

Aiden's gaze fell to the hoof-chipped cobbles under his feet. The mere mention of that night soured his belly. The horror of finding Elen and wee Hugh lying on the floor in a pool of vomitus never left him. *His* family, *his* kin, and he'd been powerless to save them. The poison had been in the eel soup, the fourth of sixteen courses the cook had prepared for their honored guest, Henry de Coleville. He knew that, because the soup was the only course he had not sampled, and it wasn't long after the soup was served that bodies began to fall. The very young and the very old were the first to stagger and convulse.

Aiden straightened his shoulders against the weight of his shame. He'd let down his clan that night, most severely. He'd passed the miserable cur in the corridor leading to the kitchens and failed to confront him. True, it had been before his kin fell ill, but still . . .

"I cannot say," he admitted.

"Then how will we prove his complicity?"

His hands formed heavy fists. "When we find the wretch, we'll force him to confess."

The other two men were silent. Like Niall, they had doubts that the man in the black cloak existed. Understandable, perhaps, given the severe beating he'd taken, but shortsighted. The theft of the necklace could not have been the act of a solitary thief in the night—it had been planned and executed to devastating effect.

"They're headed for the orchard," Duncan said. "Should we follow?"

Aiden shook his head. "Three strangers trailing in her shadow will surely alert the guards. We'll split up. You two see what information you can gather at the Crimson Kettle."

The expressions on Duncan and Graeme lightened. An evening at the alehouse with a pint in hand would be an easy one to pass.

"Rent us a room," Aiden said. "I'll meet you there when all is done."

The two warriors nodded and crossed the lane.

Aiden followed Isabail Grant, keeping enough distance to appear uninterested, but not so far that he couldn't see what she was about. When it was clear her destination was indeed the orchard, he circled around and threaded through the barren apple trees from the other side. Pretending to examine the trees, he was able to get within two rows of Lady Isabail and her party without drawing their gaze. His view was at an angle, partly obscured by tree trunks. Conveniently, a strong westerly wind carried their conversation to his ears.

"So, the rumors are true then?" Isabail asked her companion knight. The breeze whipped her cloak away from her body, and she tucked it closer. "Queen Yolande is quick with child?"

The sandy-haired soldier shrugged. "That is certainly the talk. She has withdrawn to Kinghorn with an entourage that includes a midwife, and the king has spared no expense to ensure her comfort."

"I'll pray that it is so," Isabail said. "We're in sore need of a royal prince. Such a shame that all three of Alexander's heirs passed so young. And what news of my petition?"

"The king has been in Ross these past weeks. He has not yet made his decision."

"But he'll make it soon?"

"At next decree, I'm told."

The young woman frowned. "Why would it be a weighty call? Who has a better claim than I?"

The knight offered his hand as they navigated a muddy patch of ground. "The Comyns insist the land rightfully belongs to them."

Isabail snatched back her hand, anger evident in the red stains upon her cheeks. "Based on what? We border the land to the northeast, while the Comyns would need to cross the Red Mountains to reach it. There is—"

She said something further, but only the angry tone reached Aiden's ears—the words were lost to the wind. He edged closer. Using his hunting knife, he pried a small piece of bark from the tree in front of him and peered at it, frowning.

"My claim is far superior," insisted Isabail. "It's only right that Dunstoras be granted to me in recompense. The miserable wretch murdered my brother."

Aiden jerked, slicing his thumb on the blade. *He* murdered her brother?

"If I could see him into hell myself, I would," she added. "MacCurran deserves to burn. His men freed the murderess along with their leader that night. No coincidence, I say. It's clear they were working in concert. Only the lowest of lowborn curs would murder a good man—a respected peer of the realm—to acquire a blood jewel."

"The king also mourns the loss of Henry de Coleville," the knight reminded her. He bowed and extended an arm to suggest she lead the procession forward through the grove once more. "And he must cultivate the alliances that best serve Scotland."

"That's the value of my petition," Isabail said, her eyes lighting with excitement. "If he sides with me, he can kill two pigeons with a single arrow. I can—" As they advanced down the row, the wind lifted her words away.

Eager to hear her intentions, Aiden wove between the trees, catching up the distance. But as he rounded a third gray trunk, he came face-to-face with the shiny tip of a guard's spear. A burly fellow draped in the Lochurkie colors of green and black—who moved with more grace than Aiden would have credited him— stood between him and Isabail's party.

"Name your business," the guard growled hollowly through his steel helm.

The man's hold on his weapon was careless, and it would have been easy to yank it from his hands. But as tempting as it was to teach the young pup a lesson, Aiden resisted. If he had indeed been charged with the earl's murder, getting caught in the man's domain would mean the noose for sure. No pleasant stay in the dungeon this time. Lochurkie's warden would be justified in seeing him hang.

"I meant no offense," he said, injecting a hint of nervous tremor into his voice. "I'm but a simple laborer, tasked with identifying trees tainted with black rot." He held up the piece of bark in his hand. "Like this."

The guard was wily. He made no attempt to inspect the bark—his gaze remained locked on Aiden's face. "And if you find it?"

Aiden had taken several turns about the Dunstoras orchards with Master Tam. He knew the basics of good tree management, thank heaven. "I'm to remove all infected wood, as well as any dead prunings and withered apples, to limit the spread."

The guard stared at Aiden through his helm for a long moment. Finally, he waved his spear. "Go on with you, then. Away from here."

"Thank you, sir."

Aiden spun on his heel and headed deeper into the grove. A rueful sigh escaped his lips. Hopefully, Duncan and Graeme had achieved greater success. He was no closer to finding his mysterious man in black and time was running out.

Niall toiled for hours in the cellar. Despite every effort, he was unable to rid himself of the sweet taste of Ana's lips or the searing burn in his blood. His desire for her had reached a near unbearable level.

He reminded himself repeatedly that she might be a murderess, but his gut refused to believe it, no matter how often he revisited the facts. Perhaps it was the obvious flush that rose to her cheeks whenever she lied, or the genuine concern that furrowed her brow as she tended to the injured. It might even be his memories of that night in Lochurkie, when a thin slip of a woman, her entire body atremble, had offered him a look of gut-wrenching gratitude that he did not deserve. The exact reason mattered not—he simply could not see Ana Bisset as the killer of children.

Which probably made him a fool.

As he raked scorched debris into a pile, clouds of fine black dust swirled into the air. Niall adjusted the linen scrap tied over his nose and mouth, but it was already soiled, and he coughed just the same. A thick layer of oily soot coated every inch of wall and ceiling, making it near impossible to avoid the grime.

It would take at least a sennight of solid work to set the cellars right. All around him, laborers hammered at blackened beams, carted out burnt refuse, and inventoried the remaining goods. But that was only the beginning. Once the destruction was cleared away, the repairs would start. Opportunities to pick the lock would be very rare indeed. Gaining entry to the coffers was going to require a spot of luck.

"No, no, no. I said take the undamaged goods up to the great hall." The perpetually frowning steward, Eadgar, stood on the bottom step, calling out orders and breathing into a now heavily soiled handkerchief. "Do not stack them on the floor."

The laborer obediently tossed his sack of apples over his shoulder and mounted the stairs.

Niall shoveled his pile of charred bits and chips into a pail. A very organized fellow, the steward. Aware of everything under his nose. Such a man would surely keep meticulous records, not unlike the friar. Notes on what goods were added into storage, what goods were lost, what goods were consumed. If such a notation existed for the necklace, he might be able to discover who had delivered the jewel to Duthes and prove Aiden innocent. Clearing his brother's name would be a huge victory. Well worth any additional risk.

But he did not have free run of the manor. An unfamiliar face, he would be swiftly exposed if he started wandering the upper levels in search of the steward's books.

"You, there!"

Niall glanced up.

Eadgar waved a hand at him. "Help those men remove the door."

Two workers were unhinging the heavy oak door to the armory, which had sustained serious damage. Propping his shovel against the stone wall, Niall leapt to help. Together, he and one of the other men maneuvered the inch-thick, iron-banded panel down the corridor and out through the kitchen into the courtyard. They dropped the door on a growing pile of burnt wood.

"Are you near done?"

Niall turned. Ana stood behind him, her leather pouch slung over one shoulder, a wary look in her eyes. Almost as if she feared he would snatch her to him and kiss her again. Niall almost smiled. The idea was very tempting, save for the wealth of soot that covered his body. He was in dire need of a bath.

"Aye," he said, pulling his linen mask down to take a deep breath of fresh air. The midday sun had made a valiant effort to warm the day. "The heavy work is complete. The maids and their brooms will finish the rest. Repairs will commence anon."

She nodded. "Let's away then."

"After I drink from the well."

"Can you not wait until we reach the bothy? I've water there."

Niall allowed his feet to answer her question. He crossed to the well and drew a bucket of fresh water. Although it was difficult to ignore the tapping of her foot on the packed dirt and her repeated heavy sighs, he drank his fill before turning back.

"You, lass, are too impatient by half."

"And *you* have no respect for the time of others."

He frowned. "Can a man not reward his labors with a cup of water?"

"Not the now."

Suddenly, the notion of kissing her wasn't nearly as appealing as paddling her arse. The woman was a nag. "I'll drink when I have the need."

"Och, by all means, drink until you are sated. Drink until the moon rises. Drink until the summer winds arrive. Because *your* needs far outweigh those of others."

He skewed her a hard stare. Her anger seemed excessive for such a small slight. "Who has stirred your ire so?"

"*You* have."

"Surely not. I've been occupied in the cellars these past few hours."

"Exactly."

His frowned deepened. "You speak in riddles."

"Not a quick-witted fellow, are you?" she said testily. "Did you forget that I'm promised to tend the village poor today?"

He had indeed forgotten, but her anger was still unwarranted. Taking her elbow, he guided her toward the manor gate. "You should have fetched me earlier."

"And how, pray tell, was I to do that? The guards would not let me inside the kitchen, and you chose not to come out."

"A message, perhaps?"

She snorted. "To do that, you need a willing body. I was told the work in the cellar was more important than any woman's concerns and to go about my business."

He glanced down at her. "And yet you waited for me."

A flush stole up her throat and into her cheeks. "More the fool, I."

That was a rabbit hole of a comment, if ever he heard one. Niall tightened his grip on her arm and guided Ana around a large gray pig standing in the middle of the road basking in the afternoon sunshine. "Can you read?"

"Aye, my father taught me. Why do you ask?"

The tension in Niall's gut eased. Reading the steward's books would be much easier than stealing them. Of course, relying on her to aid him meant he'd need to share a few details about what he sought. . . . "After you've ministered to the needs of the villagers, I've a task for you."

"What sort of task?"

They stepped to the side to allow a farmer with a creaking wagonload of hay to pass. Once the fellow was out of earshot, Niall said, "I need you to enter the steward's chambers and go through his records."

Ana glanced up at his soot-darkened face. "I beg your pardon?"

"Enter the steward's chambers and—"

"You cannot truly be asking that!"

"I am. I'm interested in a particular entry. It won't take but a moment to determine if the record is there. The risk of discovery is very low."

In *his* mind, perhaps, but not in hers. She was already under scrutiny. The last thing she needed was to get caught sneaking into the steward's rooms. "Absolutely not. I will not do it."

His eyebrows angled sharply. "You've no choice in the matter. If you do not fulfill my demand, I'll be meeting with the constable."

"You would threaten that, even after the kiss we shared?"

He returned her stare, not a hint of warmth to be found on his handsome face. "Aye."

A pang of something unnameable rippled through her chest. Well, there it was—the bitter truth. He felt nothing for her, not even a wee spot of fondness. What a fool she was. Once again she'd dyed the wool of reality with the colors of her imaginings. "Your threat is not as powerful as you think. If I am caught, I will find myself at the mercy of the constable anyway."

"One offense will get you a day in the stocks, the other a dance on the gibbet. I think your options speak for themselves."

She grimaced. "You are a miserable, lowborn wretch."

He released her arm. "I'm a man on a mission. That's all that need concern you." Pointing down the lane, he said, "Let us waste no more time. Walk."

Ana tightened her brat about her shoulders and walked.

It was all so simple for him, the solution so clear. But Ana could not contemplate playing the spy without her stomach rolling in protest. Ask her to clean and lance a putrid wound, and she would do it without suffering a twinge of nausea. This? Nay, she could not do it.

There had to be an alternative, some other way to review the steward's records.

She just had to find it.

"You're a popular lass today," Niall murmured.

Lifting her head, Ana studied the small crowd huddled around the door of her bothy. A mix of unwed mothers with children, lame beggars, and old men bent by long years of labor, they waited patiently for her return. Some stood, some sat, and some leaned on roughly hewn canes. All wore an empty expression forged of endless despair.

Ana took a deep breath. *This* she could do. Ease pain, apply poultices, soothe coughs. Maybe even coax a smile to a weary face.

"Is there anything you require?" Niall asked. "Any help I can provide?"

"Nay, I have all that I need."

"I'll leave you to it, then."

He spoke the words, but didn't move. Ana glanced

at him. He was staring at the treetops visible above the thatched-roof huts to the west, and her stomach sank. Although the circumstances were decidedly different— and he'd given her no cause to worry—she was transported back to the woods outside Lochurkie, to that night when he'd disappeared into the darkness. The question slipped out before she could stop it. "Will you be back?"

"Aye. Before dark."

Relieved to have escaped a comment on her odd query, Ana nodded sharply and waded into the crowd. "Do what you will."

"I always do, lass. I always do."

When she reached the door of her bothy and turned, he was gone.

A very somber group greeted Niall when he strode into the Black Warrior camp. No one spoke and no one smiled. Leod and Ivarr were engaged in a fierce mock duel that was unusually absent of taunts and slurs.

"What news?" he asked Cormac, who was seated on a boulder by the fire, fletching an arrow with pale gray goose feathers.

The bowman looked up. "We found the thieves."

Niall waited for further explanation, but got none. "Did they refuse to aid us?"

Cormac shook his head. "Nay. They were dead."

"Some kind of quarrel amongst them?"

Cormac tossed his partially fletched arrow to the ground and rose to his feet. "I think not. Every soul in the camp was slain—men, women, and even the wee bairns. None were spared."

Niall's belly knotted at the image. "Any hint of what befell them?"

"No blood and no injuries to be seen."

So, they were back to poison. And once again, the finger of blame could be pointed at one of his men. Who else knew of the thieves' camp and had reason to see them dead? Niall panned the clearing, studying the faces of his men, one by one. Cormac. Leod. Ivarr. Jamie was nowhere to be seen. Did one among them hide a bitter, blackened heart? "Did all of you go?"

Cormac shook his head. "Leod remained behind with Jamie."

As he had requested. "And did any leave the camp earlier in the day?"

The bowman frowned heavily. "Do you suggest it may have been one of *us*?"

"Only we four knew our intention to query the thieves."

An angry flush rose in Cormac's cheeks. "Every man robbed at knife point in the past several months had cause to see them dead."

"Perhaps," acknowledged Niall. "But how many would murder women and children over a lost purse?"

The bowman had no answer. He simply tightened his lips and looked away.

"Were you able to give them a decent burial?"

"Nay," said Cormac, stooping to pick up a loose feather from the ground. "We had not the time. The constable and his men were scouring the nearby woods for poachers. Instead, we allowed them to catch a glimpse of us through the trees, then led them to the camp."

Niall nodded. So long as the dead were properly laid in the sod with a few words for their souls, it did not matter who lifted the shovel. "Good."

"Have you another plan to acquire the necklace?"

"Aye."

"That's the whole of it? *Aye?*" Cormac twirled the feather adroitly in his fingers. "Do you keep your plans close because you believe I'm the blackguard?"

Niall met the other's man's gaze. "What would you do in my boots?"

"Trust in my men."

"I think not. You're the least trusting fellow I've ever met. You insist on seeing every sign for yourself when we're tracking game through the forest, and you carry your coins on your person at all times, never leaving them behind in camp."

Cormac shook his head. "This is a far more serious matter."

"Indeed." A foe willing to slay an entire camp of thieves was a *very* dangerous man. If he was right and that foe was living among the Black Warriors, then the safety of Wulf's young son was at risk. A minor risk, surely, as the lad posed little threat, but . . . "Where is Jamie?"

The bowman stared at him for a long moment, clearly reluctant to drop the subject. But in the face of

Niall's firm resolve, he eventually said, "Down by the pond. I tasked him with finding me a clutch of goose feathers."

Niall nodded sharply, then headed through the wood toward the pond.

As he walked between the trees, he unbuckled his belt and slid his dirk sheath free. The blade was a tad long for a boy, but it was light and well balanced. In a battle for his life, it would do the lad proud.

He swept aside a yew branch and stepped onto the muddy shore of the pond.

Jamie was halfway around the ice-crusted basin, foraging through reeds flattened by long departed geese. A posy of gray feathers filled his left hand. The task had seemingly distracted him from his worries, as his usual sad countenance had been replaced by a faint smile. Niall was loath to banish it, but time was short.

"Jamie."

The lad's head popped up, his eyes finding Niall on the opposite shore. As anticipated, the smile fell away and the loose excitement fled his frame. He stood stiffly, waiting on Niall's command.

"Come here, lad."

The boy circled the pond and approached.

"I've a gift for you." Niall held out the knife. "A lad your age should have a blade to call his own."

Jamie stared at the knife but did not take it.

"It's a hunting dirk," Niall said. "Excellent for carving a fish or a rabbit."

The boy's gaze dropped to his boots.

"Very helpful when faced with a tight bind, as well."

Jamie still did not reach for the weapon.

Frustration surged through Niall. He could not take the lad with him to the village. The knife was the only way to keep him safe. "You will take the dirk, and you will keep it with you at all times," he ordered crisply. "If I see you without it, I'll take a paddle to your arse. Understand?"

He thrust the sheathed blade into Jamie's hands.

Then he turned on his heel and marched back to camp.

Ivarr and Leod had completed their mock duel and they met him as he entered. Leod's limp was improving, but he still used his practice sword as an impromptu cane. Both men were sweating profusely, despite the coolness of the day.

"Cormac told you about the thieves?" Ivarr asked.

Niall nodded. "Take extra care. There's clearly mischief afoot."

"Were you able to open the lock?"

"Nay. But I'm not ready to give up just yet." Niall found his long sword amid his belongings. He drew the weapon and studied the fine steel edge with a critical eye. He'd not polished or oiled it in more than a sennight, which in his mind was a serious failing. A warrior who did not take proper care of his blade was not a warrior at all. It was sorely tempting to strap it to his back. If he slipped into the village after dark, who would note its presence?

Ana, of course.

He could already anticipate her annoyance at having the battle blade in her home, but was that cause enough to leave it behind? An image of the lecherous French soldier rose to mind. Nay, it was not. He sheathed the weapon and wrapped the leather baldric around its length.

"I'll sup with you this eve," he told his men. "Ana is tending her flock. I trust you've snared a hare or two of late."

Cormac grinned. "Better than that—a stag. Downed with a single arrow, right beneath the constable's nose."

Niall frowned. "So you're the reason they're combing the woods in search of poachers?"

"Nay," the bowman protested. "They never saw me. 'Twas some other fool who raised their suspicions. We saw the leavings of his campfire near the double-trunked oak—ashes and bones strewn everywhere."

"Nonetheless, it's not wise to taunt the constable."

Cormac shrugged. "I aim to keep my skills sharp."

"A worthy notion," Niall acknowledged. Cormac was a formidable archer, and he'd not developed his talents sitting on his hands. "But hunt only rabbits from now on."

Chapter 8

Ana knew the wound was festering before she lifted the old man's lèine. She could smell it. Easing the rough cloth over his bony hip as he lay on the ground, she peered at the jagged tear in his flesh. Red and swollen, the injury was seeping pus.

To distract the man from what she was about to do, she asked, "How did you get this, Rory?"

He promptly launched into a wild and woolly tale involving a small pig, a fence, and a bramble bush. The tale was long and rambling, and he lost track of the story threads too often for the words to be true. But he appeared to believe them.

Ana soaked a linen square in chamomile and willow-bark tea. Ever so gently, as the old man recounted his tale, she used the sodden cloth to cleanse the wound. He winced once or twice, but did not stop talking. Much of the infection came away, but some still remained, so she filled the wound with a poultice made from ramsons, calendula, and yarrow, and then carefully wrapped it in linen bandages.

"I'll need to see you again in a day or two," she told him. "This poultice will draw out the pus, but I'll need to apply some healing unguent when it's clear."

He accepted her help in rising to his feet and leaned heavily on his oak branch cane, his face pale, his eyes dark with worry. "I've nothing to trade for your care."

"Come anyway. If we don't treat the wound properly, you'll lose the leg."

"Thank you, Goodhealer," he said gratefully, squeezing her hand. Tears formed in the corners of his eyes. "You're a kind soul."

She smiled. *Tell that to the village friar*, she wanted to say. "Don't wait so long next time. Have your granddaughter fetch me if you fall again."

He nodded and hobbled off down the lane.

Fearing the old man's failing memory would distort her instructions as surely as it had the story of his wound, she made a mental note to seek out the granddaughter herself. She tossed the remains of the tea on the dirt path, then gathered up her collection of linen squares, salve pots, and dried herbs, and entered the bothy. The sun was low on the horizon, and only a faint half light lit her way. The peat fire still burned strong, and the warm hut smelled like herbal tea.

The cauldron of pottage sat off to the side, unheated.

Exhausted by the steady stream of patients she'd seen since midday, Ana did not bother to hook the stew over the fire. She simply took a piece of bannock and some cheese from her larder and flopped down on the bed. The ropes groaned under her weight, but she was too tired to care. Her fingers ached, her hands were chapped, and her eyes were dry and gritty.

Sleep was an enticement too powerful to resist.

She closed her eyes and was instantly gone.

Thanks to a blanket of heavy clouds, there was no moonlight to guide Niall's way. His only cues came from the larger landmarks along the trail—the yew stump, the half-fallen tree, the granite obelisk. But the route was becoming increasingly familiar, and he made good time down the sloping brae toward the road. The evening was young and the woods were silent, save for the occasional screech of an owl.

He never heard the arrow, only felt it plow into the flesh of his left shoulder, ripping through sinews and tendons with careless abandon. It went deep, the metal tip piercing the front of his chest just below the collarbone. The searing pain stole a ragged gasp from his throat, but it was self-preservation, not weakness, that took him to his knees. A good archer could launch another arrow in seconds.

He dropped behind a fallen log and drew his sword. The lack of moonlight would work in his favor, hiding the gleam of the steel. Forcing his thoughts away from the blood trickling from his wound, he listened for any rustle of leaves or brush.

Nothing, not even the owl. His attacker was patient, waiting.

He peered through the trees to the road. There lay the quickest path to safety, but also the quickest path to the grave. Out in the open, he'd be an easy target. The only way to survive this day was to do the unexpected. But whatever he chose to do, he had to act swiftly—he was already becoming woolly-headed.

His free hand sought the slippery metal tip of the arrow.

The shooter's aim was high, thank the gods. He might yet live. Better yet, he could tell by the angle on the arrow that his attacker was up the hill and to the right. To land an arrow in the dark, the archer would by necessity be close—perhaps as little as thirty paces.

Niall tied the bottom of his brat about his waist and quickly stuffed the loose folds with anything in easy reach—bark, moss, and dried leaves. He made low moans as he worked, suggesting his injuries were dire. A padded brat was a sorry replacement for a breastplate, but any protection was better than none.

Once he deemed the stuffing sufficient, he didn't hesitate.

He sprang from his hiding spot with a deep, guttural roar and tore up the hill in the direction of the archer. Leaping rocks and ducking under branches, he churned through the brush as erratically as possible. His legs felt like lead. Every heartbeat felt like his last. But still he plowed forward, his sword at the ready, driven by a burning desire to know which one of his men was a contemptible blackhearted traitor.

To his surprise, the second arrow never came.

He drove farther and farther up the hill, meeting no resistance. None at all.

Light-headed and at the end of his endurance, he stopped. A quick glance around verified that he was alone, and he sank to his knees in the winter loam, every breath a lance in his chest. His attacker had run. All that remained were a few broken branches indicating the haste of his departure. Bloody coward.

Niall licked his lips, his mouth dry as paste.

He was growing weaker by the moment. He had to find Ana.

Using his sword for leverage, he pushed to his feet. Thighs atremble and head lolling, he turned to make his way back down the brae. The thick root of a towering oak proved his downfall. Literally. He caught his boot tip in a deep groove and lost his footing. His sword hit the tree and tumbled from his grip, even as the darkness closed in around him and the earth rose up to meet him.

That was the last he remembered.

Everything in the windowless Crimson Kettle was dark, dreary, and dull. Aiden took a sip of his drink. Including the ale. A dozen lit torches tried but failed to brighten the hazy interior. Even the colored threads of the namesake tapestry on the wall, depicting a bubbling kettle over a fire, were lost beneath a layer of smoke and grease.

Nonetheless, it was a popular place.

From the entrance to the tapped ale kegs stacked at the back, the room was awash with laughing, cheering, ale-swilling bodies. Most were village men celebrating the end of another hard day, but several wore the green and black tabard of a castle guard, and a trio of fat merchants sat at a table near the door.

Angling his stool to give him a clear view of the front door, Aiden leaned against the wall and extended his legs. "So, none of the lads you befriended had anything of value to share?"

Duncan and Graeme shook their heads.

"We heard plenty about the quality of the last harvest, but not one word about a visitor to the castle around Samhain," Duncan said.

A sturdy, red-cheeked barmaid carrying six pitchers of ale in each fisted hand wove adroitly between the patrons, plunked one down on their table, and moved on. Aiden watched the foam on the top of the ale slosh back and forth, slowly settling. "So the lady remains our only hope."

Graeme frowned. "Did you not say her guards were formidable?"

"Aye," Aiden admitted, topping up his horn of ale. He took a long draught of the tasteless brew. At least it wet his tongue. "She's very well protected."

"Then how is she a hope at all?"

Aiden had no answer to that. But his commitment to his goal was unshakeable. "She knows who the man in black is. I'm convinced of it."

Duncan exchanged a glance with Graeme, then said, "That won't help us if we can't speak with her."

"Perhaps we can lure her out of the castle."

"How?"

"Offer her new information pertaining to her brother's death."

"But we have no such information."

Aiden sighed. "Hardly the point. Her eagerness to avenge her brother's murder will entice her outside the castle walls."

Graeme frowned. "Is she likely to come without her guards?"

"Nay, but if the time and place are of our choosing, we can arrange an ambush."

The door to the alehouse swept open and a group of men entered, brushing snow from their cloaks. Aiden recognized the tallest among them—the sandy-haired knight who'd been speaking to Lady Isabail in the orchard. Two guards from the castle hailed the newcomers and waved them toward their table.

"The difficult task will be getting the message into the lady's hand," Aiden said. The knight scanned the crowd with a slow, narrow-eyed gaze before following his brethren. Whatever he searched for, he didn't seem to find it.

"Can we pay a village lad to run it to her?"

"The risk is high. If the message is waylaid, we lose our opportunity."

"What alternative do we have?" Graeme asked drily.

"None," Aiden admitted. He traced a deep gouge in the tabletop with his finger. They might find an older, more determined person to carry the message, but a lad would ask fewer questions.

"Then I say we—"

"Move your feet."

Aiden looked up. The sandy-haired knight stood before him, his lips set in a grim line, his eyes cold as a north wind. 'Twas possible the fellow was simply making his way to the piss pots at the back of the room—this was certainly one route to take—but Aiden had a feeling the knight had come looking for him.

Based solely on a comparison of their attire—a leather-trimmed wool tunic versus a ragged lèine—the fellow had every reason to believe Aiden would move his feet. A common man did not impede his betters. But the look in the knight's eyes dared Aiden to remain right where he was. So he did.

"Step over."

The knight did not immediately react to Aiden's insolence. He smiled. "I remember you. The orchard keeper with an unfortunate talent for badgering ladies."

"Badgering?" Aiden drawled. "From a distance of twenty paces? I think not. At best you could say I was admiring from afar."

"A lady is above your station, cur. Your admiration is better directed at the pigs in the sty."

Aiden placed his horn of ale on the table. The knight was clearly spoiling for a fight. Perhaps the fool had expressed his hopes for a marriage alliance with Lady Isabail and been summarily rejected. The cause mattered not. He shrugged. "A sow, or a lady. Can you fault me for being unable to tell the difference?"

The man came at him before the last syllable left his lips.

But Aiden was ready for him. Blocking the knight's clawing hands with a purposeful forearm, he landed a solid punch in the man's midsection, just below his ribs. Air chuffed from the knight's chest, and he lost his balance. Aiden took advantage. One hard shove, and the knight was on his knees, gasping for breath.

But he didn't stay down.

With a furious roar, he surged to his feet, drawing his sword with a cold slither of steel.

The patrons around them scrambled for safety.

"Sir Robert! Put your blade aside immediately." A pair of men wearing the telltale black leather hood of the constable's company flanked the knight, their hands on the hilts of their own weapons. "The law forbids the drawing of a weapon in the alehouse."

Sir Robert glared at Aiden, his anger unabated. "This wretch insulted your lady. His insolence cannot go unpunished."

Still seated at the table, Aiden met Sir Robert's stare. One carelessly tossed insult did not warrant this level of rage. He must truly be in love with the woman.

"Many things are said in the alehouse," one of the constable's men said calmly, "most of which should be forgotten. As I am willing to forget your current breach, sir. Put down your weapon."

The muscles in Sir Robert's jaw worked furiously for a moment; then he lowered his arm.

"I will bow to the law," he said, sheathing his weapon.

The constable's men nodded and returned to their table.

Sir Robert favored Aiden with another hard stare. "As for you," he said quietly, "best stay out of my way until I accompany Lady Isabail to Edinburgh in two days time. The constable's men won't always be about to save your sorry arse."

He kicked Aiden's boots aside and strode off toward the piss pots.

Ana woke with a start.

The blanket of nightfall still lay heavily over the room, broken only by the faint orange glow cast by the fire. She lay much as she'd fallen, the bread and cheese still in her hands, her boots still on her feet. There was no way to know how long she'd slept, but sating her hunger was no longer her primary concern. Worry nagged her instead.

She put aside the food and rolled off the bed.

Niall was yet absent, despite his assurance that he'd be home before dark. She barely knew the man, but her gut insisted his failure to return was ominous.

She tossed another peat brick on the fire.

Why did she feel such a burning need to act? No one had made her the man's keeper, and he'd likely not welcome her concern. Half the time, he made her so angry she lost all semblance of good manners. And the other half . . .

A sigh escaped her lips.

Well, the other half gave her reason to worry.

She wrapped her brat about her shoulders and lifted her satchel from the hook by the door. Opening the flap, she peered inside. Bruise salve, pain relief tea, and wound liniment. Linen strips for bandages. Calendula, comfrey, and garlic. Without knowing what had befallen him, she couldn't be sure she had what she needed. He might not have taken ill at all. Although the knot in her belly said otherwise.

Ana stepped into the lane and shut the door quietly behind her. She knew what direction she was headed— Niall's gaze had given her that much—but her ultimate destination was a mystery. It was a little mad to wander into the forest in the dark without a journey's end in mind, but doing nothing was the only alternative—and that wasn't in her nature.

She followed the road to the edge of the forest, where the leafless trees stood like dark sentinels, silent and resolute. Bent arms and boney fingers stretched toward the sky, swaying with the breeze. Ana swallowed. Lord, her imagination could run wild. Forests had given her shelter more times than she could recount.

She pressed forward into the gloom.

What clue she sought, she did not know. With no torch to light her path, everything she spied was a relentless shade of gray. But an increasing sense of urgency and a certainty that she would find something gave wings to her feet.

She had been striding along for a goodly time when a low moan drew her up. It came from the right, somewhere up the hill. A sharp tingle in her hands told her she'd found what she was looking for.

Cutting through the trees, the thick brush pulling at her skirts, Ana scrambled up the incline. "Niall? Where are you?"

Another moan guided her to a dark shape prostrated beneath a large oak tree.

Much too large to be a badger. She touched the shape, reassured by the nubby texture of wool weave under her fingers—until she realized it was not only cold, but wet. She brought her fingers to her nose. *Blood*. Working by feel, she quickly located the source of the trouble: the shaft of an arrow protruded from his broad back. Fearing the worst, she slid a hand under his body and felt for the arrowhead. Only the tip of the steel had broken through his feverishly hot skin.

She grimaced.

The rest of the arrowhead was still lodged in his chest, and as long as it remained there, she could not use her gift to heal him. The little she could feel of the arrowhead also failed to tell her if it was a simple bodkin or something more troubling, like a swallowtail. If the arrowhead was barbed, there was only one way it could come out. Straight through.

He stirred again, a restless movement accompanied by a nonsensical murmur.

The more pressing issue was to get him home. Remaining here, in the frigid chill of winter, would steal away what little chance he had of surviving. Niall was a very large man—too large for her to carry—and dragging him down the hill would not only take a great deal of time, it would injure him further. She needed help.

The kind of help that came with a cart.

But who could she enlist at this hour of night? And since she had no idea what Niall had been doing, who could she trust not to run to the constable?

Gordie.

The young wheelwright from Inverness. A month ago he'd come to her, blushing madly, seeking aid in removing an unsightly and rather inconvenient wart. Once cured, he'd beamed ear to ear for a sennight and promised her the moon—though she'd been satisfied with an iron-strapped water bucket at the time.

Ana packed some dried moss mixed with yarrow around the wounds, and wrapped his chest with linen strips as best she could. She took off her brat, tucked it around Niall's shoulders, and then stood. The icy breeze immediately sent a shiver up her spine, but she had no regrets. Niall needed the heat more than she. Lifting her skirts, she hastened down the hill. Before she set off down the road, she planted a branch to mark the location. She could not rely on Niall's moans to guide her a second time.

Then she raced for the village.

Time was of the essence. She had no idea how long Niall had been bleeding into the sod, and a fever was not a good sign. It usually took a day or two for infection to set in.

Gordie lived in the upper level of the smithy, which was on the far side of the village, next to the alehouse. She made good time, thanks to the fine fit of her leather boots, but was winded when she arrived. The door to the smithy groaned on its hinges as she swung it open.

"Gordie," she called breathlessly, leaning on the door.

No answer.

"Gordie, you layabout, wake up. I've need of you."

Hay rustled in the loft. A tousled head appeared over the edge, peering down at her. "Who is it?"

"Ana Bisset." She waved him down. "Come quick now, there's a good lad. I've need of you and your cart."

He donned a leather jerkin over his lèine, then descended the ladder, leaping the last few feet to the ground. "Is aught amiss, Goodhealer?"

"Aye, but I must ask you to keep what you see this night to yourself. No word to anyone. Can I trust you to do that?"

The blond-haired young man tossed her a lopsided grin. "If you can keep silent about my concerns, I can certainly keep silent about yours. Lead on, Goodhealer. I'll not breathe a word."

Gordie harnessed a sleepy ox to the blacksmith's cart, then led the way out of the barn.

The hay-lined cart rolled with remarkable quiet down the lane, and Ana said so.

The young man smiled. "If there's one thing I do well, it's craft a fine wheel."

Almost an hour after Ana left Niall in the forest, they returned to the base of the oak tree. Ana immediately checked for a heartbeat and was relieved to feel a heavy pulse beneath the hot, dry skin of Niall's neck. Gordie helped her carry Niall down the hill to the cart, taking care not to disturb the arrow. Niall did not stir with the movement.

"Hurry, Gordie," she said, climbing into the cart.

In response, he clucked encouragingly to the ox and tapped its hindquarters with his birch switch. "Get up, Belle." The cart lurched forward at a good clip and Gordie jogged alongside, keeping the cart straight in the road with an occasional *gee* or *haw*.

Ana knelt beside Niall in the hay and checked his bandage. Moving him had caused another gush of blood, but it was already slowing. She replaced the moss and applied fresh linen strips. He was silent and still throughout, which concerned her. She would have been happier to hear Niall moan with every rut in the road, to hear him fiercely battling the injury. His silence meant he had slipped into a very deep sleep— from which he might never awake.

The cart rolled up to the door of Ana's bothy and stopped.

Ana leapt down and opened her door. "Let's get him inside."

With Ana at his feet and Gordie supporting his shoulders, they carried Niall into the hut and over to the bed.

"Sit him up," she said. "I'll need your help to dislodge the arrow."

Awkwardly, thanks to the protruding arrow shaft, they managed to get Niall onto the bed in a seated position. His head rolled forward, his chin to his chest, his dark hair matted with blood and sweat. While Gordie held him upright, Ana lit two candles. Then she unwrapped the bandages, removed the moss, and cut away Niall's lèine with her knife until his entire chest was exposed. Crusted blood covered a large portion of his skin, and the flesh around the wound was so swollen that she could no longer see the tip of the arrowhead.

Ana rolled up her sleeves.

"Hold him as tight as you can."

Picking up a steel-headed mallet from the table, she climbed onto the bed and circled around to Niall's back. Her stomach was churning, but she ignored it. This was the only way to heal him; she knew that. To keep her hands steady, her resolve must be unwavering.

Bracing her feet on the bed frame to firm her balance, Ana settled her mind and stared at the notched end of the wooden arrow shaft. She did not let herself dwell on how small the target was, or on how the arrowhead would rip through Niall's flesh. She simply took a deep breath and swung the hammer.

It struck the wood with a solid thunk and Niall jerked. But not a sound escaped his lips.

"It's through," Gordie said hoarsely.

Ana hopped off the bed and swiftly packed more moss around the now gushing wound. Her decision to push the arrow through had been the correct one—the arrowhead was small but barbed. She glanced at Gordie. His face was an alarming shade of green, and she nodded to the door of the hut. "If you've a need to empty your spleen, I'd be grateful if you'd do it outside. But come back, I still require you."

He leapt up and ran for the door.

Holding Niall gently to her bosom, his breaths shallow but even against her neck, she listened to Gordie wretch for a few moments. A man's pride did not suffer such moments well. When he returned to the hut, unable to meet her eyes, she said matter-of-factly, "There's fresh water in the bucket by the door."

He rinsed his mouth, then returned to her side.

"Hold him while I saw off the arrowhead."

Gordie was a stalwart lad—much braver than she'd been the first time she helped her mother with an arrow injury. He rolled Niall's head back to give her better access, took hold of Niall's shoulders, and held him firmly in place.

Ana's saw was small with fine, sharp teeth, and it cut through the wooden shaft with six determined glides of the blade. Then she cleared away the blood-soaked moss, tugged the arrow out of Niall's back, and repacked the wound tightly. Through it all, Niall remained silent and unmoving. Ana tried not to worry about that.

With Gordie's help, she stripped away his remaining clothes, washed off the blood, and laid him on the heather-stuffed mattress. Although her primary interest was in his injuries, Ana could not help but appreciate Niall's fine form. Few men she had treated carried their weight so well. He was truly a masterpiece of corded muscle, narrow hips, and lean limbs. She ran a finger down the long scar on his arm. Far from perfect, but still the handsomest man she'd ever seen.

"Will he live?" the young wheelwright asked.

"The wound itself is survivable," she said. "But his fever concerns me."

Gordie nodded, then picked up the arrow shaft. "I had assumed by your desire for discretion that he'd been poaching." He stroked the pale gray fletching. "But the constable and his men use only black and white feathers."

"I've no need to know who shot him or why," Ana said, draping the blanket over Niall's lower body. Given what she knew of the man, the story no doubt involved brigands and murderers. "If he lives, that might be worth exploring, but for now, my only goal is to heal."

"Have you further need of me?"

"Nay. Get along home now." Ana offered him her palm "My sincerest thanks, Gordie. You were a great help."

He shook her hand. "It's not often I have an adventure of this sort."

"A good thing, I should say."

"Aye," he agreed, smiling. "May the rest of your night be uneventful, Goodhealer." He exited, and a few moments later she heard the low rumble of the cart as it moved away.

Eager to return her hut to a tidy state, Ana scooped

up the remnants of Niall's bloody clothing from the floor. They were heavier than expected. Digging through the folds of the linen and wool, she discovered his purse. Had this been any other patient, she would have put the leather pouch aside, not even glancing at the contents. But Niall had stolen her father's ring.

This was her chance to get it back.

She thrust her hand inside and rooted around. Sensing something small and weighty, she pulled it out— but it was not the ring. It was a midnight blue stone carved with a circular symbol—a piece of northern slate, if she wasn't mistaken. An odd treasure, to be sure. Ana replaced the stone and dug through Niall's coins until she found what she was looking for.

She quickly tucked the ring back inside the tin box and hid it beneath the bothy wall.

Returning to the bed, she checked Niall's wounds. The bleeding had slowed to a mere ooze, so she cleaned the moss away and applied a liniment that included agrimony, oxeye, and yarrow. His skin was scalding hot, his cheeks flushed.

Ana brushed Niall's hair from his face. The fever bothered her. The wounds were swollen and red, to be sure, but no more or less than she would expect. The angry red coloration and clotted pus she normally associated with a wound gone sour had not made an appearance. So why then the fever? And the unusually deep sleep?

If it wasn't so unlikely, she'd almost think . . .

She bent and retrieved the arrowhead from the floor where it had fallen. The swallowtail was coated in blood and dirt, but she brought it to her nose, closed her eyes and sniffed deeply. The heavy metallic scents of blood and steel overwhelmed her senses initially, but as she took another sniff, a faint edge of bitterness surfaced. Her heart stumbled.

Poison.

Worse, it was not one she could name. And if she could not name it, she could not craft a cure.

Ana stood and laid the arrowhead carefully on the table. Her healing gift was a wonder, but it had limitations. To use it effectively, she had to visualize exactly where in the body to send the healing heat. Blood-borne illnesses—especially poisons—were extremely difficult to cure.

She turned to look at the handsome man on the bed.

Her heart thudded slow and heavy. Her healing failures were few, but all of them had been cases of blood-borne illness suffering a delay before treatment could begin.

Even if she expended every effort and drew on every ounce of her strength, there was a very good chance that Niall would die.

Chapter 9

Ana's eyes itched with unshed tears.

Damn the man. She should be rejoicing at the prospect of being free of his unreasonable demands. She should be happy to put his threats behind her. She should *not* be feeling like fate was ripping the heart out of her chest once more. *No attachments.* That was her solemn vow.

But his actions that November night in Lochurkie had changed everything.

He had saved her. And nothing he'd done since—not the harsh words, not the binding of her hands, not the cool dismissal of their kiss—had shaken her valiant view of him. Rather, a dozen little things had nurtured it, like the way he'd defended her in the cellars, the way he'd held her safely in his arms on a cold winter night, and the way he'd insisted on accompanying her home. Meaningless things. And now . . .

Now her chest felt so heavy she could barely breathe. *He could not die.*

She wouldn't allow it.

Ana rolled the loose sleeves of her sark up to her elbows. She carried the water bucket over to the bed and peeled back the woolen blanket, exposing Niall's bare chest. Digging into the folds of her neckline, she located the Rod of Asclepius pendant, drew it from around her neck, and kissed it. She dropped to her knees beside the bed and placed the bronze token in Niall's right hand. The pendant had no power—her mother had given it to Ana after her first successful healing, to welcome her as a practitioner of an ancient art—but if the gods were kind, perhaps they would watch over her efforts this night.

Then she closed her eyes and rubbed her palms together, summoning the healing warmth.

From deep inside, it came. First as a bloom of heat in her chest, then as a tingle of energy that crept down her arms toward her hands. Ana opened her eyes and watched the fine red swirls grow like crimson vines, wrapping around her forearms, curling and weaving until they reached her fingertips.

Then she placed her hot hands on either side of the wound on Niall's firm chest.

He did not stir.

Concentrating hard, she pictured the entrance to the wound in her mind's eye—the swollen flesh, the parted skin through which the arrow had passed, the blood that pumped weakly through his veins—and immediately the heat flowed into his body, mending as it went.

The track of the arrow through his body was her guide. In her mind, she gently tested the ragged edges, seeking out the dark blots of poison. First she sought to nullify the venom, then heal its rancid effects. Blackened flesh became pink. But for every healed inch, she paid a stiff price. Waves upon waves of icy chill and pain washed up her arms, evoking racking shivers.

She ignored them as best she could.

When the poison had been drawn from the immediate area of his wound, she extended her efforts, hunting deeper and broader. The easy part was done. Chasing the poison coursing through his body would be the real challenge.

Settling herself as comfortably on the floor as possible, she painstakingly searched for droplets of poison buried in every heavy muscle of his body. There were many, but they were small. It took immense concentration to hunt them out and destroy them. It also took time. Pent-up power pooled in her fingers, straining for release, and the pattern on her skin rose up like a welt. Her skin heated to an unbearable level. Fighting the odd mix of scalding hands and a shuddering chill in her torso, she lifted one hand and dipped it in the water bucket. Cold water embraced her hand, providing instant and sigh-worthy relief. With the burning in one hand temporarily abated, she switched hands.

On and on it went.

Bent to her task, Ana lost track of the hours. At some point, the starry sky gave way to the rosy blush of morning, but she knew not when. All she knew was that when she finally sat back, she could barely keep her head up. Her limbs trembled with exhaustion. Pain radiated from every joint in her body.

It had been a long time since she'd healed a body so broken.

She stared at the strong angles of Niall's face and watched the rise and fall of his chest as he breathed. The feverish flush still colored his cheeks and his breathing remained so slow and shallow that each drawn breath threatened to be his last. She'd done all she could, but it may not have been enough. He'd lain in the forest for hours. It was possible the poison had seeped places she could not imagine.

If so, his fate was in God's hands.

Her eyelids drooped.

She was so tired. So very tired. As much as she desperately wanted to stay awake to watch over Niall, her drained and depleted body would not allow it. Her head felt as if it weighed ten stone, and she could barely convince her fingers to move as she commanded. If she didn't soon lie down, she would collapse.

But she couldn't leave Niall. If he died while she slept, she'd never forgive herself.

She tucked the blanket around him, scooped some water from the bucket, and dribbled it between Niall's dry lips. Then she entwined her still-patterned hand with his and laid her head on the mattress next to his arm. An awkward position for sleeping, to be sure, but her body would not care. Not until she woke to stiff limbs, that is.

Ana squeezed Niall's hand.

"No dying," she murmured. "I will not have it."

Then she gave in to the heaviness of her eyelids and sank into a dreamless sleep.

The world tilted madly. Images rushed by—a dark snake slithering through the woods, an arrow whizzing through the air, a woman's worried face. Then someone squeezed Niall's hand and softly spoken words pierced the dizziness. "No dying. I will not have it."

The voice was sweet and familiar, and the wild beat of his heart settled.

Niall struggled to open his eyes and eventually won the battle. But the dizziness did not abate. Candles flickered in and out of his vision, and the bed on which he lay felt as if it were tipping. He grabbed the mattress as tight as he could, determined not to spill to the floor. Easier said than done, as it turned out. One of his hands was already spoken for.

He peered down his arm.

Waves of dark red hair washed over the bed, ebbing and flowing like the tide. Beyond the red sea, a slender arm covered in bright red lace entwined with his. Niall tried to make sense of the view, but could not. He just knew that it felt right that she was there. A name came to his tongue, and he spoke it.

"Ana."

She did not rouse.

He lifted his head to get a better look. The bed tipped in the opposite direction, and his stomach rolled with it. Sweat broke out on his brow. Black spots swam into view. He fought against the encroaching darkness, but to no avail. A cool numbness flooded his limbs and his head fell back.

With a heavy sigh, he sank into a dream, dancing with a beautiful, red-haired fae.

A firm hand shook Ana's shoulder. "Wake up, Goodhealer."

Ana lifted her head and blinked, her eyes gritty with sleep.

Mr. Hurley, the constable, was crouched beside her, a deep frown creasing his brow, his lips a grim line in his beard. Bold sunlight poured in through the open chimney in the roof, banishing the shadows to the farthest reaches of the room. She lay half on the floor and half on the bed, exactly as she had when she closed her eyes. But what was the constable doing in her bothy? Had something terrible happened . . . ? Her heart plummeted.

Niall!

Ana's head whipped around.

Her valiant savior lay on the bed, his blanketed chest rising and falling in a slow, steady pattern. A healthy bloom of color filled his cheeks. *He had survived.* She put a hand to his brow. His skin was no longer hot. Not just survived; he thrived.

"Is your husband not well, Goodhealer?"

Ana scrambled to her feet and faced the constable. "Indeed not. He had a fever most of the night."

Hurley folded his arms over his chest. "Did he suffer an injury?"

Not pleased with the direction of the conversation, Ana avoided the question and went on the offensive. "Was there a reason for your visit today, Constable? I do not recall inviting you inside."

"I announced myself, but got no response. Fearing for your safety, I entered."

"Thank you for your concern," she said. Given the weariness still plaguing her limbs, his explanation was all too easy to believe. "And your reason for coming to my door?"

"The baron bade me check on you." The tall soldier met her gaze evenly. "You did not oversee the baroness's meal last eve nor help her break the fast this morn."

Ana did not need to fake her dismay. She had completely forgotten Elayne. "I'll offer him my sincerest apologies. I was tending my husband and lost track of the hour. Is the baroness well?"

"She's fine. Bébinn says she's eating more." He glanced at Niall. "What illness befell him?"

"Nothing serious. A touch of the ague."

The constable nodded agreeably, but continued to study Niall's sleeping form with a keen eye. "I received a report from a citizen of good standing that a man with an arrow in his chest was carried into your abode in the middle of last night."

Ana swallowed tightly. "Your informant was mistaken."

"We've suffered greatly at the hands of poachers in recent months. I hope you won't take offense, Goodhealer, but I must verify your husband's health for myself." Bending, Mr. Hurley grabbed the edge of the blanket.

Dear Lord. What if the wound had not completely healed? What if she'd missed—

With a quick flick of his wrist, the constable bared Niall's upper body.

A wave a hot relief poured over her. The wound was naught but a dark rose stripe—the flesh had completely knitted. It now looked to be several weeks old.

The constable pointed to the scar. "How did he come by that?"

"I don't know," she said with a shrug. "He will not speak of the day he nearly died in Aberdeen."

"Come now, Goodhealer. Surely you've seen a stabbing injury before? Your husband did not acquire a wound of this sort whilst moving cargo about on the docks."

Ana put her hands on her hips. "Clearly, Constable, you've never worked the docks. If you had, you'd be aware that spears, harpoons, and pikes are regular tools of the fishing trade. Robbie is a good man who suffered a terrible injury. I will not hear aspersions against his name without due cause. You've seen your fill, sir, and he is obviously not the poacher you seek. Do not dare to tarnish his character simply to assuage your frustration."

Mr. Hurley dropped the blanket and stepped back.

Offering her a courtesy bow, he said, "My apologies, Goodhealer. 'Twas not my intent to offend you."

It most certainly had been, but Ana did not call him on the lie. She preferred to hasten him out the door before he thought to search the hut. If he found the bloody moss and the arrowhead, the conversation would turn ugly. "Please inform the baron that I will attend the baroness at noontide."

"I would be happy to pass on the message, Goodhealer." With obvious reluctance, the constable backed away. When he reached the door, he favored Ana with a steely stare. "Please have Robbie present himself to me when he is on his feet again."

"Of course."

Ana closed the door behind him and rested her forehead on the rough wood surface. How had she ended up in this untenable position? Two visits by the constable in a handful of days did not bode well. The voice in her head telling her to run buzzed so insistently she could barely think.

Had her father still been alive, it would have been his voice urging her to leave. He'd always been so careful, so protective. The slightest hint of trouble and he would be packing up the caravan. But she was on her own now, forced to make a difficult choice. If she fled, she'd be leaving Elayne and Niall behind, and that upset her mightily. But staying carried a great deal of risk. She was now under scrutiny from the baron, the friar, *and* the constable. It was only a matter of time before someone dug deeper than her charade could bear and determined her true identity.

Ana shoved away from the door.

By God. Why did she constantly indulge in such morose thoughts? Moaning about her situation would not remedy it. Only action could do that. If she was to stay, it had to be *her* choice and it had to be a *committed* choice. She could no longer blame Niall for holding her captive—the man was unconscious. And she had reclaimed the ring.

Bending to the firepit, she stirred the peat coals and set a kettle amid the flames.

Aiding Lady Elayne was the honorable thing to do. But Elayne was not the only reason she was reluctant to leave. Ana rooted through the jars on the table, lifting the lid from each and sniffing to confirm the contents. She added a liberal amount of dried willow bark to the kettle. Once the mixture had boiled for several minutes, she lifted the pot from the fire with her hook and set it aside to steep.

Then she returned to the bed and stared down at her patient.

He was much easier to admire when he was sleeping. Without the stern lines and the icy blue glare, his face was as bonny as any she'd seen. Like this, it would be a simple matter to dismiss her feelings for him as mere infatuation. The truth, however, was more complicated. Infatuation could not explain the horrible feeling of dread she'd endured when she thought he might die. Nor could it account for the warmth that filled her chest each time he publicly claimed her as his own.

Nay. She might as well admit it.

She cared for the blackguard. 'Twas a foolish and pointless love, but it was love just the same. Why else would she even consider entering the steward's chamber in search of the records he desired? The mere notion set her belly atremble with fear. Yet, her thoughts had returned to the possibility several times as she tended the villagers yesterday. Why? For the hope of earning a smile from Niall. Because she wanted to do him proud.

If that was not love, what was?

Not that anything would ever come of it, of course. Ana turned and packed her satchel with herbs. She could not drag another person—especially one she loved—into the mess that was her life. Not when she knew what fate held in store for her. Watching her mother burn at the stake had tortured her father like no amount of running had been able to do. His heart had broken that day, and he'd never been the same.

To some, it would seem an easy solution to simply cease healing—to live a quiet life in a hut in the woods, far from those who would do her harm.

Her hands tightened on the satchel. She'd even thought the same, back when her own healing powers were weak and unfocused. But healing wasn't a choice. A healer could no sooner deny aid to an injured person than cut off her own arm. Having the power to save a life made it impossible to stand back and do nothing—even when the risk of discovery was high.

She was a healer, and that would never change.

Niall would find some other woman to love. A

woman who could make him a home and bear him children, not drag him from hamlet to hamlet, one step ahead of a fiery justice.

Ana heaved a sigh. She would stay. She would help Lady Elayne deliver her son and help Niall recover from his injury, but she would not give in to the demands of her heart. When all was well, she would disappear into the foggy moors, just as she and her parents had disappeared many times before.

It was for the best.

Friar Colban was visiting with Lady Elayne when Ana arrived.

The sight of his voluminous black robes soured her belly, but Ana pasted on a smile and joined them by the fire. "Good day to you, Your Ladyship. I beg your forgiveness for my absence. A pleasure to see you as well, Friar."

Elayne returned her smile. "Is your husband recovered, Goodhealer?"

"He's on the mend," Ana said. "Thank you for your concern. I understand you've been eating better."

She wrinkled her nose. "The turnip broth is all I can manage."

"The cook will try some other soups once the kitchens have been repaired. In the meantime, the broth is a fine meal." Ana put a hand on Elayne's forehead, then on her rounded belly. No clamminess and the babe moved with vigor. "You fare well."

"Indeed." Elayne glanced at the friar. "Friar Colban

has encouraged me to resume my duties as chatelaine as soon as possible. The baron's affairs need tending."

"Childbearing is only a portion of your wifely duties," the friar said, nodding.

"Lady Elayne is still far too weak to be exerting herself," Ana responded firmly. "Directing a stronghold of this size is a formidable task. I believe she requires a few more days of healthy eating to regain her strength."

"We don't have a few days," Elayne said, her smile broadening. "A messenger delivered the news this morn—weather has delayed King Alexander's travels, and he will now stop in Duthes on his way to Edinburgh from Balconie Castle. He arrives two days hence."

"The *king*?"

Elayne nodded happily. "A king under my roof. Is that not the greatest honor?"

Ana glanced at the friar. "I must still recommend rest for Lady Elayne."

He shook his head. "For the next few days, none of us will have the luxury of rest. Lady Elayne must stand at her husband's side as the king rides through the gate, and she must ensure he is properly welcomed. Every detail must be perfect. Such an opportunity may never come again. She must do her husband proud."

"I fear she may collapse."

"Nonsense." He smiled at Elayne. "I believe the lady is much stronger than you suggest, Goodhealer." His gaze slid back to Ana. "Lady Elayne has been a charming hostess this morn. I have lacked for nothing this past hour, including entertainment. She's been regaling me with several fascinating tales."

Ana's stomach rolled. "Oh?"

"I was particularly interested in her description of your serpent pendant. May I see it?"

She swallowed. *Thank the Lord*. The pendant still lay in Niall's hand. "I'm afraid I do not have it with me today, Friar."

"How unfortunate," he said coolly. "I trust you'll bring it with you when next you pray in the church?"

"Of course." A hot flush rose up her throat. *Liar*. She could never show him the pendant. The blackfriars were renowned for their zealous condemnation of pagan beliefs. "They were laying out the noontide meal as I passed through the great hall, Friar. Perhaps you'd like Bébinn to accompany you to the high table?"

He favored her with a hard look, then stood and held out his hand to Elayne.

"I think it best that you resume your duties immediately, Your Ladyship. Take your seat at the baron's side. Show the gillies that you are strong and in control, and they'll deliver finer work."

Elayne placed her thin hand in his and rose awkwardly to her feet.

Ana frowned. "Are you sure you wish to do this, Your Ladyship? The scent of certain foods still causes you grief."

The young woman nodded. "I must try. The baron has been ever so patient with me these past few months. He deserves my fidelity."

Emptying her spleen in front of a large crowd of people would not do the baron any great service, but speaking so frankly in front of the friar would only embarrass Lady Elayne, so Ana held her tongue. On that subject, at least. "I do not recommend you sample the food served to your husband, Your Ladyship. Shall I have your page bring you a bowl of broth?"

Elayne tossed her a grateful smile. "Yes, Goodhealer. That would please me."

They left the room, Bébinn trailing along behind. Ana sighed heavily, then followed.

Chapter 10

"Bloody stupid fool. What possessed you to wear the pendant whilst visiting the manor? You should have foreseen the result. No one to blame but yourself."

Niall opened his eyes. He was lying on the bed, the thatch roof over his head. Bright sunlight streamed in through the chimney hole—midafternoon, judging by the angle. Slowly, he turned his head to look at Ana. No tipping or tilting of the bed this time, thank the gods. She was bent over the iron cauldron, scraping out the contents with a wooden spoon. Her brèid had been removed, and her dark red braid hung over one shoulder, the tip swaying with every angry jab of the spoon.

"Now what will you do?" she muttered. "You know he'll keep asking for it. How long can you deny him?"

Encouraged by his clear head, Niall pushed to his elbows so he could better see her. A stab of pain shot through his shoulder, but it was bearable. "What happened?" he asked.

Ana dropped the spoon into the cauldron with a loud clatter and darted to the bed. Putting a warm hand to his forehead, she smiled. "Finally. You've awakened. How do you feel?"

"Well enough. Where's my lèine?"

Her hand dropped back to her side. "Do you recall what befell you?"

"Aye," he said, remembering the events with bitter clarity. "A craven cur shot me in the back with an arrow. Where's my lèine?"

"I burned it." She sank to the edge of the bed—so close that her sweetly feminine scent filled his nose. "'Twas little more than a rag, I'm afraid. We had to cut it off, and it was thoroughly stained with blood."

He frowned. "We?"

"Gordie, the wheelwright's apprentice, aided me. Fear not; he'll hold his tongue. He's a trustworthy sort." She sighed. "Unlike my neighbor, the candle maker. I earned a visit from the constable, thanks to that scurrilous rat."

"Is Mr. Hurley the cause of your current black cheer?"

"Nay. The constable was appeased for the moment."

Niall replayed the night in his thoughts. The last thing he remembered was falling into the thicket some ways up the hill from the road. "How did you find me?"

"A wee bit of luck."

"But I gave you no inclination as to my aims for the day."

She shrugged. "You told me you would be back before dark, and you were eyeing the forest at the time. I took a risk."

A wave of weariness hit Niall, and he fell back on the mattress, his gaze drifting over every gentle curve of Ana's face. "Why? Had you left me to die, you'd have been free to depart Duthes."

"It's not in my nature to leave a man to die. Even you. Although I will admit, I took advantage of your weakened state and reclaimed my ring."

A faint smile rose to his lips. "How unexpected."

She adjusted his blanket, tucking it close around his chest. "You'll be unusually weary for a day or two. I wasn't able to get all the poison out."

"Poison?" Niall glanced down at his shoulder. Neat strips of linen were wrapped around the injured area.

"Aye. Whoever shot you was determined to kill you."

"I owe you a great debt, it would seem." Niall tucked a wayward strand of her hair behind her ear. It was just as silky as he remembered. "Thank you."

A pretty blush filled her cheeks. "No thanks are required. I was merely fulfilling the necessities of my profession."

He could have argued—she'd done far more—but he let the matter drop. "What pendant do you fret over?"

"You were not meant to hear that." She looked away. "'Tis nothing."

"Your dismay was evident. I would know the cause."

"Truly, it does not matter. Apply your efforts toward regaining your health."

Annoyed that she would deny him, he tore the blanket off and sat up. Ignoring the wave of dizziness that assailed him, he cupped her delicate face in his hands and forced her to look into his eyes. "I will not allow anyone or anything to distress my wife. Explain the situation and I will deal with it."

A frown settled on her brow. "What will you do? Slay all my detractors with the great sword we found at your side in the woods? I need no such aid. What kind of healer would I be if I willingly invited death to solve my problems?"

Niall found the softness of her skin distracting. She was so damned beautiful. His fingers itched to explore, rather than simply hold. It took all his willpower to leave them where they were. "Some men deserve to die."

"That's your belief. 'Tis not mine."

He snorted. "Clearly, you've not seen the things I've seen."

"Most men are redeemable. If you kill them, that opportunity is lost."

Niall shook his head. "Leniency is for good men gone astray, not for craven curs."

She opened her mouth to argue further, but Niall was weary of the debate. He only wanted the name of her antagonist. *And to kiss her.* Which was as good a place to start as any. He tugged her toward him.

She did not protest. Not as the heat of their bodies slowly mingled, nor as he lowered his mouth to hers.

Her lips were soft as flower petals, and his first instinct was to avoid crushing them. But when she slid her arms about his neck and returned the kiss without any hint of shame or fear, his good intentions fell victim to a surge of white-hot desire. His blood thrummed insistently through his veins, consuming all rational thought. He forgot that his intent was to coax a name from her; he forgot that he was freshly injured.

Swift and sure, he took her to the mattress, pinning her with his weight.

He freed his hands from their self-imposed tethers and dragged them over the sweet curves of her body, plumping and squeezing, memorizing every dip and hollow. He fully intended to revisit each spot with his tongue.

But only after he was done ravishing her mouth.

Ana knew she should stop him. A man so recently injured should not be making love to a woman—the risk to a knitting wound was too great. Except, there was no partially knitted wound beneath the bandages on his shoulder. No scabs, no ooze, no sundered flesh. She'd covered the area with linen to hide the truth, to avoid his questions. If she wanted to maintain the illusion, she should push back.

But she didn't.

The sensations pulsing through her body were too delightful. Too thrilling. Gooseflesh rose on her skin in the trail of his touch, and shivers ran down her spine.

Hot, heady desire pooled between her thighs. Instinctively, she arched her back, closing the gap between the muscular ridges of his chest and her belly, trying to satisfy the exquisite ache in her core. But it wasn't enough. She needed him closer. Deeper.

Almost as if he read her mind, Niall's hips ground against her mons, his erection thick and hard. Sensation exploded inside her. Delirious with pleasure, Ana writhed underneath him, increasing the friction to a fever pitch. A wanton mewl vibrated in her throat.

He answered by yanking up her skirts and slipping a hand between her legs. He sucked in a sharp breath as his fingers met a warm, wet welcome.

"Sweet Jesu," he muttered shakily.

"Take me," she encouraged. "Take me *now*."

He lifted his head and looked in her eyes. His incredibly handsome face was dark with passion, the crests of his cheekbones flushed, his nostrils flared. "Are you truly a widow?"

"What does it matter?"

He groaned and dropped a hard kiss on her lips. "I do not make a habit of deflowering maidens. Have you been with a man before, or no?"

"The time to ask that question was *before* you kissed me."

"Agreed," he said, his voice strained. "I'm a fool, and I beg your forgiveness. Now answer the bloody question."

"I'm not a maiden." Ana took a deep breath and waited for the inevitable demand for details. Men never liked knowing they were not the first. But it never came.

"Good," he grunted. He stole another scorching kiss. Then he lifted her hips, positioned his cock at the well of her femininity, and drove into her. Full and deep and hard.

Ana gasped and clutched the blanket.

Her sheath clenched around him. She'd never felt so completely and utterly taken. So consumed by the flames of desire. Pleasure sang through her body, carrying its vibrant melody to the very tips of her fingers and toes. Perspiration beaded on her chest and trickled down between her breasts.

He gave her but a moment to catch her breath before he began to rock in and out.

Ana's eyelids drifted down. Each intimate stroke was strong and sure, and each tapped just the right spot to spawn shudders of ecstasy. Tension built in the core of her being, tight as a bowstring, promising a release of untold joy. She wrapped her legs around Niall's torso, giving him even greater access, and lifted her hips to meet his pounding tempo.

The sound he released was half groan, half deep-throated growl.

His powerful arms caged her on the bed, and his mouth swooped down to capture hers once more. Sweat slickened every taut muscle of his body, and Ana slid her hands up the ropes of his arms, over the dark pattern of his tattoo, and down the planes of his chest to his incredibly honed belly. She'd never seen a man so beautiful. Or met a man who could tempt her so sweetly and drive her to the edge of insanity with his glorious body.

Her hands slipped around to his lean, clenching buttocks.

"Faster," she urged.

And he obliged.

The bed squeaked and groaned under the force of their movements, and as the exquisite hum of her body reached a fever pitch, she added short, breathless squeals to the chorus. "Oh, oh, oh." Ana's fingers dug into Niall's buttocks as her excitement grew unbearable. And then she flew apart. With every pulsing overture, a sweet wave of weariness stole the strength from her limbs and left her floating in a sea of bliss.

Niall sensed her release and drove into her one last time. Then he lifted his head, uttered a deep, primal roar, and found his own shuddering fulfillment.

Niall collapsed on the bed beside Ana, utterly spent. Something hard and metal dug into his hip, and he reached into the folds of the blanket to secure it. He glanced at the pendant briefly, but it could not hold his attention. Staring at Ana's passion-flushed face was far more interesting.

"You are a very beautiful woman," he said.

She shrugged. A languid movement that bespoke deep satisfaction.

"Would you rather I admired your wit?"

She turned her head to look at him. A tendril of red hair curled damply against her brow. "When you die, what words do you hope will be said over your grave? That you were comely? Or that you were an honorable warrior who met his responsibilities well?"

"The latter, of course. But women prefer to be seen as desirable."

"Not all women." She smiled. "I'd rather be remembered for my healing."

He ran a finger over her soft lips. They were still pink and full from his kisses. "I must admit you heal with exceptional skill. I felt nothing but a twinge or two."

The glow of her cheeks deepened to scarlet. "I should probably check the bandages for bleeding. Despite the lack of pain, you may have torn the wound open again."

"Later." He cupped her chin and leaned in to kiss her again. She tasted like sunshine and sweet summer wine. "First you must tell me who has been vexing you. Is it the friar?"

"He does not like me."

"He does not like anyone," Niall said with a snort. "To him, we're all sinners with scant chance of passing through the pearly gates. What did you do with my sword?"

Her gaze lifted to meet his. "You can't run the village priest through."

"Why not?"

"If I have to answer that question, you are not the man I thought you were."

He smiled slowly. "Careful, lass. That was almost a

compliment. Fear not. I have no intention of slaying the wretch. But neither will I stand back while he makes threats against my wife."

"I am not your wife."

He kissed her again. Hard. "My lover, then."

"I'm not your lover, either." She straightened her skirts. "This was a sweet interval, but it cannot be repeated."

Niall watched her scoot off the bed, his eyes narrowed. "You care for me."

Standing, she turned to face him. "Nay, I do not."

"A woman does not risk everything to save a man she does not care for," he said softly.

"She does if she owes that man her life," she retorted. "You saved me from certain death in Lochurkie, and I returned the favor. A life for a life. It was nothing more."

Niall studied the twin flags of color in Ana's cheeks. The brazen chit was lying to him. She *did* care for him—she just preferred not to admit it. Well, he could live with that. "And why, exactly, are we not to repeat the lovemaking?"

"It will muddy the terms of our agreement."

He bounded from the bed, naked as the day he was born, and met her toe-to-toe. "The agreement where you do anything I ask, or I inform the constable of your unsavory past?"

Her lovely lips tightened. "Aye."

"You truly want to limit our relationship to that?"

"Aye."

He shook his head. "Be careful what you wish for, lass."

Ana swallowed tightly. Niall was just as intimidating stark naked as he was fully clothed. Perhaps more so. There was raw power visible in every flexed muscle. "Your sword is under the bed."

He stared into her eyes for a long moment, then turned and retrieved his weapon. Ana was treated to a breathtaking view of his lean backside as he bent—and of the ten red arcs caused by her fingernails. *Lord*. She'd quite forgotten herself.

"What's this?" he asked, pulling out a small burlap-wrapped bundle.

"The arrow that felled you. Gordie thought the fletching might give you a clue to the shooter, so I held it."

He laid his sword on the bed, then peeled back the layers of burlap. His face darkened as his fingers ran over the pale gray fletching.

"Are you familiar with the color?"

"Aye."

"So you know who shot you?"

"Aye." He rewrapped the arrow and thrust the bundle at her. "Bury it in the woods. The constable should not discover it here."

Ana placed the rolled burlap on the table. "An unlikely event. I convinced Mr. Hurley that you were sick with the ague, not injured by an arrow."

He tilted his head and looked at her. "He took you at your word?"

"More or less." Ana found it hard to concentrate with Niall's unclothed body an arm's reach away—her gaze constantly strayed from his face, drifting downward. He had the rangy, rippling sinews of a large wolf. Not an ounce of softness to be found. *Anywhere.* "Do you have another lèine?"

"Talk will not hold the constable off for long," Niall said. "He'll be back. You must search the steward's rooms today."

She blinked. "Today?"

"You are promised to return to the manor for the evening meal, are you not?"

"'Twill not be so easy as you suggest," she said. "The king arrives unexpectedly in two days time and preparations for his visit are under way. The manor is abuzz with people. 'Twill be impossible to enter the steward's chambers without notice."

"King Alexander stops here?"

She nodded. "Just for the night."

"Then we've no choice—we must act swiftly. With the king will come his personal guard. It will be doubly difficult to move about once they arrive." He raked back the long dark strands of his hair, the honed muscles of his arm flexing.

Ana thrust her hands behind her back. No matter how tempting, she would not touch. "Perhaps we should wait until after they've departed."

"Nay." He crossed to his bag, which lay next to the bed, and dug through the contents. "Time is short. I cannot wait. You will do it this eve, while most are enjoying their supper."

Ana was silent as Niall tugged a dove gray lèine over his body and pinned a darkly hued brat over his shoulders. She struggled to find some argument that might sway him. She had no talent for sneaking about. "If I knew what information you seek, perhaps I could find an alternative way to acquire it."

"I told you—I seek a particular notation. There's no other way to discover it, save to ask the steward's permission to peruse his records, which I am loath to do."

"And what notation is worth such a risky endeavor?"

He lifted his head and pinned her gaze with his. "The date a gold and ruby necklace was delivered into the baron's hands."

"A necklace?" Disappointment dropped like a stone in her belly. For some reason, she'd imagined his motivations were loftier.

"A very unique necklace."

"Of course." No matter how *unique* a necklace it was, his pursuit of it still made him a treasure seeker, not the chivalrous defender of hapless young women she wanted him to be. "And what will you do once you have verified this notation exists?"

"Leave."

"Leave Duthes? Without the necklace?"

He frowned. "Do not concern yourself with my actions. Concentrate on your own."

Ana stared at his handsome face and his fully

clothed body. While she would not label the intimate moments they'd shared a mistake—they'd been far too enjoyable for that—there was no question she'd crossed a line from which it would be nigh on impossible to retreat. Having thrilled once to the delights of his flesh pressed against hers, her body now hungered for it again. Memories of every exquisite touch and taste plagued her thoughts. Resisting him would be incredibly difficult.

Unless he was gone . . .

She drew in a tight, painful breath.

"Fine, I'll do it."

Niall frowned. The haste with which she'd changed her mind had been positively unseemly. Almost as if she was eager to be rid of him. Yet she cared for him; he was convinced of that. But he couldn't argue with her decision—getting inside the steward's chambers was paramount.

"Perfect," he said crisply. "Let's away, then. The sooner 'tis done, the sooner you can have your freedom."

With a hand to the small of her back, he escorted Ana down the lane.

As they approached the manor, excitement over the king's impending visit was palpable. Preparations were under way everywhere they looked—people scurrying to sweep the grounds, clean the midden, and hang new banners. Soldiers were polishing their armor and their weapons. The stables were mucked, barrels were rolled behind the kirk, and the cook had set up tables in the close to lay out his growing collection of baked goods. Pages were scrubbing the outer walls of the dovecote. The laundresses were hanging clean linens on ropes strung between the manor house and stables. An equal mix of broad smiles and worried frowns decorated their faces.

It was pandemonium.

The volume of people moving about the keep would make their task much more challenging, but Niall could not summon any rancor. A visit by the king was an unimagined opportunity. If he could gain the evidence he needed tonight, he could approach the king on his arrival and prove his brother's innocence. Niall's family would be avenged.

The nightmare might finally be over.

Niall held the heavy oak door open so Ana could pass. Everything hinged on the steward's records. He could only pray they held the information he needed.

Inside the manor, the rushes had been raked from the floors and the bared wood planking was being vigorously scrubbed. Women were beating the dust from the tapestries on the walls, and men were replacing every candle stub with a long, fresh taper. A handful of servants polished the baron's silverware to a mirror shine, and several more were sweeping cobwebs from the corners. Lads with armloads of wood and lasses piled high with linens scurried in every direction.

He shepherded Ana through the great hall and up the stairs. At the door to Lady Elayne's chambers, he paused. "Visit with the baroness briefly, then excuse yourself. I'll determine which room belongs to the steward."

Ana nodded.

Then she entered, leaving Niall to his task. Had he thought to track the steward's movements earlier, locating the right room would have been easy. But regret was a fruitless emotion. He'd have to do it the usual way—by spying.

In truth, finding the right room was the least of their problems. Getting into the room without drawing notice was a far more ambitious endeavor.

Niall leaned against the stone wall, folded his arms over his chest, and adopted the bored mien of a man waiting. When a rosy-cheeked maid with a mop and a bucket shuffled past, he followed. She entered the room two doors down, and as the door swung open, he peered inside. A huge chamber with a platform bed, currently being tidied and rearranged. Probably for a guest. Possibly even the king himself.

Definitely not the steward's room.

It took the arrival and departure of five more servants for Niall to make a decision. Two rooms had not been entered—the small one at the end of the hall and a larger one immediately beside Lady Elayne's chambers. The steward was a senior retainer deserving of a well-appointed room, but he was not a noble. He would not have a gaggle of personal attendants. The smaller room was the most likely candidate.

Now to figure out how to get in.

Niall glanced around. Near the top of the stairs, a gillie was oiling the hinges on the doors. Farther down the hall, another fellow was repairing a door latch. A distraction of some sort was in order.

But what?

Chapter 11

Lady Elayne was not well.

The young woman sat in a chair before the fire, her skin white as the snowflakes drifting past the window, her eyes dark with distress. "I've not been able to eat anything since morn. Nothing stays in my belly. Not even the soup. My only blessing has been that I did not empty my spleen in the great hall."

"You've simply overtaxed yourself," Ana reassured her. "A little rest and your belly will settle."

"But I can't rest. Not now. Not with the king's arrival imminent."

"You must do what's best for the bairn, Your Ladyship." Ana offered Elayne her arm. "Come. Take to your bed for a short while."

"Nay," said Elayne, waving her off. "I cannot. This is my husband's moment to shine. I need only be strong for two days, and then I can rest. Help me remain on my feet these next two days and you'll have my eternal gratitude."

Bébinn looked up from the tapestry she was mending. "You are an inspiration, Your Ladyship."

The young baroness smiled at her handmaiden. "I only do what I must."

With a shake of her head, Ana acknowledged defeat. "This is against my better judgment, but if you insist on carrying on, I recommend drinking plenty of well water and taking a seat as frequently as you can. Cease chasing down the cook and the ale wife and the laundresses. Set up a table in the great hall and have them come to you. Have one of the baron's pages record your thoughts on the removes and wines that will be served at each meal, and have Bébinn fetch the spices from the larder. Continue to consume the broth, even if your belly rebels—some meager portion might remain and offer you strength."

Elayne nodded. "I can do all that."

"If you must walk, have Bébinn escort you. If you feel light-headed at any time, sit."

The baroness took the advice meekly. "I will."

Still not satisfied, but unable to summon an argument that might sway the noblewoman to take better care, Ana added, "This eve, I'll fetch a manchet from the kitchen for you to nibble on. With any luck, 'twill calm the heave in your belly."

At the word *heave*, Elayne turned a shade of green.

Bébinn set aside her stitchery and grabbed the pail next to the chair. She lifted it to Elayne's lap and brushed the young woman's hair back. An instant later, the baroness was retching into the bucket.

Ana wet a cloth in the ewer of water standing on the side table and washed the young woman's face. "Slow, deep breaths, now. There's a good lass."

"Sometimes, I wish I were dead," moaned Elayne, slumping back in her chair.

"Hush, Your Ladyship," Bébinn said sharply. "Such words are an invitation to the devil. The Lord gave us life and to deny that gift is to deny Him."

"He tries me sorely with this illness, He does."

"Then prove yourself worthy of his challenge." Bébinn jabbed a needle threaded with bright green floss through the coarse weave of the tapestry. "Be firm in your devotion now, and you will be rewarded in the afterlife."

A lecture on sanctity did not hold great appeal for Ana, so she took advantage of a brief lull between comments and said to the baroness, "I'll fetch your bread."

She nodded. "Bring it to me in the great hall. I will attend my lord husband at the high table for supper."

Ana left the two women to their discussion and ducked into the corridor.

Niall was waiting for her, leaning nonchalantly against the wall, the arrogant tilt of his head more reminiscent of a lord than a farmer. He straightened. "Ready?"

She glanced at the gillie repairing a latch two doors down. "Nay."

"The door you want is at the very end of the hall," he said quietly.

"I cannot do it," she responded. "Not while someone is watching." Frankly, she was a bit relieved. This inauspicious adventure went against her every instinct.

"His eyes will be elsewhere in a moment," Niall assured her. "Just walk toward the steward's door."

"Now?"

He nodded.

Ana took a hesitant step. What did she have to fear? Walking the hall was hardly a crime. And if the gillie made note of her presence, what did it matter? She was not about to steal anything—just read a few notes. She took another, firmer step. If she got to the end of the corridor and the gillie's eyes were still upon her, she'd simply turn around and come back, citing a cramp in her leg and the need to walk it out.

Her shoulders straightened.

She could do this.

Adding a slight hobble to her gait and rubbing her leg for effect, Ana ambled down the corridor. How Niall would draw the gillie's attention was a mystery. One she didn't care to solve. She kept her gaze locked on the door in front of her and kept walking.

Five paces from the door, the mystery solved itself.

A warbling coo and the mad beat of wings echoed off the walls of the corridor, and then something swept across the top of her head. Ana screamed and flung her hands up to ward off the pigeon trapped at the end of the hall with her. The bird flew frantically from wall to wall, desperately trying to find an exit.

The gillie ran toward her, shooing. "Away wie ya, ya barmy bird."

As Ana remained half-crouched in front of the steward's door, the gillie waved his arms and sent the bird flying in the opposite direction. He followed the bird down the corridor, shouting down the stairs to his fellow workers to fetch a broom. Niall used his great size to block the corridor once the bird had flown past him.

He tossed her a meaningful look, then returned to the pigeon chase.

Ana opened the door and slipped inside.

The room was small, only a narrow gap of wood floor visible between the bed on one side and the desk and chest on the other. A faded tapestry hung above the desk—a bucolic scene involving rolling hills of heather, grass, and sheep. There was no fireplace, but heat radiated from the rear wall, suggesting the flue from the hearth in the great hall rose up directly behind it.

Eager to complete her task and retreat, she set to work.

The desk to start, obviously. It was piled high with stacks of parchment. She pulled the stool from beneath the desk and sat. The first pile appeared to be taxation accounts—the entries were individual names accompanied by a number of shillings or goods delivered in lieu. She put that stack aside. The next tower of pages proved more interesting. A lengthy list of items, mostly foodstuffs, with two columns labeled *In* and *Out*.

Ana ran her finger down the *In* column. No dates.

Just quantities. She flipped through the pages to be certain none of them included dates, then put that stack aside, too. It seemed doubtful she'd find notice of a necklace buried amid the inventory of apples, corn, and flour. More likely, the steward kept separate records for the items stored in the baron's coffers.

She sifted through the remaining parchment sheaves, but found nothing.

Frowning, she swiveled on the stool. Where else might Eadgar store such a record?

In the chest? She lifted the brass-hinged lid and dug quickly through the contents. A collection of lèines, tunics, and hose, but no parchment. Under the bed? She dove to her knees and peered beneath the bed frame. A fat hairy spider waiting patiently for prey and a forgotten slipper, but no records.

Still on her knees, she slowly spun around.

Her eyes widened as she spotted the chair beside the door. It had arms with handholds, a beautifully carved backrest, and a smooth, crescent-shaped seat—a birthing chair. An odd item to find in the possession of the steward, to be sure. As the healer, it would be better placed in *her* possession. Or at least given to Lady Elayne. Nonetheless, it was not what she was searching for this eve.

Her gaze moved on, stopping at the lumpy heather-filled mattress. She'd hidden a thing or two under her mattress in the past. Might not the steward do the same?

She scooted to the bed and slid her hands beneath

the mattress. Sure enough, her hands met several sheets of stiff parchment. She smiled.

Catching the pigeon Niall let loose inside the manor took an amusing amount of time. Only after they ceased chasing the bird, and one of the pages tasked with caring for the birds coaxed it from the rafters, were they able to remove it to the dovecote. All the while, Niall kept lookout for the steward.

Fortunately, Eadgar was very busy with preparations for the king's arrival. Niall glimpsed him twice, jogging from one household crisis to another, keys jangling at his hip.

Ana had been in the steward's room for nigh on ten minutes when Niall saw Eadgar for the third time. Niall was chatting up the gillie who'd been repairing the door latch, keeping the lad occupied, when the steward swept by them, his tunic sodden and reeking of midden. He was headed for his room.

"Eadgar," Niall called, hoping to stall him.

The steward halted and turned, a dark scowl on his face. "You'd be a fool to utter another word, lad. At this moment, I don't care if the roof is collapsing over our heads. I'm going to peel these wretched garments off, wash the shite from my face, and don clean clothing. Only then will I consider your request. Is that clear?"

"Aye." Very clear.

The steward stalked to his chamber, threw open the door with a crash, and stepped inside.

There was no opportunity to warn Ana.

*   *   *

Ana had her nose between the pages of a fascinating list of valuables currently owned by the baron when she heard the stomp of boots on the wood planking outside the door. She thrust the sheaf back beneath the mattress and rose to her feet.

The door swung open with such force that it hit the wall with a loud bang.

Eadgar marched into the room, but drew up short when he spied her.

"What are you doing here?" he snarled.

The stench rolling off him was thick and sour and near unbearable. Ana's nose wrinkled. "My apologies for not consulting with you before entering, Eadgar. I must have temporarily lost my head. But when I heard the description of this chair from one of the maids, I had to see it for myself." She pointed to the birthing chair.

His scowl did not ease. "You stole into my room to view a piece of furniture?"

"Aye. Such an item would be a godsend for the Lady Elayne when her time comes."

The dark look became confusion. "Why?"

"'Tis a birthing chair," she explained, trailing her fingers over the thistle pattern carved into the backrest. "And a lovely one at that. I've never seen its equal."

The confusion cleared. "Ah. 'Twas a gift to the baron from Laird Leslie. We had no idea of its purpose."

"May I take it, then?"

He nodded.

Ana hoisted the chair and backed out of the room, giving him as wide a berth as the room would allow. He really did reek. "The Lady Elayne and I thank you mostly profusely, Eadgar. I'll leave you to you ablutions."

His scowl returned and he slammed the door behind her.

Niall took the chair from Ana. "Well?"

"I found one notation that might be of interest," she said, as they descended the stairs to the great hall. "A gold and ruby necklace was delivered to Baron Duthes on the seventh of December."

"Roughly a fortnight after I freed Aiden from Lochurkie." The timing was right. As was the description. Niall lifted the chair over his head to avoid colliding with a bevy of servants carrying platters of food and piles of trenchers for the evening meal. "Any mention of who delivered it?"

"I've not the time to discuss this now. I'm very tardy fetching Lady Elayne's bread."

He shouldered open the heavy door to the manor and allowed Ana to pass. "How long would it take to say aye or nay?"

"The answer is more complicated than that." She headed across the courtyard to the kitchen. They paused at the entrance, brought up short by a wave of sticky heat. Repairs were furiously under way inside. The sounds of hammers and saws mingled with the shouts of the cook and his bakers, who had reclaimed the ovens. The cook's two apprentices were adding glaze to a salmon subtlety, while gillies loaded up a dozen tureens with vegetable pottage and sent pairs of sturdy pages on their way with the food. Younger pages were handed large baskets of barley and rye bread.

"Don't be contrary. Tell me what you found."

She stopped and confronted him, hands on her hips. "I'm not contrary. *You* are impatient. Go home. I'll meet you there after the supper."

Niall frowned. Allowing an hour to waste away did not sit well—not with his brother's fate hanging in the balance—but a proper discussion would be difficult with so many ears listening. Reluctantly, he nodded. "Have one of the pages accompany you home."

"Pages do not escort servants." Catching the look in his eye, she added hastily, "I'll find someone else." Then her attention turned to the bread table, piled high with rounds and loaves of every shape and size.

"Lass?"

Ana glanced at him, one brow arched.

"You did well."

She smiled, then dove into the crowd.

Ana hunted high and low for a manchet of white bread. With the king arriving soon, numerous fine breads would be on the menu, but there were none in sight. She could have asked the bakers, but they looked sweaty and disgruntled after a very long day of work.

Unfortunately, too, her hunt was hindered by distraction.

She could not stop thinking about what she'd discovered in the steward's records—not only had the necklace Niall sought arrived in Duthes on the very same day that she arrived, according to the notation, *she* had delivered it. An outright lie, but how was she to dispute ink on parchment? Written by one of the most highly respected men in the barony?

What was she to tell Niall?

Not the truth, that was for certain. The bitter twist to his lips when he asked if the notation identified the courier did not bode well. Although she did not know what importance the necklace held for him, any association between it and her would surely taint her in his eyes. He already questioned her knowledge of poisons. Yes, he might see reason and accept that any one of the persons traveling with the merchant caravan could have brought the necklace. But what if he did not?

Ana spotted a tall willow basket in the corner and skirted two assistants wielding cleavers on haunches of spiced mutton to reach it. The basket was brimming with small rounds of white bread. Gathering her apron into a makeshift carryall, she appropriated several.

Then she made for the door.

Staying silent was not an option. Niall would hound her until she gave him an answer. Of course, since he'd seen nothing with his own eyes, she was free to make up any tale she liked. The challenge was coming up with a story that would satisfy his thirst for information.

She had a feeling Niall wouldn't be easy to satisfy.

Niall polished his sword while he waited for Ana to return.

Using wet sand, he rubbed the blade from tang to tip, removing tiny spots of rust that speckled the steel and leveling out the nicks and scrapes. Then he stroked the blade along a large whetstone, honing the cutting edge to lethal sharpness. When the sword could whisper through a piece of leather, he lightly oiled the steel and wiped it down with a soft linen cloth he borrowed from Ana's medicinal stores.

The weapon was leaning against the wall, reflecting the blaze of the fire in its smooth surface, when Ana returned to the bothy.

She glanced at it and frowned. "Can you not put that away?"

"Nay," he said. "Leaving it in the leather sheath causes rust to form. A good sword deserves a seat around the fire."

"There's no such thing as a good sword," she muttered. Crossing to her chest of foodstuffs, she pulled out dried beans, barley, and onion. A quick chop at the table and then all went into the freshly cleaned cauldron, along with some water and black pepper. She nodded to the food chest. "Best ease your hunger with bread. The pottage will not be ready for some time yet." A blush rose in her cheeks and she looked away. "I should have put the pot on hours ago."

Although the memories of what they'd been doing *hours ago* were sweet and tantalizing, Niall's need to know what she'd found in the steward's records was keen. "Tell me what the notation read. Word for word. Leave nothing out."

Ana swung the cauldron over the hottest part of the fire, then turned to face him. "On the seventh day of December, in the thirty-sixth year of the reign of Alexander III, king of Scotland and the Islands, one gold necklace set with three matchless rubies was delivered to Baron Duthes by"—she hesitated ever so slightly— "Laird Leslie."

It was a challenge to watch those lips move without dwelling on how sweet they'd tasted, but her lie made it easier. "Laird Leslie?" he pressed softly. "Are you certain?"

Her gaze flickered to the thatched roof. "Aye."

A tight spot of anger bloomed in his chest. He had begun to think he could trust her. Now this. Rising from the bed, he slowly advanced on Ana. Using his size to full advantage, he herded her back until she collided with the table. "That's a lie."

"Nay." Her slender, elegant throat worked as she swallowed.

Planting a hand on either side of her, caging her against the table, Niall pinned her gaze. "Laird Leslie was in France in December, celebrating the Yule with his daughter and new grandson."

"I can only tell you what the record stated. I cannot attest to its veracity."

He stared at her, hard. Whose name was truly recorded? "Who are you protecting?"

"No one."

He ran a thumb over the bright red crest of her cheek. "Lying to me is a grave mistake."

Her gaze met his. "After all that I've done, after all the risks I've taken to see your goal gained, why would I lie now?"

Why indeed? "Perhaps the name is that of a family member."

Her face fell. "My mother and father are both dead. I have no siblings, and I never knew my grandparents. I have no family to protect."

Her response, though delivered without a hint of self-pity, stirred him. More than most, he knew what it was like to be alone. But a lack of family did not mean she had no one to protect. "I am not so easily gulled," he said. "I suspect it is your lover that you protect."

"My lover?" She snorted. "*You* are my lover."

He shook his head. "The previous man you welcomed into your bed."

The flush in her cheeks deepened to a fiery scarlet. "You think me a faithless wench who jumps from one man's bed to another?"

He preferred to think nothing of the kind. But that just made him a fool. "You are lying to me. I would have the truth."

"The truth is this interrogation has naught to do with the necklace," she said hotly. She placed both hands flat on his chest and shoved. "You are simply jealous."

Her push, even as furious as it was, could not contend with the strength of his thighs. Niall held his position with ease. "You think too highly of your charms, lass. I've never been a man who clings to a lover. You could invite a hundred men into your bed—I would not care. Only one name matters."

"The name of the *man* I'm so determined to protect."

His grip tightened on the table. "Aye. Confess it now and we'll be done."

Her hands dropped limply to her sides. "We're already done."

He scowled. "You've not yet given me the name I seek."

"I've given you everything I have," she said quietly. "There is no more. Now let me pass."

Anger Niall understood. This cool, unemotional response he did not. "Laird Leslie did not bring the necklace to Duthes."

"Then you must look past the name and seek other evidence. Let me pass."

He studied her lovely face. Resolution was written in every gentle angle. Whatever name was written in the steward's records, it was clear she believed it a lie. He could accept that. But he could not accept her insistence on keeping it from him. It suggested she was more loyal to another than she was to him—and that wounded him more than he expected.

"I have no desire to let you pass." He bent his head and stole a quick, hard kiss.

She held herself stiffly, unyielding. "If you wish to sup, you'll let me be."

"Perhaps I've a hunger for something other than food." He nibbled his way along her jaw to her earlobe. Drawing that tender flesh into his mouth, he suckled. His hands left the table and sought softer, gentler terrain.

Her eyes drifted closed. "And if I don't share that same hunger?"

He smiled. She now gripped the front of his lèine tightly, holding him to her. "Say nay, and we'll go no further."

Confident that her lips would never utter that word, he blazed a trail of hot kisses down her neck to her collarbone. "Last chance for dissent, lass."

Her answer was to tip her head back to give him greater access to the silky skin of her throat.

With a grunt of satisfaction, he scooped her up and carried her to the bed.

Ana slipped out of bed before dawn and pulled on a clean sark. Niall had given her another taste of heaven, another aching glimpse at a life anyone but she could enjoy. But a glimpse was all she could endure.

Studiously averting her gaze from the temptation

that lay large and naked on her bed, Ana built up the fire. Without her body curled alongside him and with only one thin blanket, he would soon grow chilled. Last night had been a perfect example of why she needed her freedom. Even as he had boldly stated he cared not one whit for her, she had succumbed to her desire to have him. Had she no pride?

The coals in the pit eagerly embraced the added peat, bursting into flame.

He had invited her to take a hundred lovers. What kind of woman allowed such an indifferent man to feast upon her body? She flushed in the dimness. And he *had* feasted. No doubt about that.

She glanced at the bed.

The blazing fire cast a golden glow about the room and the rugged angles of his face were clearly visible. She was helpless against the sincerity of his desire. He displayed no shame in wanting her, made no effort to hide the need that coursed through his body. And she felt like a goddess in his arms. She had only to spy the heat in his eyes and the sinful curve of his lips and her resistance melted like snowflakes.

And it would happen again. As surely as the sun would rise.

No matter how much she prayed for more strength, no matter how much she convinced herself that holding her distance was the only way to keep him safe, she would allow it to happen again. When it came to Niall, she was as weak as day-old tea leaves.

Despite his overbearing and mistrustful nature, she wanted desperately to believe in a future together. She loved the rotter.

She grimaced. Not that he'd given her reason to think he wanted such a future.

Ana padded barefoot over the packed dirt floor to her clothing chest. Careful to lift it without the wood creaking, she gathered her meager collection of sarks and overdresses and stuffed them in a canvas bag. Her comb and a pair of snow white wimples went into the bag, as well. Desperation had forced her hand. She could not leave Duthes while Lady Elayne still struggled with illness, but she had another option—she could take the baron up on his offer to house her in the manor.

Inconvenient? Definitely. She would need to be especially vigilant around Bébinn.

But succumbing to Niall's seductive charms was proving to be the greater risk.

She dragged a woolen dress over her sark and rammed her toes into her leather shoes. It would be better this way. Even now, her traitorous body was urging her to return to the bed, snuggle close to his warm body, and lose herself in the dream. Unless she was strong now, she had no hope of resisting him. Leaving was the wise thing to do.

But it was not an easy thing to do.

Her feet dragged as she walked to the door, her belongings in one hand and her healing satchel in the other. Ana unlatched the door and slid it open a crack.

Before the heat of the hut could escape into the dark winter night, she squeezed through the gap and quietly shut the door behind her.

Leaving him felt a little like betrayal, but she tried not to dwell on that. With her breath a white fog in the moonlight, she strode down the lane toward the manor.

Chapter 12

Niall woke with a bitter taste in his mouth. The bothy was bright with a new day—so bright, it hurt. He jammed his eyes shut. Rolling to the edge of the bed, he sat up, trying to tame the wicked pound in his head. His maladies were consistent with a night spent overindulging in wine. Except he'd not had anything to drink.

He scrubbed his face and squinted around the room.

He was alone. The fire in the pit had died to a low yellow blur, suggesting Ana had been gone for an hour or more. Pushing to his feet, he made a beeline for the water pail. His tongue felt woolen and his feet were unsteady. He poured icy-cold water down his throat, but anger boiled in his belly just the same. *By God*. The bloody wench had drugged him.

She'd added something to his soup.

As he lowered the water pail, his gaze fell on her clothing chest. A small corner of white linen hung over the edge. Knowing in his gut what he would find, he set the water on the ground and crossed to the chest. Raising the lid, he stared inside.

Save for a lone, threadbare shift, it was empty.

The vixen had run.

A low growl escaped his lips. The woman was determined—he'd give her that—and a shade more devious than he had imagined. She'd lain in his arms, apparently at peace, all the while plotting to poison him and run off.

But run off where?

East lay Aberdeen, which she admitted to knowing quite well. West lay the Red Mountains, a decidedly harsh region during the winter months. South would take her to Fife and north would put her on the road to Elgin. With no knowledge of her past, other than her brief story about the ring, he had little to go on. Of course, his imagination insisted on detailing all the possible mishaps that could befall a woman traveling alone—wolves, brigands, starvation. *Damn it*. Any other man would curse her existence and forget about her. *He* was making plans to go after her.

Niall tugged on a fresh lèine and pinned his multi-hued brat over his shoulders.

One small mercy—she couldn't have gotten far in an hour.

He slammed the door behind him. Crouching in the lane, he studied the marks in the dirt. An overnight thaw had softened the ground, leaving a telltale imprint of her leather boots—and a clear indication of her direction. She'd gone left, deeper into the village. His gaze lifted to the parapets of the manor visible above the thatched roofs of the neighboring bothies. Perhaps it would be easier to find her than he thought.

With raw determination in every stride, Niall gave chase.

Inside the walls of the manor, activity had reached a fever pitch. With only a day left to prepare for the king's arrival, there was much to be done and done swiftly. Gillies ran about with arms full of linens and kindling. The ladies sat before the fire, stitching at a frenzied pace, hoping to repair any tapestry or clothing trim that did not shine.

Niall shouldered past a gillie sweeping the rushes and marched up to Eadgar.

"Have you seen my wife?" he asked the steward.

The very nature of the conversation was intriguing, and all around him, people paused to listen. The steward met his gaze, quiet and firm. "Goodhealer Ana has requested a pallet in the manor so that she might better tend the Lady Elayne."

"Given the king's imminent arrival, it was very generous of you to agree."

The steward correctly interpreted the chill in Niall's voice and took a step back. "All I could offer her was a spot in the lady's chamber."

Niall headed for the stairs.

"I trust this matter will be swiftly resolved?" Eadgar called after him.

"Count on it."

Mounting the stairs two at a time, Niall reached the

baroness's chamber in short order and knocked. The door was opened by the same maid he recalled from his first day in Duthes. He pushed past her and entered. His eyes found Ana immediately, over by the fire, placing a damp cloth on the lady's forehead.

Niall acknowledged Lady Elayne with a bow. "Your Ladyship."

Then he turned to Ana. "Where are your belongings?"

Her eyes narrowed. "It matters not. I am not leaving."

Spotting her healer's satchel and a burlap bag next to the bed, Niall snatched them up. "I never took you for a coward. And yet, rather than deal openly with our concerns, you chose to run away."

She scowled. "My duty lies here at Lady Elayne's side."

"A woman's first duty is to her husband." He smiled at the baroness. His most charming grin. "Is that not so, Your Ladyship?"

Elayne returned his smile. "Indeed."

"I will not go," Ana said darkly.

"Your will is irrelevant," he said. He tossed her bags over one shoulder, then swooped in to scoop Ana over the other. She shrieked, but he ignored her. "Lady Elayne's house will soon be filled to the rafters with royal guests. She does not need another mouth to feed."

"Put. Me. Down." Ana pounded his back with each word.

Niall offered the Lady Elayne another bow. "Good day to you, Your Ladyship." Then he carried Ana out the door and down the stairs. She struggled against him, kicking and punching, but he held her tight.

"This is unseemly," she hissed. "People are staring."

"I care not. The next time you poison me, I promise I'll do more than drag you home before a gawking crowd."

She suddenly ceased her struggles. "It wasn't poison. It was a sleeping draught."

"Call it what you will," he said coldly. "But abuse my trust again at your own peril."

A heavy sigh flowed from her chest. "You've made your point. Now put me down. You'll reopen the wound on your shoulder."

He did not slow his pace.

Only when they were back inside the bothy did he lower her to the floor and release her. "Understand this and understand it well. When I said nothing would stand in my way, I meant it. If you attempt to leave again, I will hunt you down, no matter how far you have run. Am I clear?"

He met her gaze with steely purpose.

"But you can enter the manor at will now," she protested. "The guards recognize you. You no longer need me."

"Am I clear?" he repeated.

"Aye."

He hooked her satchel over the peg by the door. The

movement drew a wince. His shoulder was very unhappy with his activities of late.

"Let me have a look at that shoulder," she offered.

"And have you lay me low again? I think not."

"Were I the blackhearted wench you paint so well, I'd have left you to die in the woods," she said drily. "The sleeping draught was necessary because you seem to sleep with one eye open. I feared you would wake up and stop me from leaving."

He grunted and removed his brat. "Why the need to run at all? We suit well enough."

As he peeled off his lèine, she said softly, "I've no desire to suffer heartache, and you, sir, are a breaker of hearts if ever I saw one."

He dropped his arms and stared at her.

Her gentle hands unwrapped the linen from his shoulder, but as he tried to peer at the wound, she pushed his chin aside. "I cannot do my work with your head in the way."

"I wish to see the injury."

"Can you not tell it is healing by the minimal pain? Let me do my work."

"At least it's my left shoulder," he said, shrugging. "If I end up lame, I'll still be able to wield a sword."

"You'll not end up lame."

The chill of unguent slathered on his skin followed her words. It was an act of faith to let her ply her medicines on him—he had no knowledge of what she put in her salves. Still, when he looked at the earnest expression on her face as she tended him, he could not summon any fear.

"The baroness did not look well," he said, his gaze trapped by the delicate hue of the skin that ran along her jaw to her ear. Pale as a winter moon. Not a freckle to be seen.

She frowned. "She insists on being involved in the preparations for the king, but she is not strong."

Ah, yes, the king.

Niall glanced up at the chimney hole. In less than a day, the trumpets would blare and the huge coterie of retainers that regularly accompanied the king would descend on the keep. Yet the necklace that determined his brother's fate still lay beyond his grasp. Failure did not sit well upon his shoulders.

"Be quick," he told Ana. "I've work that needs be done and done swiftly."

Tonight he had a chance to redeem himself. Best not waste it.

Ana was thankful that Niall's thoughts, although clearly dark, kept him occupied. He did not try to examine the wound again. She quickly covered up his shoulder with fresh linen and tied a neat knot.

As she finished, he frowned. "Your hands are cool now, but the night you found me in the woods, they were very hot."

She stiffened. Had he been conscious? "It may have seemed thus because your flesh was bitter cold. The winter night very nearly took you before I returned with the cart."

He nodded, his expression thoughtful. "No doubt."

Ducking her head to hide the flush in her cheeks, she stuffed the remainder of the linen strips in a small chest by the table and replaced the wax stopper to her salve. Putting order to the table was far easier than reining in the chaotic tumble of her thoughts.

"I also recall," he said slowly, "that your arms were dappled with a red pattern not unlike autumn vines."

Ana choked out a sharp laugh. Dear Lord. He *had* been awake. "What a curious vision. Delirium had set in, obviously."

His gaze met hers, serious as sin. "Perhaps."

Ana's heartbeat slowed to a breathless pace. "Are you satisfied that I healed you with all due care?"

He glanced down at the bandages. "Aye, I am."

"Then all is well."

He nodded. "For now."

Niall found her response to his queries decidedly flimsy, but pursuing the truth of what happened that night was far less important than retrieving the necklace. At least, for the moment. Tonight might well be his last opportunity to break into the baron's coffers. Once the king's guards descended upon the keep, every corridor would be closely watched.

After the eventide meal, the repair work in the cellars would cease, and he would have an excellent opportunity to pick the lock. Assuming he could get past the guard at the gate.

"I need a tabard and helm," he said to Ana.

She frowned. "Like the ones worn by the constable's men?"

"The very same."

"And why do you mention this to me?" she asked, bristling.

"The size of helm I require is a fine match to the guard who carried your neeps back to the castle the day I arrived in Duthes. That helm also had a telltale dent in it that others would be quick to recognize."

She planted her hands on her hips. "And what? You want me to waylay the poor fellow in some alley and rob him of his accoutrements?"

"Nay. Visit him in the guardhouse on pretense of tending the guards' training injuries and make good use of those nimble fingers."

Her eyes grew round as targes. "Snatch the items right before his eyes? In the middle of a troop of armed men? Are you mad?"

Niall smiled. She definitely had no sense of the distraction she posed. "'Twill be easier than you imagine."

"I think you've lost your wits."

He handed her the leather satchel and pointed to the door. "Make haste. I need the garb by gloaming."

Glaring, she grabbed the satchel and stomped out.

Niall rooted through his purse and found his meager supply of coin. Three silver pieces and a dozen pence. One of the more valuable scraps of information he'd gleaned from the stable hands was the name of the local whisky maker—One-Eyed Thomas. A useful fellow to know, to be sure.

An hour later, he returned to the hut with his booty.

Ana was waiting for him with a triumphant grin on her face and a heaping basket of bread in her hands. "They traded bread for my services and were most appreciative." She dumped the basket on the bed, and a gleaming silver helm rolled out amid a scattering of loaves.

Niall shrugged, unsurprised. "We're all fools before beauty."

She tilted her head. "You really think me beautiful?"

"Lovely enough to tempt a dead man from the grave," he admitted. "But as beauty proved the downfall of Samson, Julius Caesar, and Achilles, it's hardly the most admirable of traits."

She tossed a round of rye at his head. "Wretched cur. I risked my life and this is how you reward me? With insults?"

He grabbed her wrist before she could lob a second loaf, and yanked her to his chest. "If I admit that I'm as beguiled as any, would that temper the offense?" he whispered. Then he fiercely claimed her lips, goaded by a burning desire that refused to be satisfied any other way. She might be devious, she might be a liar, but at that moment, it didn't matter. He wanted her, and that was enough. Temporarily lost in the soft press of her body against his, and the responding pound of blood through his body, he took everything she was willing to give.

After he pulled away, her eyes still held shadows. "Do you truly believe me capable of murder?"

He shook his head. "A murderess would not have tended Aiden's wounds while he was in Lochurkie's dungeon."

She blinked. "You knew about that?"

"Not as fact. I knew someone had treated his wounds. He wore poultices on several of his more severe injuries. Once I knew you to be a healer, it was an easy leap to make."

"Then why let me believe you thought me a poisoner?"

Niall's gaze roved the sweet curves of Ana's face. "I've been led astray by a pretty face and gentle ways before. Expect the worst, and you're prepared for anything."

"So you still do not trust me."

"Take no offense," he said, donning the tabard. The two front panels hung to his knees, the sides open. "I trust no one. Not even my brethren in the Black Warriors."

"The Black Warriors?"

"Those men who aided me in freeing Aiden." He buckled his sword at his side, enjoying the familiar weight and the knowledge that, for a short time at least, he was once again a knight of Scotland.

"What of your kin? Surely you trust *them*?"

He snorted. "My mother was perpetually lost in her cups. She'd have sold me for a keg of ale had anyone expressed an interest."

She passed him the helm. "And your father?"

"Fed me and clothed me, as he deemed just dues

for his bastard, but he could barely remember my name."

"Is there no one upon whom you rely?"

He held up a hand. "Enough, lass. There's no value in this conversation. Trust makes a man weak."

She touched his sleeve. "I disagree."

He slid the helm over his head and stared at her through the eye cutouts. The metal was cold against his ears and he briefly coveted a hooded gambeson. "The only thing I trust is that you won't willingly reveal your past to the constable. That's enough for me."

Her hand dropped away.

Niall felt her withdrawal as decidedly as his hearing was made hollow by the helm. A coolness settled over her features and she stepped back.

"Then there's little more to say."

"Agreed," he said. Then he spun on his heel and left the hurt look in her eyes behind.

As the door snapped shut, Ana mentally kicked herself. *Why?* Why had she continued to press him for details of his past? Wasn't it enough that she refused to let go of her valiant image of him? Now she also had glimpses of him as a young lad, barely recognized by his father and abandoned by a drunken mother. What boy deserved such a fate?

How lucky she'd been to enjoy the close bonds she'd shared with her father and mother. No, their lives had not been easy. Far from it. But through it all, they'd had each other. Niall had had no one.

She should be grateful that he'd driven a wedge between them.

He deserved so much better than she could offer him. He deserved a wife who could give him a steady, uncomplicated life full of children and laughter and love. He deserved all the things his childhood had denied him. He did not deserve the miseries a lengthy association with her would bring.

Aye, she thrilled to his kisses. Aye, she warmed to the look of desire in his eyes. And aye, she would leave a piece of her heart behind when she ran.

But it was undeniably, unequivocally for the best.

Niall was of two minds. Part of him wanted to return to the bothy, scoop Ana into his arms, and take her to bed. With dedicated effort, he could sweep the wounded look from her eyes. But time was short.

He had but one chance left, and this was it.

He picked up the sack he'd left outside the door and marched toward the manor. He affected the stiff-legged gait of a patrol soldier and approached the gate in a steady, relentless fashion. As was the norm for this hour of the night, the portcullis was down. A solitary guard stood just inside the iron grate, rubbing his hands and stomping his feet to ward off the chill of the icy mist that had filled the glen and crept up the hillsides to the manor.

Boldness won the day, not reticence. Niall strode up to the guard with confidence. "Bloody cold night."

"Aye, I'm freezing my bollocks off." The guard

peered at him through the portcullis. His eyes lingered on the dent in Niall's helm. "Garret, is it?"

"It is." Best keep the conversation limited. The echo of his helm would only take him so far.

The guard's gaze slipped to the misty road behind him. "What were you about?"

Niall held up his burlap sack, the contents rattling on cue. "Paid a visit to One-Eyed Thomas."

The guard grinned. "That old bugger makes the best whisky in the Highlands."

"That he does."

A hopeful gleam appeared in the young man's eyes. "Would you be willing to spare me a wee dram?"

"I can do better than that, if you and the gateman are willing to omit my unsanctioned foray from your report to Mr. Hurley." Niall dug into his sack and pulled out a flagon of whisky. Holding it aloft, he asked, "What say you?"

The guard grinned. "Consider yourself unseen."

Niall handed the man his whisky and waited while the gateman on the wall above winched up the portcullis. Once inside the close, he headed for the kitchen entrance. The faint rosy glow emanating from the archway told him the baking was done for the night and the coals in the ovens were banked. The kitchen gillies would return before dawn to bake fresh bread for the king's visit, but at the moment, stillness reigned.

The inner walls of the kitchen were still black from the fire, but several new beams—their wood pale against the dark ceiling—had replaced the charred rafters.

Niall wasted no time.

He strode through the baking area and down the corridor to the coffers door. Laying the burlap bag on the ground, he dug through the contents for the hoof pick and needle. The lock was a simple enough mechanism, but it had been many years since Niall had relied on his ability to break one.

In the years before his father reluctantly took him in, thieving had been his primary source of food. With his mother ever flat on her back or drinking away the coin she earned in a fruitless attempt to forget who and what she was, he was alone more often than not. He'd learned early that a meal only came to he who was brave enough to fight for it.

He slid the pick into the keyhole and felt for the latch that held the lock secure. So focused was he on the inner workings of the mechanism that he failed to note the five shadows standing in the lee of the stairwell—until the slither of steel alerted him to their presence.

Niall dropped the pick and spun around, drawing his own sword as he turned.

Before him stood Constable Hurley and four of the manor guard, all with their weapons at the ready.

"I knew there was something off about you, Bisset," Hurley said.

Niall did not respond. There was a good chance Hurley was bluffing about knowing his identity. If he spoke, the game would be over for certain. He quickly assessed his opponents, sizing up their strength by the way they held their bodies and their weapons. Hurley was by far the most formidable foe—his stance was loose but brimming with energy, and the hand that held his sword was steady and sure. But all of the men were trained soldiers. This would not be as easy as thwarting the thieves in the woods.

"Step away from the door," Hurley ordered.

Niall held his ground. The door protected his back and he had no intention of giving up what little advantage he possessed.

There was only one way for this to end well—he had to escape with his helm intact. Hurley might suspect his identity, but as long as his helm remained on his head, the constable had no proof. That lack of proof was the only protection Niall could offer Ana at the moment.

All was not lost, though—this time he had his sword.

By God, the blade felt good in his hand. The calluses on his palm and thumb fit smoothly against the leather-wrapped hilt. So familiar were the heft and balance of the great sword to his arm that his muscles bunched with excitement. The entire length of his body knew what came next and was primed to act. Wielding a sword was what he did best.

"Come now, Bisset," taunted Hurley. "Why risk injury? Come along quietly and you'll enter the dungeon a whole man."

For Ana's sake, Niall might have considered surrender. But he wasn't a fool. The punishment for attempting to rob the baron would be severe. If he saw the inside of the dungeon at all, it would be as a bruised and battered replica of the man he was now. Worse, the instant Hurley confirmed his identity, he'd send a troop of soldiers to Ana's bothy and have her arrested.

Surrendering was not an option.

Feigning a nervous hold on his weapon, Niall hid his intent until the last possible moment. He let silence increase the tension. Only when the eagerness to do battle got the best of his opponents did he make his move. As the soldiers' blades wavered with restless anticipation, he leapt.

Hurley's conviction that Niall was a simple peasant betrayed him. His defense was not as rigorous as it should have been. The pommel of Niall's sword pounded Hurley's hand, knocking the constable's weapon loose. Before the blade had time to hit the dirt, a fist to the man's temple dropped the thinner man to his knees.

Niall blocked a sword thrust from one soldier with his blade and booted the exposed knee of a second opponent. A sharp yelp echoed in the corridor. Metal slid along metal, and sparks flew. One of the guards pulled a dirk from his belt and dove into the fray with two lethal blades, slashing and stabbing. Niall took a long slice to his left arm before he had a chance to step clear.

Pain ripped up his arm.

He ignored it. Pain wasn't nearly as inconvenient as death. And he was no stranger to pain. In battle, the man who won was the one who remained on his feet.

Pressing two of his opponents with a fierce attack, he took down a third with a hooked foot.

Spinning away from a pair of arcing blades, he struck the prostrated man with the flat of his blade, knocking him unconscious. His left arm was dripping blood, and as he dodged another slashing blade, he slipped.

Niall quickly righted himself, but took a jarring blow to his helm.

Ears ringing and head pounding, he pivoted. He met the next blow with his sword and used his considerable size and strength to push his attacker back a foot. And another. When his chance came, he took it—he buried his blade in the guard's exposed thigh. His success came at a price. As he yanked his sword free, he felt a sword edge slide along his ribs.

Very aware that blood loss would end his campaign for freedom if he did not swiftly bring the battle to a halt, he summoned every last reserve of might he possessed. With a low growl, he went on the offensive.

Clang, clank. Kick.

His third opponent fell.

Gaining strength from the knowledge that the odds were now two to one—odds he knew he could win—he jabbed and feinted and sliced with all the finesse and power he possessed. He fought like an animal caged. He scored a slice on one man's right arm, and the fellow's blade spun off into the darkness. Niall finished the man with a solid head butt.

Ears ringing, blood dripping, he faced his last foe.

The man with two blades. Beneath his helm, the fellow's teeth were clenched in a raging snarl. Clearly not about to surrender or run, despite how the battle had turned.

Killing the man would be simple—Niall outweighed him and outmatched him. But he'd come this far without slaying any of the baron's men and it behooved him to maintain that record. The intensity of the hunt for him after all was said and done would be commensurate with the insult he delivered. Why put Ana at increased risk?

Better to let the man live.

Unfortunately, his foe made that choice a difficult one. He attacked with a furious roar. Every swing of his blade was followed by a slash or jab of his dirk. Smaller and uninjured, his movements were nimble and quick. Opportunities to drive a fist into his face or pummel his head were rare, but Niall pursued every one, determined to end the encounter.

His foe was brave and fierce.

But eventually, the right opportunity arose.

As he dodged one of Niall's kicks, his right arm lifted a tad too high, exposing his ribs. Niall smacked his torso with the flat of his blade so hard he heard the air huff from the guard's chest. As the man instinctively crunched forward, Niall hammered his head with his fist. The man's eyes rolled back in his head, and down he went.

For a moment, the only sound was Niall's labored breathing.

He eyed the lock.

Then surveyed the bodies at his feet.

Hurley was stirring. Once the constable awoke, the chase would be on. Even without proof that Niall had attempted to rob the baron, Hurley was likely to be ruthless in his search for vengeance. Niall needed to warn Ana before he escaped into the woods.

But did he have time to snatch the necklace *and* warn Ana?

Boot steps on the stairs behind him answered his question.

Niall sheathed his sword, gave the lock one last rueful look, then loped down the corridor to the kitchen. From there, he hooked left and headed for the postern gate, located behind the stables. Disappointment was a boulder on his chest. His best chance at redemption was lost.

After tonight, the baron would be a fool to leave the necklace where it lay. Niall could only hope that wherever the ruby ended up, it was easier to pilfer.

For now, his job was done.

Chapter 13

Unable to sleep for worry, Ana was mixing a new batch of unguent when Niall burst through the door. She glanced up. His grim expression set her heart to racing.

"Constable Hurley and his men will be here anon," he said, removing his helm and tossing it aside. "If you wish to run, pack a bag as swiftly as you can."

Her throat tightened. "He knows about Lochurkie?"

Niall shook his head. "I'm not sure what he knows, but his men were lying in wait for me when I arrived at the manor." He peeled off the tabard.

That's when Ana noticed the blood. How she could have missed it she did not know—the sleeve of his lèine was soaked a dark crimson. She snatched up a handful of dried moss and ran to him. "You're wounded."

He shrugged her off. "We've no time for that. Did you not hear me?"

"Hurley is coming," she repeated, pressing the moss against his arm. A surprising calm settled over her—

she was about to be dragged back to a dungeon cell, and instead of trembling hands and wild-eyed panic, deliberate actions and cool thoughts prevailed. It was a miracle, really. "But he may not know that I was tried and condemned for murder at Lochurkie."

Niall frowned. "He was expecting me—that's cause enough for worry."

Ana spied a second slice along his ribs. A shallower cut than the one on his arm, but bleeding just the same. Why did men insist on solving all their problems with a sharp blade? "Even if we run, we won't get far. Did they see you without the helm?"

"Nay, but Hurley will come here first. He called me by name. He's convinced it was me."

If Hurley had not seen Niall's face then there was still a chance. But a very slim one. Ana's heart thumped in her chest. "If his search turns up no helm, no sword, and no injured man, will he not be forced to rethink his assumption?"

He stared at her. "What are you suggesting?"

"Under the woodpile, on the left side, there's a hole. We can hide the helm and tabard there." She glanced around . . . and then up. "The sword can be hidden in the thatching."

He snorted. "And the injured man?"

Ana took a deep breath. Her belly quivered with nervous tension. She had not shared the truth about her healing talents with anyone since . . . Could she truly do this? Heal Niall before his very eyes? How would she bear the look on his face if he thought her an abomination? She straightened her shoulders. If it meant saving his life, she could bear anything.

"Let me deal with that," she said. "Hide your accoutrements."

"Nay. Running is the wiser option. If they find me here, it will not go well for you."

She met his gaze, the calm returning. "If I do not treat these wounds, running will not save us. I must ask you to put your faith in my abilities. Would it not be better for Hurley to discover us asleep and unharmed?"

Niall gathered up his belongings, doubt a deep furrow in his brow. "Perhaps."

"Then go. Hide your belongings and return swiftly."

Despite his obvious reservations, he did as she bid. Once the helm was hidden and the sword was buried in the heather thatch above their heads, he sat down on the bed and offered up his arm. "Do your worst."

She dropped to her knees before him. "Are you a brave man?"

He said nothing, just stared at her.

"Because what I'm about to do will strike fear in your heart—but you must hold fast."

The steel in his gaze did not bend. He rolled up his sleeve to reveal the whole of his injury. A parting of flesh from elbow to wrist that ran along his previous scar. "Time marches on, lass."

Ana rubbed her hands together. Immediately, the healing heat bubbled up in her chest and poured down her arms. The delicate red pattern rose on her skin, twisting and twining its way to her fingertips.

Niall's gaze dropped to her hands and he frowned. But he did not pull away.

Ana took that as permission to continue. She laid her hands on the torn flesh, one above the other, covering most of the wound. Niall did not flinch when her hot hands touched him, nor draw in a sharp breath. He simply waited.

She pictured the sundered flesh knitting together, from one end of his forearm to the other. Inch by inch, along every carved thew. He had marvelous arms— lean and roped with muscles—and she drew easily from her memory the image of a successful conclusion.

"Hurry, lass," he said softly.

She lifted her eyes. The frown still haunted his brow, but his attention had shifted to the door. "You hear something?"

"The clink of ring mail."

"Toss your lèine into the fire and blow out the candle." Once he had stripped, Ana closed her eyes and tried desperately to focus. If she did not have enough time, if even a portion of the wound remained open . . . Nay, she mustn't think like that. She shifted her hands to the cut on his ribs, sent the healing heat into the wound, and prayed. Then she quickly cut away the bandages on his shoulder—the ones she no longer needed to hide the healed arrow wound—and peeled off her overdress.

He doused the light and the bothy sank into darkness.

Ana leapt into the bed and felt his weight slide alongside her. He threw an arm around her and pulled her close. Shutting her eyes, she tried to savor the strong warmth of his embrace, but the drumbeat of fear in her chest was too great.

A minute passed. And then another. The flare of fire from the burning lèine died away.

Then, without announcement or warning, the door flew open, hitting the wall with a loud crash. Ana shrieked and sat up.

Several men stepped into the hut, all wearing ring mail, one carrying a torch. A helmless Constable Hurley stood at the forefront, a large bruise blackening one eye. Niall leapt from the bed, his body forming a barrier between Ana and the soldiers.

"What is the meaning of this?" There was a rough edge to his voice, much as one might expect if he'd been roused suddenly from a deep sleep. Ana applauded his creativity.

Hurley's gaze ran the length of Niall's naked body, then shifted to Ana in the bed. She drew the blanket up, covering the thin linen of her sark. He did not answer Niall's question. Gesturing to his men, he said, "Search the hut."

To Niall and Ana he snarled, "Outside. Now."

Fearing the discovery of the hidden items, she slid from the bed, dragging the blanket with her. As inappropriate as it was to stand before a group of strange men in her small clothes, if they were to stand outside, Niall needed the blanket more. She tossed it over his shoulders as they walked to the door.

"Nay," Hurley said, snatching the woolen cover away. "I must examine him tip to toe."

Ana glared at him. "It's winter."

He glared back. "I'm under orders from the baron. If you have a concern, take it up with him."

"I will. Be assured of that."

Outside in the lane, another half dozen men waited. Hurley sent several of them inside to help with the search, then grabbed a torch from one of his men and strode over to Niall.

"Hold your arms aloft," he ordered.

For a moment, Ana thought Niall would refuse. The look on his face was dark and strangely still. But he lifted his arms away from his sides. Wise decision. She'd patched too many holes in the man already. Including that one along his ribs. . . . Tilting her head ever so slightly, she risked a quick look. *Thank God.* Nothing remained of his injury save a long pink scar.

Hurley peered closely at each of Niall's scars. He frowned as he tested the gash on his ribs with a jab of his finger. "I do not recall seeing this scar the other day."

"Your attention was centered on his upper chest, as I recall," Ana said.

He grunted and circled around to Niall's back. When he'd looked his fill, he thrust the torch at one of the guards, clearly disappointed to find no open wounds.

Behind them, disconcerting sounds emanated from the bothy. Rattles and crashes. The tinkle of broken pottery. The creak and snap of breaking wood. She grimaced. It seemed she was going to need that new bed after all.

A soldier scurried from the hut to Hurley's side. He handed something to the constable—too small to be the sword or the helm. Hurley nodded sharply to the soldier, dismissing him, then marched over to Ana and Niall. He held out a handful of moss soaked in blood. *Niall's* blood. "Explain this."

Ana's guts turned to water. But she knew if she failed this night, both she and Niall would hang. "I'm a healer, Mr. Hurley. I use such items to tend my patients."

He shook the moss. "And from which patient did this blood come?"

She dug through her mind for a name. She'd treated no serious injuries today, other than Niall's. If he questioned her patients, as he would surely do, he'd quickly discover her lie. Unless she named a person who might not recall which day he had visited her. "I tended a wound on Rory's hip today. It's his blood."

Hurley studied her face in the flickering half light. "You'd best hope his accounting matches yours."

"The man is losing his wits. He might say anything at all." The cold ground was already numbing her toes, and she shifted to her feet to keep them warm. "Just check his hip. You'll see that I tended it."

The constable's gaze dropped to her shuffling feet.

"Mr. Hurley," Niall said quietly. "I have a great respect for the law, so I'm willing to overlook the rousting of my wife and I in the middle of the night. I'm sure you have good cause. But my wife is barefoot and shivering with the cold. I will not see her suffer."

Hurley turned to Niall, his expression sour. "Your will is of no importance to me."

Niall stood taller, bristling with menace, despite his nakedness. "Allow my wife to return to the fire."

"Nay."

"Then give her the blanket and a pair of shoes."

"You do not dictate my actions," snarled the constable, rubbing his bruised temple. "I do as I please."

Niall took a step forward, but was immediately halted by several sharp pikes. "She has done nothing to warrant this abuse."

"But you have?"

Niall stood silent, his hands fisted at his sides.

Hurley closed the gap between them, coming toe-to-toe. "Go ahead, goodman. Attack me. I can see that you want to."

Niall shook his head. "I've no desire to see the inside of the baron's dungeon."

"Then hold your tongue."

Ana saw her opportunity and stepped between the two men. She put one hand on Niall's chest and the other on the constable's sleeve. To Mr. Hurley, she said, "If I catch chill, I will be unable to tend the baroness on the morrow. Perhaps you would allow us to beg the hospices of a neighbor while you complete your search?"

He scowled. "You can go, but not him."

A childish comment worthy of a sigh. "Robbie has not fully recovered from the ague. He should not be standing naked in the night, unless the baron's intent is to bury an able worker."

"Constable!"

A guard had appeared at the door to the hut.

Hurley tossed them a triumphant look and spun away. He marched to the bothy, where he exchanged a few words with the guard, then disappeared inside.

Ana shivered. She carefully avoided looking at Niall, afraid that her fear for them both would be written all over her face. Had they found the sword? The blade alone would not be enough to prove Niall a malefactor, but it would surely incite Hurley and his men to tear the house apart looking for further evidence.

The constable returned to the door and waved to them. "Goodhealer Ana, your presence is required."

She frowned, but obeyed. Niall was held back by three armed guards.

Stomach tight with worry, she entered the blissful warmth of the bothy. Inside the hut, all of her pots of herbs and unguents had been set on the table. One of the guards—a rather beefy fellow with sallow skin and a deep shadow of beard on his chin—was opening each one and sniffing the contents.

"Hamish here," the constable said, "once worked

for an apothecary. He has informed me that you are in possession of some very concerning items. Namely nightshade and foxglove."

"If he worked in an apothecary, then he must also have told you that those herbs have medicinal value." She edged closer to the fire pit and felt a tingle of life in her numb toes.

"Do you deny they are poisons?"

Ana crossed her arms. "Foxglove is used to settle an uneven heart and nightshade is used in an unguent for gout."

"The baron has placed a great deal of faith in you," said Hurley, "trusting you with the care of his wife and unborn child. He'll not be pleased to discover you are in possession of such dangerous physics."

"I possess a knife and a saw, as well. Does that make me a murderer?"

"Time will tell," he said darkly.

Anger bloomed in Ana's chest, but she tamed it, all too aware of how easily rational people could fall victim to misunderstanding about herbs. "Mr. Hurley, there has not been a single death in the village since I became the healer. Why would you accuse me of misusing these medicines?"

He stared at her for a long moment. "Auld Mairi died."

"She was four score," Ana pointed out.

"But hale and hearty before you descended on the village."

"Auld Mairi was aged," she repeated firmly.

Perhaps the surety of her voice convinced him, or perhaps he simply realized how ridiculous his accusation was—she could not be certain—but he nodded sharply and turned away. Addressing a senior guard, he asked, "Was anything else discovered?"

"Nay."

The constable rubbed his bruised temple again, deep furrows of disappointment on his brow. "Let's return to the manor, then." To Ana, he said, "We'll be taking your husband with us."

"Why?"

"I do not answer to you, Goodhealer. I answer to the baron."

"And did the baron demand my husband's presence?"

"Nay," Hurley admitted. "Baron Duthes has retired for the night."

"Then you have no reason to hold Robbie."

The constable's eyes narrowed. "Have a care, Goodhealer. Unless you want to join your husband in the dungeon, you would be wise to cease your insolence." He turned to leave.

"Wait." Ana dug through the pile of clothing the guards had left in the middle of the room and located a brown lèine. She thrust the garment at Hurley. "Please see that he gets this."

After a brief hesitation, the constable accepted the clothing. "Good night to you."

She leaned against the doorframe as Hurley handed Niall the lèine. They gave him a moment to pull the shirt over his head, then prodded him forward with the butts of their pikes.

Niall gave her a long, even look before he acquiesced to their demand.

Then they marched off toward the manor, and an empty silence fell upon the bothy.

Niall was beaten repeatedly en route to the manor. By the time they dragged him down the stairs to the dungeon and shackled him to a stone wall, he had welts and bruises too numerous to count. But he still held himself strong and sure.

The constable tugged off his gloves, handed them to a guard, and then rolled up his sleeves. "You're not truly Ana's husband," he said nicely. "That much I know. Tell me your real name."

"Robbie Bisset."

Hurley shook his head. "Lies will only earn you pain."

He signaled to another guard—a tall Frenchman whom Niall recognized as Ana's harasser from the cellar—and was handed a sturdy wooden club. With a finesse clearly born of regular practice, he swung it at Niall's ribs. The wood collided with his flesh with a dull thud and a rush of mouth-souring pain. His shoulders instinctively curled.

"Let's try again." Hurley stood back. "What is your name?"

"Robbie Bisset," Niall said, through clenched teeth.

His answer earned him another blow, this one on

the opposite side. "Why were you trying to break into the baron's coffers?"

"You have the wrong man," he said, barely able to draw a breath.

The constable paced the ground before him, the club resting on one shoulder. "I knew you were trouble the moment I laid eyes on you," he said. "You look like no common laborer I've ever seen."

Niall straightened against the wall.

"You think I don't recognize the calluses of a trained swordsman?" Hurley used the club to flatten Niall's right hand and expose his palm. "I'm not a fool. Now tell me who you truly are."

"Robbie Bisset, husband of Ana Bisset. Dock-worker."

Hurley smiled—a tight, thin-lipped grimace. Then he swung the club again, this time at Niall's knee. Wood crunched into bone with a sickening flash of agony. "The body is a remarkably frail piece of equipment," the constable said. "This knee, for example, will be nothing but broken bone and swollen tissue after five or six solid blows."

Surfacing from a sea of red-hazed pain, Niall accepted those words as fact. If he left this dungeon at all, it was likely to be as a crippled man—because he sure as bloody hell wasn't going to speak the truth. Ana would pay the price of every word.

"You have the wrong man," he repeated hoarsely.

There was a commotion outside the dungeon door;

then the portal swung open, revealing a very angry baron. The nobleman wore a rumpled sleeping robe and his hair was widely askew. "What in the name of our Exalted Father is going on?" he demanded. "The healer roused my wife and me from a good night's sleep, insisting her husband has been falsely accused of some crime."

"He is not her husband," Hurley replied. He pointed the club at Niall. "This man was caught trying to break into your coffers."

The baron's eyebrow's soared. "Really?"

"That's a lie," Niall spat out. His only hope of surviving lay with his ability to sway the baron. "Ask any witness. The constable dragged my wife and me from our beds this night. He did not find me here in the manor."

Duthes shifted his attention back to the constable. "It appears we have a difference of opinion. Did you catch him in the cellars, or not?"

"In a manner of speaking," Hurley said. "We found a helmed man in the cellars, but he escaped. I know this man to be other than what he says, so I sought him out immediately." Hurley went on to explain the calluses and the scars on Niall's body that he swore were battle injuries.

The baron listened, tapping his finger against his lips. When Hurley was done, he said, "If you are convinced he is not the goodhealer's husband, that should be easy enough to prove." He strode over to Niall. "How long have you been wed to Ana Bisset?"

Niall experienced a sharp pang of regret. Perhaps he ought to have rehearsed a few lies with Ana after all. He was about to dig himself a very deep hole. "Five years," he lied.

"And where were you wed?"

"Aviemore," he said smoothly, as if his words were not about to cause both him and Ana a heaping midden of grief. Aviemore lay on the other side of the Cairngorm Mountains and it would take a week or two to prove him wrong. But, of course, proof was the least of his worries.

"The name of the priest who wed you?"

"Brother Ben."

The baron nodded. "We'll ask these same questions of the healer in the morn. I trust your answers will match."

Unlikely. But certainly worthy of a mote of hope.

"I'm for my bed," the baron said. "Mr. Hurley and his men will entertain you until the morrow."

"How very kind of them," Niall said drily. Hurley was caressing the club with an expression of barely disguised glee. "Am I expected to be alive in the morn?"

"Of course." Duthes exchanged a pointed look with the constable, then addressed Niall. "The questioning always goes better on the second day, once the original bruises have had time to spread and swell."

Lovely.

And the night had started with such promise.

* * *

Ana waited in the empty smithy for Gordie to return. He slipped through the door just as dawn was breaking, his older brother, Simon, in tow. Wearing his guard's tabard and standing a good four inches taller than Gordie, the sandy-haired Simon was quite imposing.

Ana held out her father's ring. "No one must ever know what we discuss this night. May I rely on your discretion?"

Gordie's brother examined the ring, then tucked it away. "Aye."

"Then tell me what you know."

"Robbie is holding up well," Simon said, as he shut the door. "Lots of bruises and a few painful ribs, but naught that will cripple him."

"That's hardly reassuring," Ana said sharply. "Can we free him?"

Simon shook his head. "He's shackled to the wall. The constable holds the only key."

"How goes the interrogation?"

"Now that the baron is gone, they don't seem eager to pose questions. Mostly they just taunt him. The big Frenchman has taken a dislike to him, I think."

"Did the baron query him?"

"Aye."

Ana prompted Simon. "What of?"

The young man's face twisted thoughtfully for a moment, then cleared. "The baron asked him a question or two about you."

"What sorts of questions?"

Simon scratched his head. "When and where you were wed."

"Did he answer?"

"Aye."

"Come on then, lad, spit it out. What did he say?"

"That was several hours ago. I don't recall."

Ana took Simon's big hand in hers and squeezed reassuringly. "This is very important. I must know what Robbie said. Think hard."

The young man looked down at his feet. "He may have said five years."

"We've been wed five years?"

He nodded.

"And where did he say we were wed, Simon?"

Simon heaved a sigh. "I'm sorry, Goodhealer. I don't recall."

Ana named a few towns, hoping to prod his memory. "Elgin? Rothes? Old Meldrum?"

He shook his head.

"Braemar? Alford?"

He frowned. "None of those. But it may have been a bit like Alford."

"Aboyne?"

"I think not." He groaned with frustration. "But I was fetching a pail of water for the constable at the time. Perhaps I didn't hear proper."

"Aviemore?"

His face lit up. "Aye, that's it! He said Aviemore."

Ana smiled and gave Simon a tight hug. "Good lad. I owe you both more than I can ever repay."

When morning came, Ana donned her best gown for her meeting with Baron Duthes—a midnight blue twill with white trim on the bodice. She neatly brushed, plaited, and covered her hair to banish any image he might have of her as a crazed harridan from the night before.

After the fast was broken and the tables in the great hall were put away, one of the baron's young pages escorted her to his chair by the hearth. The baron was speaking with the steward, so she stood quietly, waiting for him to address her.

Her heart was thudding in her chest.

She could not afford any mistakes. If Simon had misheard any of the information, or she stumbled in the recounting of it, not only would she have failed to free Niall, she'd be joining him.

The baron nodded to Eadgar, then faced Ana.

"Let us dispense with your claim, then. King Alexander will arrive in a few short hours. You say that your husband, one Robbie Bisset, has been falsely imprisoned. Mr. Hurley insists that the man he holds is not your husband. What say you?"

"Mr. Hurley is mistaken. Robbie is most definitely my husband."

Duthes nodded. "Then it should be an easy matter to settle. Your husband has answered several questions regarding your wedding. Answer those same questions with matching answers and he can go free."

Ana smoothed her damp palms down her skirts. "Thank you, Baron."

"Thank me when all is done," he said. "How long have you been wed?"

"Five years."

"Where were you wed?"

Ana discreetly crossed her fingers. Please, *please*, Lord. "Aviemore."

The baron nodded. "And what was the name of the priest who wed you?"

Ana stared back at him, her mind blank. Simon had not said anything about a third question. Her eyes darted to the young man standing several feet behind the baron's chair, hoping for a miracle. Simon nodded ever so slightly to the left. Her gaze drifted in that direction—and found the pimply face of the young man's good friend Ben.

Her gaze swung back to the baron, who was now frowning.

"My apologies, Baron," she said, as an icy droplet of sweat ran down between her shoulder blades. "Five years is a long time to remember a name."

His expression hardened. "Either you know who wed you or you do not."

Ana swallowed her trepidation and prayed she was correctly interpreting Simon's nod. "Brother Ben," she said, cringing as she spoke the words. "I believe his name was Brother Ben."

A broad smile broke on the baron's face. "All is well, then. You may collect your husband." He waved to two of his guards. "Escort the goodhealer to the dungeon and help her retrieve her mate."

Chapter 14

The grate of a key in the lock brought Niall to his feet, despite the pain and sapping weariness that beleaguered his body. He swallowed the bile that rose in his throat and shook off the queasy turn of his stomach. He'd be damned if Hurley would see him hanging in his chains.

As the door creaked open, he peered through his knotted and blood-soaked hair at his tormentor. He blinked. Then blinked again. It was not the constable. It was Ana, looking positively regal in a dark blue gown and pristine white brèid. A vision, clearly. But why had his imagination conjured her with that glorious red hair bound and hidden?

"Unshackle him immediately," she ordered the pair of guards who had accompanied her.

The two men hastened to do her bidding, proving she wasn't a figment of Niall's distorted imagination. Unlocking his bindings, they released his wrists and stood back.

Despite being given his freedom, Niall made no attempt to push away from the wall. His legs were trembling. He did not trust them to hold his weight. Not yet. "Am I free to leave?"

"You are," Ana said. "The baron has apologized on behalf of Mr. Hurley for this very unfortunate misunderstanding."

Niall snorted. "Truly?"

"As we both had identical answers to his questions, he could not help but side with us on the issue of your identity."

"Ah," said Niall, as if he understood. Which he did not. How could she possibly have known what answers he had uttered in complete desperation? He took a deep breath, gritted his teeth, and straightened. His badly bruised knee and bludgeoned ribs protested mightily, but by some small miracle he held his own.

"I think he's quite happy to have the dungeons empty for the king's visit." Ana wrapped an arm about his waist and lent him support as they walked slowly through the door toward the stairs. "Duthes will be a shining example of Scottish society, without a single miscreant serving time in the bowels of the keep."

"The king is a very observant man. He'll not be swayed by a solitary fact."

She glanced at him. "Have you met King Alexander?"

"Once." Niall used the wall to help him mount the narrow stone stairs. "A number of years ago."

"I've heard he's quite handsome."

He smiled. "So the ladies are wont to say."

When they reached the top of the stairs, he un-hooked Ana's arm from his waist and tucked her hand in his elbow. He would not enter the great hall looking like an invalid.

The sparks in Ana's eyes told him she did not approve, but she said nothing.

They traveled thus, slowly and steadily, all the way back to the bothy. Only when the door was closed behind them did he allow himself to sag. "Bloody hell."

Ana thrust a bowl of steaming pottage at him and prodded him toward the mattress. The frame of the bed was now a pile of splintered kindling next to the fire pit. Damn Hurley's soul to hell and back.

"I'll speak to the carpenter after I sup," Niall said, sinking onto the soft pallet with a sigh.

She studied him with a critical eye. "It doesn't appear that they broke any bones."

He shoveled a spoonful of soup in his mouth before answering, relishing the savory taste on his tongue and the warmth in his belly. The dungeon had been cold and wet, not a single comfort to be had. "Hurley was under strict orders to keep me alive, thanks to you."

Ana chewed her bottom lip for a moment.

On any other day, Niall would have happily taken on that chore himself, but today, he ached from head to toe, and the soup had greater appeal. "What bothers you?" he asked, after swallowing another spoonful.

"I think the time has come for us to be completely honest," she said.

He peered up at her. "There's more? I'd have thought your confession to being a witch was honesty enough."

"I'm not a witch!" she refuted hotly.

"Call it what you will, but you cannot deny your healing skills are derived from some sort of magic."

She pursed her lips. "I do not worship the heathen gods, nor call upon the devil to invoke my healing talents. If it's magic, it comes from no unholy source."

Niall finished his soup and held out the bowl for more. "You condemn the worship of the old gods?"

"Nay, not condemn. I know many a soul who still hold the old gods dear, but I myself have accepted the Christian god." She ladled more soup into the bowl. "You are surprisingly tolerant of my healing talents."

He shrugged. "I've seen many strange things in my time."

She was quiet for a while, allowing him to eat his fill. When his belly was full, and the bowl put aside, she favored him with a solemn stare. "Are you one of the painted ones?"

Niall blinked. The question was completely unexpected. "A Pict? Why would you think that?"

She pointed to his left shoulder and the tattoo that lay there. "I saw similar markings on standing stones in Alford. My father said they were Pictish."

"The Picts are a dead people. They no longer exist."

"They were conquered by the Gaels several centuries ago," she agreed. "But a proud history does not die so easily, I think. Monuments attesting to their battles and beliefs lie all over the north and east. To my mind, that means some might still hold their Pict heritage dear."

"Inkings do not a Pict make."

"Of course not. But combined with your possession of this, it does leave room for wonder." She opened her hand to reveal the midnight blue stone from his pouch. The disk carving lay faceup.

He met her gaze.

There was no judgment in her eyes. No condemnation. Just honest curiosity. It was a risk to tell her the truth, but certainly no greater risk than she had assumed by healing his injuries right before his eyes.

"Aye, I'm descended from the Picts."

A serene calm settled over her beautiful face, as if the answer somehow satisfied all of her concerns. She dropped the piece of slate into his outstretched palm. The stone was warm from her skin. "Why does a Pict seek a ruby necklace?"

"I seek to right a wrong. The necklace was stolen while under our protection and as punishment our lands were seized."

"Did Duthes steal it?"

"Perhaps," he said. "Or he may have acquired it without knowing its history."

"You think him innocent?"

He nodded slowly, reliving a portion of his misadventures during the night. "Not one of the questions I was asked last eve pertained to the necklace. Nor was

I asked anything about the events that transpired at Dunstoras the night the necklace was stolen."

Her eyebrows lifted.

"Dunstoras is my home," he explained.

Ana sank onto the mattress beside him. "I would ask you not to assume the worst."

With her soft curves pressed against his side, he struggled to keep his mind focused. "About what?"

"The name in the steward's records." Her fingers picked at a nubby thread in her gown. "It's mine."

"Yours?" he said hoarsely.

"I can promise you, I did not deliver a ruby necklace to Duthes. Had I been in possession of such a valuable gem, I'd have headed for Aberdeen. I know a man who'd have given me a goodly sum of gold coin for it, no explanation required."

Her honesty made him smile. "Is the date of the entry a match to your arrival in Duthes?"

She nodded.

"How did you arrive? Alone, or with a party?"

"I traveled with a merchant caravan. For a price, they allowed me to sell my herbs and unguents in their stalls."

Closing his eyes, Niall massaged his forehead. A pounding ache had begun behind his eyes. The price of his insistence on walking home unaided. "How many merchants?"

"Eight." A hot hand tugged his fingers away from his temples, and then gently touched his head. Instantly, the throbbing pain receded. "Eleven, if you include the wives."

"Describe them to me."

"All of them?"

"Aye."

"Do you hope to recognize someone?"

Niall opened his eyes and stared into Ana's eyes. "The arrow you pulled from my chest was shot by one of my own men. The more I know, the better."

"All but three of the merchants were Flemish."

He picked up her hand and lightly traced the crimson pattern on her flesh. Her own form of inking. Much finer and more feminine than his. "Then start with the ones who were not Flemish."

"Thomas of Oban was the leader of the group," she said. "Large, portly fellow with white hair shorn to his ears."

Niall followed a delicate swirl to the center of her palm.

"Archibald of Atholl was a leather goodsman." Her voice was thick. "Short and round. With the biggest arse I've ever seen on a man."

He smiled.

"Miles of Northumberland traded silks and spices from the Outremer. He was dark haired, small, and thin as a willow switch. Oddly pale, except for a large port wine stain on the left side of his chin and neck."

None were a match to any of his men or Duthes's men. He was no closer to discovering who had murdered his kin and stolen the necklace. "Did you meet any other Scotsmen of note along the way?"

"I don't recall," she said. "My first few days with the caravan are a blur—I lived in constant fear that the caravan would be swarmed by Lochurkie's men."

He brought Ana's hand to his lips and kissed the spot where the vine ended on each of her fingers. "Did any of the merchants meet with Duthes when you arrived?"

"It was Yule," she said on a light breath. "I did not see the baron meet with anyone, but it's possible he visited one of their stalls."

"Continue to think on it. If you recall anyone who seemed out of place, inform me immediately," he said, lying back on the mattress. With a sharp tug on her hand, he pulled her atop him.

"Nay," she protested. "You're injured."

Sliding her brèid back, he freed her hair to his touch. Burying his fingers in the soft tresses, he held her firm. "Then heal me," he said softly. And he claimed her lips.

Ana had a thousand excellent reasons to resist Niall's seduction. But the moment he kissed her, she struggled to remember what they were. Not just because the sensations spinning though her body left her breathless and dazed . . . but also because it was the first time she'd ever been so fully and completely accepted by a man.

Niall knew of her healing skills—and they did not concern him. If anything, he embraced them. She could count on one hand the number of people who'd offered her similar acceptance—her mother and father, of course, and her childhood friend Aifric. Although that last had not ended well.

He rolled her onto the mattress and with masterful lips and fingers wrought her stiff resistance into soft, pliable submission. She released a deep sigh of delight. For the moment, at least, the worry that had been her constant companion since birth was banished. He had not denounced her as the spawn of Satan or recoiled from her in fear. He knew all there was to know, and his eyes still blazed with admiration and desire.

Niall's lips scorched a damp path down her throat to her collarbone. His tongue dallied in the divot there—teasing, promising, exciting her. As she shivered with need, his fingers nimbly untied her leather belt and shucked her body of the twill overdress. To her surprise, he did not immediately remove her sark—instead, his hands roamed her flesh through the voluminous folds of the lightweight linen shift. With her blood pumping heavily through every inch of her body, her senses were roused to incredible intensity, and the slide of linen weave over her skin was exquisite torture.

She moaned and dragged her fingers down the hard planes of his chest.

Adrift in the sweet chaos of her desire, Ana almost missed Niall's flinch. But the healer in her reacted instinctively. Her eyes popped open and she drew aside the material of his lèine to look at his ribs. They were a shocking palette of black and blue.

"It's nothing," he said.

Pushing him gently away and rolling him back onto the mattress, Ana ignored his protest. She rubbed her hands together, rekindling the heat of her gift, then placed one hot hand on each side of his ribs. As the chill of his injuries flooded into her body, she shuddered. The bones of his chest had taken a brutal beating—it was a wonder he could breathe without pain.

When the last of his bones were mended and bruises healed, she bent over him and kissed him deeply on the lips. Her reward was a low growl of pleasure in his throat—the first truly uninhibited sound he'd released since she found him in the dungeon.

He took her then, hard and fast.

It was a primitive and thoroughly satisfying mating of souls. Every deep stroke and every wet slap of their bodies blending brought her closer and closer to fulfillment. Ana's release came swiftly and with all the swells and crescendos of a piper's call to arms. As the last ripples of bliss racked her body, Niall increased the tempo of his thrusts until he, too, reached the pinnacle.

He collapsed to the bed beside her and gathered her back against his chest.

"You're unusually quiet."

"I am unusually replete," she answered honestly.

Although her back was to him, she felt his grin all the way to her toes. "A fine answer."

"Do not take all the credit," she chided him. "I had a hand in it as well."

"Aye," he murmured into her ear. "Two, if recall. Both very . . . nimble."

Ana lay in the cocoon of his embrace, as close to happy as she had ever been.

"This changes nothing, of course," she told him later. "Once you recover your necklace, we will part ways."

Niall frowned. While he might have uttered those very same words had she not spoken them first, they did not sound nearly as appropriate on *her* tongue. He ran a hand from the satiny curve of her hip to the warm swell of her breast. "Why so eager to see me gone?"

"I travel best with little baggage."

He snorted. "Did you just liken me to a millstone about your neck?"

She shifted in his arms, clearly uncomfortable. "You have your ambition, and I have mine."

Wrapping his hand in a silky tangle of her hair, he tugged her head back so he could look in her eyes. The molten passion of moments ago had been replaced by cool solemnity. "What *is* your ambition?"

"To stay alive," she said. "And tying my wagon to yours would be a poor way to achieve my desires. You are a dangerous man with dangerous goals."

He couldn't deny her assessment. But, for some reason, he felt compelled to argue the facts. "Any man worth his salt could be labeled as dangerous."

"Not every worthy man is plotting to steal a valuable necklace from a powerful baron."

"True," he agreed. "But once I reclaim the necklace, all will be well."

"Will it?" She turned in his arms, facing him. Their legs instinctively entwined. "Will you then settle into a simple life of working the land and providing for your family?"

Nay, he would not. He would return to his task of guarding the perimeter of Dunstoras, fending off any and all who would dare unearth her secrets. Normally, a fairly peaceful existence. But of late, it had become more dangerous work.

He shook his head. "I am a soldier, not a farmer."

She laid a slim finger on his lips and favored him with a bittersweet smile. "Exactly."

Then she let her hand fall to his heart, relaxed against his body, and closed her eyes. "Sometimes," she whispered, "no matter how much you wish it could be different, the only answer is no."

Aiden fed a dull winter apple to his horse. He had paid a pretty price for the fruit in the village, thinking to consume it himself, but the knots in his stomach made eating impossible. They'd spent the last two days trying to find some opportunity to waylay Lady Isabail, to no avail. "Our only recourse is to snatch her on the road to Edinburgh."

Duncan and Graeme both frowned.

Duncan, always the more outspoken, said, "Did you not hear Sir Robert say he and his men would be accompanying the lady to Edinburgh? That means there will be seven well-trained soldiers, along with her usual guard."

He nodded. "But their path will take them south through Gildorm Pass. The ravine near the waterfall is narrow and rocky—perfect for an ambush."

"They'll outnumber us four to one," Graeme pointed out.

"And we'll be fighting mounted men on foot—the horses will not be able to climb the walls of the ravine."

Aiden stared at Niall's two men. He'd never heard them naysay his brother in such a manner. Enough was enough. He'd let morose thoughts hold sway for too long. Aye, it was his fault Wulf's wife and son were dead and the necklace was gone. He'd failed to protect his clan. But clinging to his guilt would not win him the day. It would only prevent him from reclaiming Dunstoras. He couldn't let that happen.

"It *can* be done, and it *will* be done. Gather your belongings. We ride for Gildorm."

The king arrived in Duthes amid great pomp and ceremony.

Alerted by the trumpets to his impending arrival, the villagers lined the streets, many of them carrying one of the colorful red and gold banners sewn in haste by the wardrobers and distributed by the steward. As the king passed, the people cheered with enthusiasm, awed by the splendor.

Ana stood just inside the manor gate, as enthralled as any.

Riding at the head of his huge entourage, swathed in a sable cloak and perched upon a pure white steed, Alexander III was everything she had imagined, and more. His gold crown was simple, but he wore it with such natural confidence, no one could take him for anything but a king. As the king rode under the inner gate and halted in the close, the baron's stable boys rushed to place a gaily painted mounting box next to his horse.

Baron Duthes and his young wife stood at the head of the greeting line and, as the king dismounted, both bowed deeply. Ana prayed that Elayne would right herself without incident. The poor woman had worked day and night to ensure all the preparations went smoothly, and her exhaustion was evident. Dark smudges lay under both her eyes, and her skin was as pale as bleached linen.

"Welcome, Your Grace. My humble home is yours for as long as you require."

"Your hospitality is welcomed," the king said.

The baron waved King Alexander into the manor, and then followed him inside. The rest of the people in the courtyard quickly followed suit.

The crush of attendees for the feast was so great, Ana was pushed to the back of the line. By the time she filed into the great hall, almost every table was full. She was lucky to claim a spot by the door, which had a very poor view of the king. Were it not for the fact that the high table was mounted on a dais, she'd have seen nothing but the plump, balding head of the village swineherd.

The high table was draped with fine white linen, and the table set with pewter wine goblets and silver spoons. Ana couldn't see the spoons, but she'd heard Elayne speak of them. The baroness had made a special request of the blacksmith to craft them, and sacrificed a pair of silver candlesticks to make it so.

A warm body slid onto the bench next to her, and she glanced up.

Niall smiled at her. "You neglected to mention that you were attending the feast."

"*Everyone* is attending the feast." Ana ducked as a page leaned over the table and quickly filled every horn with a splash of ale. "They are serving venison," she said, saliva pooling in her mouth even as she imagined the roasted meat.

"And why are we sitting so far at the back?"

She shrugged. "I've not the social standing to demand a closer table."

Niall edged closer as a last-minute straggler begged a corner of the table. Ana felt his thigh press against hers, the heavy firmness of his muscles warm through her skirts. She picked up her ale and took a cooling sip.

"He's surprisingly young," she said, staring at the king.

"Two score and five."

"Do you think the rumors of Yolande being with child are true?"

He grimaced. "I sincerely hope they are. 'Tis a bitter shame that all his previous children found an early grave."

One of the king's knights, a large raven-haired man draped in ring mail and a red tabard, strode down the aisle toward the dais. Niall lowered his head as the fellow passed and diligently studied a knife mark etched into the wooden tabletop.

"Do you know him?" she whispered.

"The king's half brother, William Dunkeld."

"The bastard?"

He pitched her a hard look. "Careful how you throw that word around, lass."

She flushed. "My apologies."

A red-faced, sweating gillie dropped a heaping platter of roasted venison on the table, then leapt out of the way as everyone grabbed for a portion. "Bloody rooting pigs," he muttered as he turned away.

Ana's arm was gouged repeatedly as she tried and failed to score a slice of meat.

Frustrated, she sat back. Niall held out his dirk, upon which was skewered a sizable chunk of venison. He smiled faintly at her look of awe. "The advantage of long arms and legs," he said. "And a childhood spent wrestling the hounds for table scraps."

He placed the meat on Ana's trencher and cut it into several bite-sized morsels. "Eat," he said. "I've likely eaten venison more recently than you."

"Then I feel no guilt at all for robbing you."

She took her time consuming the meat, savoring every chew. Although cold, it was the best tasting meat she'd had in months.

The meal was a long but merry affair. Lady Elayne outdid herself, serving twelve removes to the high table, including an elaborate marzipan subtlety that no doubt cost the baron a year's supply of almonds. But if the smile on King Alexander's face was to judge, the effort was worthwhile.

The outer tables filled their bellies with bread and cheese and watched the foods delivered to the high table with wide-eyed wonder and applause. The ale flowed freely, which led to a raucous but celebratory air.

Late into the evening, the baron stood up and spoke to the crowd before him.

"In honor of His Grace, King Alexander, there will be a hunt in the western wood on the morrow. Sir William Dunkeld, one of the king's men, spotted a splendid twelve-point stag there just this morn. A hunt truly worthy of a king."

The crowd dutifully applauded, although few of them had ever been on a hunt.

Niall scowled.

"Isn't that where your men are camped?" she asked quietly.

"Aye."

"How very unfortunate."

He pushed to his feet. "Indeed."

Ana felt the chill of his departure and frowned. "You can't mean to go now."

"I must. The baron's huntsmen will be up at dawn, flushing the game toward the western wood."

She swallowed the last of her ale and stood, her legs a wee bit wobbly. "I'll go with you."

He put out a hand to steady her. "I think not."

Ana shook off his hands. "A short walk in the fine Scottish air and I'll be right as rain."

"Will you now?"

"Aye." She headed for the door to prove her point. She stumbled over someone's boot and scowled at the offending appendage. "Bloody bampot."

"Drunken wench," came the rejoinder.

"I am *not* drunk," she said hotly to Niall. "I had only one horn of ale."

"Filled repeatedly to the brim by the baron's very able pages," he pointed out.

"True." Ana grabbed the great iron door latch with both hands and tugged, but the door wouldn't budge.

Niall reached past her and pushed it open. "I'll walk you back to the bothy before I head into the woods."

"I would be vexed, were I you." Ana halted at the top of the steps, trying to make them stop spinning. "The king is ruining everything."

He wrapped an arm around her middle and lifted her down the stairs. At the bottom, he carefully released her. "I find myself strangely lighthearted about it all," he said.

"Well," she said, gripping his lèine with a tight fist. "That's good."

"How's your head?" he asked sympathetically.

"Not so good."

"Would you like me to carry you home?"

Ana sagged against him. "It's quite a distance."

A laugh rumbled through his chest. "Are you suggesting the task is beyond me, lass?"

She ran her hands up his arms, squeezing the thick bands of muscle that hid under his lèine. "Nay. I think you capable of just about anything."

"That's a fine answer." He scooped her up and started walking.

Ana tried closing her eyes and resting against his chest, but the rolling gait of his stride made her dizzy. She opened her eyes and studied the solid shape of his chin. It was a very fine chin. "Did I ever offer you my thanks for freeing me from that stinking dungeon?"

"Not in so many words," he said, amusement thick in his voice.

"Thank you."

"You're welcome."

They walked for a while in silence. Then Ana said, "I'm very tired."

"A gallon of ale will do that to you."

"Aye," she sighed. She tried closing her eyes again. This time they stayed shut.

Chapter 15

Niall poured Ana into bed.

He'd done the same for his maither more times than he could recall, and removing Ana's boots invoked the same fierce feelings of protectiveness. Not that the two women were anything alike. Ana never shrank from her problems—she confronted them or she moved on. He could not envision her regularly drowning her sorrows in a cup of ale.

He covered her with the blanket, then stared down at her for a long moment. The longer he spent with her, the harder it was to imagine leaving her behind. Holding her felt as natural to him now as breathing, and caring for her when she was lost and defenseless stirred the very heart of him.

It was an exercise in self-discipline to walk away from her.

But walk away he must. He had to alert his men to the royal hunt. With a bit of warning, they could elude the baron's huntsmen. They might have to temporarily disband the camp, but it could be rebuilt in short order.

Returning to the camp might also provide him with the identity of his traitor—whomever had shot him must think him dead. A surprised face would tell a valuable tale. It was also long past time he checked on Jamie.

Niall left the bothy and slipped into the woods.

He had to act swiftly. Soon after the hunt, the king would depart for Edinburgh. Upon his arrival at the palace—or perhaps after a brief respite—he would hold court and dispense honors to his faithful lords and ladies. Those honors would include Dunstoras. To have any hope of clearing Aiden's name, he had to trace the necklace back to Lochurkie and prove the jewel lay in Baron Duthes's coffers. *Today*.

It would simplify his task enormously if he could name the traitor.

The fletching on the arrow that struck him pointed to Cormac. But the inaccuracy of the shot made him think twice—Cormac never missed. If the bowman had wanted him dead, the arrow would have gone right through his heart. And poison wasn't Cormac's style. He took great pride in a quick death.

Which suggested someone else—Ivarr or Leod. Both men were good archers and both would have had access to Cormac's arrows. Leod's injury would have hampered his escape through the woods, but Niall had not been able to give serious chase, so perhaps that wasn't relevant. Ivarr had a volatile temper and was the easiest to imagine holding a grudge, but Niall was at a loss for why any of his men would desire him dead.

Niall approached the camp quietly and downwind.

He stood in the lee of a large oak tree and spied on the occupants for a short while. All but Ivarr were seated around the fire, enjoying a late-night meal of bread and ale. Even young Jamie. Ivarr was on watch, slowly walking the perimeter of the camp, listening intently to the noises of the forest.

Niall wanted to see the faces of all as he walked into the camp. One of the three men did not expect him to return, and with any luck, surprise would give the rat away. With Ivarr so distant, however, it would be difficult to judge his reaction.

The only option was to draw the big warrior out first.

Leaping carefully from root to rock to snow-covered patch of moss, Niall slipped through the trees. When he was about twenty paces from Ivarr's position, he purposely snapped a twig.

The big warrior frowned and his hand immediately dropped to the hilt of his sword. Peering into the thicket, he held himself perfectly still. Niall knew what he was doing—using the corners of his eyes to detect movement. But Niall did not move. He waited.

After a long moment, Ivarr stepped toward him. His multihued brat of browns, grays, and white made him difficult to spot amid the winter trees. But not impossible. Niall waited until the warrior was nearly on top of him, before revealing himself. He stepped out into the open. With the sparest of movements, he drew his sword and settled into a ready stance.

The instant he spotted movement, Ivarr reacted. He drew his sword and his powerful arms swung the blade in Niall's direction. As recognition dawned, his eyes widened. He grinned and pulled back on his sword.

"Bloody fine way to get yourself killed," he said with a laugh.

"Good to know you're awake," Niall said, smiling. Ivarr did not seem overly shocked to see him, just a little miffed to have someone slip past his guard.

"Did you get the necklace?" Ivarr asked, sheathing his weapon.

"Nay," he answered. "I'll explain all in camp."

No longer caring whether he made any noise, he marched through the brush toward the glow of the fire. He eyed the group steadily as he broke from the trees.

Jamie sat on the fallen log, chewing his bread with a melancholy expression. Cormac was describing a pair of foxes he saw cavorting down by the stream. All three looked up as he crossed the camp.

Only Jamie looked shocked to see him. Paling, the lad leapt up from his seat and dove for the horses. Niall did not suspect the lad of trying to kill him, so he directed his attention to the two men seated before the fire. Cormac did not display any emotion whatsoever. He simply ceased talking and waited for Niall to reach the fire. Leod, on the other hand, stood and smiled. He was still favoring his wounded leg, and one hand unconsciously rubbed his thigh.

"Good news?" asked Leod.

Niall let his gaze drift from Leod's face back to Cormac. Of the three, Cormac seemed the least eager to see him. Perhaps he'd been too hasty in deciding the arrow wasn't his.

"Nay," he confessed.

"Have you been sitting on your arse the whole time, then?" asked Cormac, breaking his bread in half and offering the dark rye to Niall.

Niall took the bread. After the bowman bit into his half of the round, Niall tore off a chunk and ate it. Leod offered him a swig of ale, and he washed down the dry bread. "The baron's men were waiting for me when I attempted to break into his coffers."

Cormac looked over Niall's shoulder and frowned. "Are they chasing you still?"

He shook his head. "But come morning, there will be a veritable sea of soldiers in the woods. The baron is hosting a hunt for the king."

The bowman snorted. "The baron's huntsmen are fools. They talk while they hunt and they make no effort to disguise their movements. It's no bloody wonder why that poacher is still on the loose."

"The king's men will not be so easy to elude," Niall said. "We'll have to pack up camp for a time. Walk with me, Cormac."

The other man rose to his feet. He tossed what remained of his bread to Jamie, who was watching them from behind the horses. Then he followed Niall to the edge of the clearing.

Niall held nothing back.

"Two days ago, on my way back to the village, I was shot with an arrow."

Cormac's eyebrows disappeared beneath his mop of curly hair. "You look fit enough."

Digging into his pack, Niall produced the arrow. He thrust it at the other man. "This arrow."

All expression left Cormac's face. "This is mine."

Damn the man for being so difficult to read. "Did you shoot it?"

The bowman's gaze lifted. "I'm insulted that you need to ask, but I'll answer it true just the same. Had I shot you, I'd be standing over your grave at this moment, not exchanging pleasantries in the merry woodland."

The same conclusion Niall had already reached. But could he be certain? "You might miss apurpose if you wanted to shift the blame."

Cormac ran a finger along the gray fletching. "Then I'd have likely chosen a different color of feather, as well. Leod uses black feathers. Ivarr uses spotted. 'Twould have been easy enough to raid their belongings."

Niall stood silent. A valid point.

"It begs the question of who among us would want to see you dead."

"Indeed."

"We've stood alongside each other a long time." Cormac's gaze slipped to the other two men. "It makes no sense."

"The facts speak louder than our history together."

Cormac shook his head. "We were as solid and sure as can be until last summer."

Niall stiffened.

Cormac glanced at him and grimaced. "It was not my intent to lay the blame at your door."

"And yet, there it lies."

The bowman handed the arrow back to Niall. "You had a brief lapse of faith. It happens to the best of us."

If only the truth were as kind as Cormac's words. When his father passed away at midsummer, the chains holding Niall to Dunstoras had finally been broken. Always on the fringe of the family circle, never truly accepted, he'd felt no allegiance to Aiden, despite their common blood. It had been surprisingly easy to turn his back on his role as the captain of the Curaidhnean Dubh and make plans to join the gallowglas mercenaries in western Scotland. "You need not soften the truth," he said quietly. "I broke my vow."

The bowman shook his head. "Nay. You returned the moment you learned the necklace had been stolen and the clan was in jeopardy. And you freed the laird. You did all that needed to be done."

"It matters not," Niall dismissed. "Until we right the wrong done to our clan, until we prove our honor intact, we cannot rest. Nothing can be allowed to interfere."

"Even a traitor in our midst?"

Niall pinned the other man's gaze. "Especially that."

"Do you still believe it could be me?"

His gut said no, but his gut had led him astray before. "I cannot discount the possibility."

Cormac nodded slowly. "Well, it may not mean anything, but you have my word that I did not loose that arrow. And if I glean any information that suggests who did, I'll inform you immediately."

Believing him was tempting. Of all the Black Warriors, save Aiden and Wulf, he respected Cormac the most. He honed his craft for endless hours, never resting on his laurels. He consistently offered excellent suggestions for the defense of Dunstoras, and never wavered in his resolve, even against challenging odds.

Niall accepted the bowman's promise with a nod, then crossed the camp to the wooden cage that held a half dozen cooing pigeons. There was another source of information he must pursue—the merchant caravan that had likely brought the necklace to Duthes.

"Sending a message to Dunstoras?" Cormac asked.

"Aye." Using a quill and a small strip of parchment, he scribbled the descriptions Ana had provided and asked his men to search for the merchants. "To urge them to be vigilant. Someone willing to murder an entire camp of thieves may be seeking a bigger prize than one necklace."

"You think the secrets of Dunstoras are at risk?"

The contents of his message was a lie, but not the concern. Niall truly did wonder whether the theft of the necklace was part of a larger plan. "It's possible."

"But the caverns beneath the old keep are well hidden. Who would know they exist?"

"Our traitor, for one." Niall opened the cage, selected a pigeon, and tucked the parchment inside the band on the bird's leg. Then he tossed the gray bird into the air and watched it wing across the cloudy sky, headed west to Dunstoras.

Cormac flushed. "I suppose that's true. But even the Black Warriors do not know all the secrets of Dunstoras."

"For good reason, it would seem." Surely, such a flush of embarrassment could not be faked? If Cormac was *not* the traitor, he was left with Leod or Ivarr.

Both men were formidable warriors when healthy, but Leod was the weaker of the two at the moment. His injury was real enough—Niall had gotten a good look at it the last time he supped with the men. The gash was healing slowly, the flesh still red and angry. Ivarr, on the other hand, was as fit as Niall had ever seen him. Big as a brown bear and able to swing that sword of his with enough power to make the air hum. As for his ability to handle a bow—it had been Ivarr who downed the boar that gored Leod, with a shot right through the eye.

Niall helped the men pack up the camp. As he dismantled the lean-to, he caught a glimpse of Jamie behind the rump of Ivarr's roan. The dirk Niall had given him was hanging on his belt. Straightening, he turned. "Come here, lad."

Jamie edged out from behind the horses.

"I need you to do something for me," Niall said.

Jamie's gaze lifted, a hint of curiosity in his eyes.

"You're ten and three in a month, are you not?"

The boy nodded.

Niall was far from a traditional knight. He'd earned his spurs just as Aiden had and served his required days in the service of the king, but beyond that, he had little tolerance for formalities. Rather than take on a squire or two, as was the custom, he trained newcomers to the ways of the Black Warriors. He neither needed nor desired the attendance of a young lad. But if Wulf had been here, he would have taken the boy under his wing. Niall could do no less.

"Time to move on from tending the pigeons," he said. "You're of an age to start training in the art of soldiering."

Jamie's eyes widened.

"From this moment on, you'll be my squire. Start by ordering all my belongings. Put everything in its proper place and clean my weapons. Can you do that?"

The boy nodded.

"If you don't know what an item is or where it ought to go, ask Cormac."

Jamie nodded again.

"If you do a fine job, on the morrow I'll teach you some basic combat skills," Niall said, pointing to the dirk. "A knight must be as skilled at close combat as he is with a lance. Your father is the best knife-wielder I've ever met."

The stiffness of the boy's shoulders eased, just a little. He said not a word, but his hand slid to the hilt of the dagger and Niall knew the gesture had meaning. What boy did not aspire to be just like his da?

"In a short while, the forest will be teeming with soldiers," he told the lad. "Cormac will keep you one step ahead of the huntsmen; your job is to look after the horses. Remove all their trappings and keep them from snorting at the first sign of trouble. I'm counting on you, lad."

Jamie stood a little taller. For the first time, his gaze lifted higher than Niall's chest. "Yes, Uncle."

He wasn't the boy's uncle. He was his second cousin, actually. But *Uncle* was the title Jamie's younger brother had bestowed upon him, and Niall acknowledged the honor with a nod. "Good lad."

The hunt was a huge success. The king took down the twelve-point stag that was driven toward him by the baron's men, and he left Duthes at midday, with the antlers as a trophy. By late afternoon, the Black Warriors were once again settled in their camp.

Niall was no closer to discovering the identity of his traitor, but he had made giant strides with Jamie. The lad no longer trembled in his presence, and he actually spoke more than one or two words when pressed for the answer to a question. Niall's horse gleamed from repeated brushing and his clothes were folded neatly in his chest.

All the lad's doing.

As Niall watched Jamie diligently polish the brass rivets on his targe, he saw a hint of his cousin Wulf in the determined cant of the boy's shoulders and his meticulous eye for detail. The fierce warrior would be proud of his son this day.

If he were alive.

Yet that was unlikely. Wulf was a force to be reckoned with. When raised to anger, there was very little that could hold him back. Niall couldn't imagine anyone or anything being able to contain his cousin's rage over the death of his wife and son for three long months. Only the cold hand of death could do that.

The time had come to acknowledge that in his absence, Niall would have to raise Wulf's son.

He just hoped he was a fine enough man to do the task well.

The sun was warm—a herald of spring. Ana kept the door to her hut open as she worked to take advantage of the light and the heat. Despite the enjoyable weather, she had to start her batch of pain relief salve a second time because she forgot an ingredient. She was too busy reliving her journey from Lochurkie to Duthes, identifying the faces she'd met along the way.

She'd met up with the merchant caravan a sennight after her escape from the dungeon. By then, she was no longer experiencing dizzy spells from her head wound and she'd regained a wee bit of weight—thanks to an excellent growing season for nuts and seeds. But she'd still been looking over her shoulder, fearful that she'd be discovered.

It had not been easy to earn her seat in the caravan. The merchants had been highly suspicious of her dirty clothing and tangled hair. Only by showing her familiarity with the ways of a merchant and correctly naming one merchant's supply of unguents merely by the smell was she permitted to join them. Even so, they'd watched her carefully for weeks.

"Goodhealer?"

Ana looked up. A red-faced young page stood at her open door, breathing heavily. "Aye?"

"Lady Elayne has taken a tumble," the lad said. "She said it weren't naught to worry about, but there's blood. I thought it best to fetch you. She's in the chapel."

She grabbed her satchel from behind the door. "You did the right thing. Lead on."

They took off at a run. The wind cut through her clothing, but the icy feeling in her veins came less from the weather than from the direction of her thoughts. The chapel had a stone floor. A tumble there could have serious consequences. Had it been any other woman with child, she'd not have worried overmuch. Lady Elayne was no ordinary case, however. She was much thinner and frailer than the norm.

Ducking into the kirk, she stood for a moment to adjust her eyes. The instant she could see Lady Elayne at the back of the room, she pressed on. The baroness lay on the slate floor, curled in a ball and moaning.

Friar Colban held her hand and murmured words of encouragement.

"Be brave, Lady Elayne, and our Lord God will look after you."

Ana dropped to her knees beside them.

"The babe does not stir," the friar whispered.

Elayne's pale blue skirts were darkened with blood—not a lot, but enough to be concerning. "What happened?"

"She stood up after confession, and then promptly fell."

That did not sound as if the friar had offered her a helping hand to rise from her knees after prayer. Chivalry was apparently not his strength. "Had she eaten anything of late?"

Friar Colban frowned. "How would I know this? Food is forbidden in the kirk."

Judging by the sallow color of her skin, the answer was no. Ana ran a quick hand over the woman's belly, prompting a low moan. The friar was right—there was no immediate sign of life—but that did not mean there was no hope. It wasn't appropriate to lift the noblewoman's gown while in the presence of a man, so she turned to the Friar and said, "Thank you for tending her so well, Friar. Please send a lad to fetch me the baroness's handmaiden, Bébinn. And a litter."

With a frown, he rose to his feet and walked away.

Getting the woman off the cold stone floor was imperative, but the first priority was stopping any bleeding. Gently lifting the baroness's brocade skirts, she peered at the rounded expanse of Elayne's belly. A huge bruise had spread across her left side, from rib to hip. Blood was seeping slowly between her thighs.

Turning to her satchel, Ana retrieved a length of linen and a handful of moss. She wrapped the moss in the linen and then carefully placed the soft padding between the baroness's legs.

She glanced around. "Did she strike something as she fell?"

Colban returned to her side, nodding. He pointed to an elaborately carved oak stool near the wall. "The stool on which I sat as I took her confession."

So he had sat, while a woman heavy with child prayed on her knees. Ana bit her tongue to hold back what would surely be a disastrous retort.

The friar frowned. "I cannot help but wonder if the Lord was displeased."

Ana glanced at him. "Why?"

"She fell asleep while giving her confession," he said, his tone clearly disapproving. "Twice."

"Such events are to be expected," Ana responded brusquely. "She has expended every effort to ensure the king's visit was a glorious reflection on her husband. When she's unable to hold food in her belly, her strength is severely depleted."

"Confession is a requirement of the soul."

"And food is a requirement of the body."

He stared down his long, thin nose. "The soul takes precedence over the body."

"Of course," she said. She disagreed, but she also knew she'd never persuade the friar to her way of thinking. "I am merely explaining why the baroness had cause to sleep, and why she might have lost her footing. Her body needs rest." Not a walk in the frigid winter air to give her confession to the priest. "Perhaps you can take her next confession at her bedside."

Two castle guards arrived with a decorated wooden platform suspended between two poles. The litter was used infrequently—it had belonged to the baron's mother and was meant to hold a chair—but it would deliver the baroness to the manor with a minimum of fuss.

The baron and Bébinn arrived at the same time, both wearing similar masks of worry.

Elayne was lifted carefully onto the litter and Bébinn covered her with a thick woolen blanket. The trip to the manor was made in short order, but the litter ran afoul of the stairwell inside. The corners were too tight to navigate. Displaying admirable strength and a clear sense of urgency, the baron carried Elayne up the stairs himself.

"Will my son survive?" he asked, as he laid his young wife on the bed.

"As soon as I have news, I'll relay it," Ana assured him.

Bébinn escorted him to the door and returned at a run. "What do you need?"

"Let's start by changing her into a nightrail. These heavy garments are making it harder to tend her."

Together, they made short work of the task. Elayne's moans intensified as they shifted her, and as they removed her linen sark, Ana noted that the bruise had grown much larger. It now extended past her navel. A very unfortunate sign.

"Fetch a bucket of cold water and some rose oil," she ordered the handmaiden. She'd seen similar bruising on corpses. If she did not use her gift, there would be dire consequences.

Bébinn left her side and Ana rolled up her sleeves. The door opened and closed. Aware that she might have little time to save the babe, she rubbed her hands together and drew energy from the depths of her being, the telltale tingle of her gift blooming in her chest.

"The guard will return anon with your requested items, Goodhealer."

Ana clasped her hands tightly together, willing the tingle in her arms to cease. She glanced over her shoulder at Bébinn. The handmaiden met her gaze evenly.

"The baron asked me not to leave the room while you are tending the baroness," the woman said quietly. "Mr. Hurley expressed his concerns about some of the herbs in your hut."

Damn.

"Play the chaperone if you must," Ana said roughly, "but stay out of my way. Take a seat by the fire."

The energy of her gift continued to flow down Ana's arms. She had no idea if it was possible to stop it now. The vines crept out from beneath her rolled sleeves and wound toward her elbows. A sweat broke out on Ana's brow. Bébinn had not yet moved. She glared at the handmaiden, praying her bottom lip did not tremble with her fear. "Sit."

Clearly reluctant, Bébinn obeyed. She ignored the needlework lying on the chair next to her and made a point of watching Ana. "No herbs."

Angling her body to shield her arms from view, Ana scooped a bunch of fur pelts from the end of the bed and tucked them around the expectant mother. Then she thrust her hands into the pile of furs, flattened her palms on Elayne's belly, and mentally followed the flow of energy into the young woman's body. The babe stirred weakly at her touch. It was pressed hard against the cradle of her hips.

Ana searched for the cause of the bleeding and found it. A major blood vessel in Elayne's belly was leaking heavily, damaged by the collision with the stool. Ana repaired the tear, and redirected as much of the blood as she could, easing the pressure on the babe. She immediately felt its movements strengthen.

There was a knock at the door, and Bébinn rose to answer it. She carried the bucket of water and the flagon of rose oil over to the table beside the bed.

"Is the babe alive?" she asked.

"Aye." Ana pulled her hands back sharply and turned in the opposite direction. "Feel for yourself." While the handmaiden leaned over Elayne, she thrust her hands in the cold water and pretended to wash them. The frigid water cooled her hands, and the crimson vines faded away.

Bébinn looked, but did not touch the baroness. "The bruise is gone."

Too observant, this one. "I banished it with a firm

massage. If you catch it early enough, you can hasten a bruise away."

"I've never heard of such."

"Each healer has her own methods."

As the handmaiden watched, Elayne's belly moved with a strong kick from the babe. She frowned. "The friar said the babe was no longer stirring."

"Perhaps the winter chill had slowed its movements." Ana removed the pad from between Elayne's thighs and gently washed her flesh with a wet rag. "It moves quite vigorously now."

Bébinn stepped back and genuflected. Under her breath, she muttered the words of the Lord's Prayer.

"The babe is healthy," Ana reiterated firmly. "The baroness, however, has injured her hip and must remain abed until the bairn is born."

"A full fortnight?"

She nodded. "The lady is very weak and we cannot risk another fall."

There was a second knock at the door, and Bébinn retreated to answer it. Her dark eyes still reflected concern, but Ana was at a loss as to how to banish it. She could hardly explain how the babe had come to stir again.

The door opened to reveal a gillie with a carved rosewood box in his hands.

It was a one-of-a-kind box, finely decorated with a woodland scene that included a red hind with a spotted fawn at her feet. The instant Ana caught sight of the box, a memory of her journey returned to her in a flash.

Only a day or two after she joined the merchants, the caravan met a lone man upon the road. The caravan did not usually stop between burghs for fear of being attacked by brigands, but much as they had with her, the merchants decided a solitary traveler posed no real threat.

Ana had never seen the contents of his wooden box, but it had been the subject of a lengthy and hushed exchange with Thomas of Oban. The merchant had finally accepted the box, but his reluctance had been clear.

She tried not to stare as Bébinn carried the box into the chamber and placed it atop the chest by the window. Surely there could not be two such boxes in the world?

"A gift from the baron to his wife," Bébinn said. "With hopes that she finds the strength to keep his son alive."

"I'm sure she'll thank him when she awakens."

Was the ruby necklace in the box? If it was, this might be as close as they would ever get to it.

She had to tell Niall.

He'd gone into the forest again, to meet with the other Black Warriors. She could wait until he returned, but by then the box might be once again under lock and key. Nay. The sooner he knew, the better.

She had to go now. Lady Elayne was recovering and could spare her attentions for a short time.

"You may feed her clear broth if she awakens," she said to Bébinn, as she tucked the furs snuggly around Elayne. "But do not let her out of bed."

The handmaiden frowned. "You are leaving?"

"The baroness is sleeping well. I'll return later to check on her."

The challenge would be finding Niall in the forest. Never having been to the Black Warrior camp, she could not say for certain where it was located. But she knew where to start looking—the spot where she'd found Niall's body.

Ana gathered her satchel, nodded to Bébinn, and exited the room.

No stranger to the forest herself, she would just keep walking up the hill. If his men were as skilled in the woodland as he implied, surely they would find her before she found them.

Chapter 16

Ivarr snared a hare for supper.

The meal was a familiar if rowdy event. Cormac taunted the big warrior over the puny size of his catch, Leod disparaged the taste of Cormac's fine stew, and Ivarr recounted the tale of how a man renowned for his woodland stealth had managed to get himself gored by a mother boar defending her young. As they laughed and ate and downed copious quantities of ale, Niall found it hard to imagine any of them trying to kill him.

He tipped his bowl to his mouth and swallowed the last drops of his stew.

If he could determine why, then he could determine who. Why would anyone want him dead? To prevent him from recovering the necklace, obviously. But why? All of the Black Warriors had sworn a blood oath to protect Dunstoras. As the sun rose and fell each day, they trained hard, their primary purpose to ensure the secrets of the caverns beneath the old fortress were never revealed. How would any of them gain from stopping him?

Leod sat on the log next to him and offered him a

horn of ale. "Life with the healer appears to agree with you. I've rarely seen you as hale and hearty."

Niall washed the stew down with a swig of ale.

The other warrior pointed to his own bandaged calf. "Think she could rid me of this damned lameness? I've little patience for hobbling about."

An innocent enough question, and perfectly logical, given Leod's injury. Still, it raised the hairs on Niall's neck. Other than Cormac, the only person who knew he'd been injured and then healed by Ana was the man who had shot him. "No doubt," he said. "She seems to know her craft well enough."

"Perhaps you could bring her for a visit."

"Perhaps."

"Three sennights is overlong to be coddling a weak leg," Leod said, pushing awkwardly to his feet. He slung a bow over his shoulder and picked up a plump wineskin. "It makes every watch a bleeding misery."

Niall watched Leod limp off. The slim warrior's shoulders were hunched, his head low. After several hours on guard duty, he'd be even more exhausted. Could the injured man have trekked through the forest in Niall's footsteps, maintaining the pace Niall kept? It seemed unlikely.

His gaze shifted to Ivarr.

Which left only one serious suspect. How could he test the big warrior?

Ana got as far as the half-fallen tree before acknowledging that she might have to turn back. The wood had thickened as she advanced, the heavy underbrush tugging at her skirts and making every step treacherous.

She paused and slowly pivoted.

She'd been careful to note landmarks as she passed, and was confident she could return to the road, even if darkness fell. But the forest deepened in every direction from here, with no obvious path or landmark. No wood smoke hung in the crisp air, no flickering firelight beckoned her gaze between the gray tree trunks. Pushing on would only get her lost, and getting lost would be foolish.

She was just about to turn and head back when she spotted a large rock in the distance. Its gray shape blended with the surroundings, making it difficult to see, but the lighter circles of lichens told her it was a rock. One more landmark to guide her.

Left it was, then.

Batting aside a low-hanging fir bough, she pressed on. How much farther could the camp be? Surely it must be around here somewhere? Her eyes scanned the trees ahead, hopeful.

When she reached the obelisk, she rested for a moment against the weathered stone.

Her legs would be full of scratches by now had she no skirts to protect them, but the effort to drag the heavy material through the underbrush was immense. Sliding her brèid off, she let the cool wind feather through her hair. It was not enough to dry the beads of sweat on her brow, so she patted those with her brat as she looked around. Still no sign of the camp.

Disappointment tugged at her shoulders.

Why had she been so convinced she could find it? Aye, she knew the forest well. But not every inch of the woodland. Had she stayed in the village, she might be speaking with Niall this very moment. Instead, she had a very long trek ahead and a good chance she'd be supping after dark.

Ana pushed away from the rock and headed back the way she'd come.

Two steps along, she drew up. The subtle scent of wood smoke drifted past her nose. Faint, but unmistakable. She grinned and pivoted, nose in the air. The smoke was too thin to easily determine its source, but it came from a general westerly direction. With her goal in reach, Ana found renewed enthusiasm. Her legs plowed through the brush, snapping twigs and tugging withered leaves from branches as she passed.

Eagerly looking through the trees for a campfire, she failed to notice a lean man standing in the shadows. When he stepped out in front of her, only a few feet away, she shrieked in surprise.

He tilted his head as he studied her.

Ana swallowed. The look on his face made her stomach knot with nervous tension, though she couldn't say why. He was one of Niall's men, surely?

"Are you the healer?" he asked.

She nodded.

He removed the bow from his shoulder. "You've been a wee thorn in my side," he said, as he drew an arrow from his quiver. "My troubles would be long over, were it not for you."

Their gazes met in the fading light.

Ana's heart pounded.

The urge to flee was a strident bell in her head, but what chance did she have against a man with a bow? A sense of doom held her fast in her tracks—until she noticed the bandage on his left leg. It went against her beliefs as a healer, but the opportunity presented to her was her only hope—she gave him a vicious boot in his wounded calf. When he doubled over in pain, she yanked the bow from his hands and ran for her life.

Niall lifted his head and listened.

"Did you hear something?" Ivarr asked.

"Aye." The sound did not repeat, but he did not need to hear it twice to know what it was—a woman's scream. And there was only one woman he could imagine traipsing this far into the woods. Ana. He grabbed a bow and a full quiver of arrows. His sword, sadly, was still hidden in the heather thatch of Ana's bothy. "Pack up the camp. It's time to end this. If I don't return shortly, meet me at the stone bridge at Kildrummy. If I can come, I'll be there within a day or two. Take care of Jamie."

Ivarr looked unhappy with his orders, but he nodded. "Watch your back."

Niall slipped into the woods, heading east toward

the sound. His gut was tight and his blood pumped vigorously through his veins. Leod had headed in this direction only a short time ago.

He traveled swiftly and silently, scanning the trees for any sign of trouble. Night was falling and the gloaming blurred the landmarks into their surroundings. Eerie shadows clung to every trunk and branch. Still, he had no difficulty tracking his prey—a clear path was mowed through the brush and snow, as wide as a woman's skirts. Her boot prints were several feet apart, suggesting she was on the run.

Weighted down by swathes of twill and linen, Ana had little hope of outrunning a pursuer.

A sudden vision of her body, lying broken and bleeding in the forest, spurred him on. He charged through the trees at a breakneck pace. Ana wasn't the sort to scare easily. If she had run, she'd surely had reason.

Ana raced through the woods, resisting the urge to look over her shoulder. She wasn't entirely certain the man was following her—she couldn't hear the pound of his footsteps—but her gut told her to keep going. Retracing her path, she made good time through the brush. She had almost convinced herself she'd escaped unharmed when a heavy weight struck her back, knocking her to the snow-covered ground. Air chuffed from her lungs as she fell.

A hand looped around her braid and yanked her head back.

"Hold still, you damned wench."

Ana grabbed the knife sheathed at her waist and swung it, determined to free herself at any cost. He knocked it away with a heavy fist that numbed her fingers. The blade spun off into the brush, and Ana's hope went with it.

Her attacker wrenched her braid again. "Another witless move like that and I'll break your neck."

She believed him. She ceased struggling.

The hold on her hair eased. "Whatever magic you used on Niall's shoulder, use it now, on me," he said. "Heal my leg."

"I used no magic."

The yank on her hair was so full of vehemence and hate, it brought tears to her eyes. "Liar! I know I hit him true—I saw him fall. The arrow struck him right through the back."

"I cannot speak to what you saw," Ana said thickly. She eyed the ground for something—*anything*—she might use as a weapon. "I can only describe the wound I treated. 'Twas a scratch, no more. He'd filled his lèine with bark and leaves—the arrow barely broke his skin."

"Nay," disputed her attacker. With a sharp yank on her shoulder, he forced her to face him. "That's not possible. And even if it were, your accounting does not explain how he survived—the arrow was dipped in poison."

Ana briefly considered admitting the truth, but decided the feral gleam in the man's eyes did not bode well for her survival either way. Her death was written in those eyes, of that she had no doubt.

She shrugged. "He was delirious for a time, but I attributed that to fever, not poison. It would seem too little of the poison found its way into his body."

"You lie," he accused. His fury had abated, replaced by cold determination. "Heal me now, as you healed him, or you'll be a fine winter's meal for the wolves tonight."

She met his gaze, one hand creeping toward a nearby rock. "You'll slay me either way, I think."

"Perhaps," he said, with a harsh laugh. "But you'll live a wee bit longer if you heal me. Aren't those minutes worth anything?"

She shook her head. "If I heal you, you'll present a more formidable challenge to Niall, who will surely skewer you upon his blade anon."

His narrow face darkened.

"I have no intention of returning to camp to face the bastard." He bent to whisper in her ear. "So your hopes, sweet vixen, are for naught."

Ana struck him hard.

The rock hit him in the temple with a dull but surprisingly loud *thunk*. He groaned and his eyes rolled back in his head. Taking advantage of his unsteadiness, however temporary, she yanked her braid free of his hand, pushed him aside, and rolled to freedom. She scrambled to her feet and tore off through the trees.

Although it left no secret as to her route, she again took the path she'd already beaten. Speed was more important than secrecy.

The lichen-crusted obelisk loomed in front of her and she veered right. Somewhere up ahead in the gloom lay the half-fallen tree, and beyond that, the road. Her survival depended on reaching those landmarks. Hiking up her skirts, she threw all she had into the dash for safety.

Her lungs burned with every breath, but she did not slow.

Onward, Ana, onward.

This time, she did not ease up as the silence behind her grew steadily longer. Her attacker had surprised her once—she would not be fooled again.

Rivulets of sweat trickled down the sides of her face. Her heart pounded. Ana reached deep and forced her legs to churn through the brush. Compared to the last time she'd run for her life, she was strong as an ox. If she could succeed then, she could definitely succeed now.

She just had to keep going.

When Niall came upon the bloodied rock, his heart dropped into his boots. Sinking into a crouch, he picked it up and studied it for strands of long, dark red hair. Thankfully, there were none. But that did not mean the blood was not hers.

He had to find her pursuer.

Which was quite likely Leod. Niall stood and looked

around. Leod's unique ability to blend into the shadows made him a dangerous opponent, even injured. He could be here, watching him, and Niall might never know.

The trick to finding Leod was to become one with his surroundings, to absorb every clue the forest had to offer. Niall closed his eyes. Shutting out the visual world heightened his other senses—the scent of pine and rotting leaves filled his nose, and the distant burble of the burn reached his ears. Amid the noises of the woodland, he heard the almost imperceptible swoosh of a blade cutting through the air. Instinct made him duck.

The sword arced downward—through the spot where his head had been only moments before—and struck Niall's thigh. Not full on, thank the gods, because he was moving. But the steel sliced into his flesh just the same, and blood streamed down his leg. He pivoted, his dirk at the ready.

Leod was nowhere to be seen.

Niall spun slowly, waiting for the next attack. A hunting dirk was an inadequate weapon against a great sword—especially a great sword wielded by a man he couldn't see. He shrugged his bow off his shoulder. It wouldn't be much of a shield, but if it could gain him an extra second or two, it might be enough.

"Show yourself, Leod," he taunted. "Fight like a man instead of a coward."

He got no response.

Nothing stirred the dried leaves and thin snow of the forest floor. Taking advantage of the deepening shadows, he stepped to the left, putting a solid trunk of a tall elm tree at his back. Leod's first attack had come from the left. With his injured leg, he wouldn't have traveled far—Niall guessed he was somewhere to his right.

Niall closed his eyes again and listened deeply.

As a young boy, he'd spent many a night in the forest, hunting for the food his mother could not afford to put on their table. In those days, failure had meant a belly cramped with hunger, so he'd learned to listen well.

Tonight, he heard a light breeze dance through the barren branches above his head and the harsh screech of an owl taking ownership of the night. He sifted past those sounds, seeking more subtle noises—the rush of air flowing in and out of lungs, the whisper of loam cradling a man's feet. Nostrils wide, he drank in a taste of the night . . . and the faint scent of unwashed clothing. Gathering every bit of information the forest was willing to give up, he pinpointed Leod's location.

Then he attacked.

He swung the bow first, fierce satisfaction spreading through his veins when the wood struck an unseen object and elicited a grunt of pain. Then he stabbed, sinking his knife into the familiar firm resistance of muscle—probably an arm.

Quickly, before Leod could dart away, he yanked

the blade free and slashed again. He tried for a third jab, but his blade met nothing but air.

Leod was now badly injured.

But still one with the shadows.

"It's over, Leod," Niall said, spinning slowly. When his ears caught the sound of ragged breathing, he stopped. His gaze could not penetrate the curtain of obscurity that lay beyond a knobby birch tree, but he was confident the other man stood there. "Go to your grave with an easy conscience. Tell me why you betrayed me."

Leod shuffled into view, a huddled shape leaning heavily against the tree. His left hand clutched his sword arm, black blood soaking the sleeve of his lèine. His face was twisted. "You want to know why? Blame our father."

Our father?

Leod smirked at the expression on Niall's face. He dropped his sword and sank slowly to the ground. In addition to the cuts on his arm and torso, a dark stain of red marred his temple. "Did you think you were the great man's only chance-bairn?"

Niall stiffened.

"Apparently you did," Leod said, choking out a short laugh. "But I was the first. He brought me to Dunstoras when I was ten, much as he did with you."

A deep breath lifted Niall's chest. "Does Aiden know?"

"Nay." Leod closed his eyes. "I felt no kinship for a boy born with everything when I had naught."

Niall sheathed his dirk and crossed to the dying man. "Why did you not tell me?"

Leod opened his eyes again. "*You?* You were the old man's pride and joy—a big, strapping lad with a gift for the sword. You excelled at every task he gave you. I had no reason to befriend you."

That wasn't the history Niall remembered, but who was he to argue with a dying man? "Indeed, you were willing to slay me. For what? The necklace?"

Leod lifted his hand away from his arm and stared at the dark stain of blood. "All I wanted was for the wretch to call me son. Even if it were only on his death-bed. But he told no one, not even his confessor."

Niall sensed the end was nearing, yet he still had no answers. "Why did you try to kill me?"

"After the laird's death, I sought new meaning in my life, and I found it. In the form of a new master willing to give me everything I desired in exchange for my loyalty."

"What new master?"

Leod's next breath was a shudder. "He bade me to watch you. . . ."

Niall waited.

"He was certain you would find the necklace," he said. "And he was right."

"Who asked this of you?"

"Once Aiden was arrested, it was my task to recover the necklace from the earl of Lochurkie, but the righteous sot believed Aiden's proclamations of innocence and secreted it out of the castle with a faithful guard.

We lost the necklace after that." He choked out another laugh. "Until your determined hunt tracked it down."

Niall frowned. "'Twas you who stole the necklace at Dunstoras?"

Leod coughed, and a dribble of blood ran down his chin. "Nay, my master did that. Henry de Coleville was a very careful man. Mine was not a face the king's courier would trust near the necklace."

But his master's was? "Who is your master? Tell me now."

Leod's head fell back against the trunk of the tree. "Do not think to press me," he said, as his eyelids drifted down. "I will . . . never . . . betray . . . him."

The last word came out softly, as Leod gave up his last breath.

A deep silence settled around them, the forest's requiem for a lost life. It didn't last long—the busy chitter of a red squirrel in search of nuts soon broke the quiet. Niall was still unsettled by all that Leod had revealed, but he thrust his turbulent thoughts to the back of his mind. He closed Leod's eyes, said a quick prayer, and stood. Then he scooped up the man's discarded sword and turned on his heel. A burial would have to wait.

Ana was still out there, alone in the forest.

Reaching safety was all Ana could think about. Even after she stumbled out of the wood and onto the road, she kept running. Her attacker knew she was the village healer and could no doubt track her to the bothy. The only truly safe place was the manor.

She arrived at the gate utterly breathless and sweating profusely. As was the norm after dark, the portcullis was down and an armed guard stood in the center of the arch, challenging any who sought to enter. Usually, upon spying her face the guard ordered the portcullis raised and ushered her inside. But not tonight. Perhaps she looked more disheveled than she knew.

"I'm here to tend the Lady Elayne," she said to the stony-faced guard. Ana knew him, but could not recall his name. She'd once had to lance a boil on his buttocks.

He stared at her for a moment, then walked to the iron gate and hailed another guard on the other side. The two men exchanged a few whispered comments, and then the second guard walked away.

"You're to wait here," her guard said.

"Why?" she demanded, peering over his shoulder. She could see a group of men gathered in the inner close, a number of them carrying torches. A loud voice was exhorting the crowd, but she couldn't make out the words. "The baroness needs my care. I can hardly deliver it from here."

He didn't respond.

Ana glanced behind her. The road was empty, but it might not remain that way for long. "Please," she begged the guard. "Grant me entry. I promise you the baron will vouch for me."

He said nothing, just stood at attention, his eyes straight ahead.

Through the portcullis, Ana saw the second guard reach the throng in the courtyard. The loud voice ceased, and a strange quiet fell over the night air. She shivered and drew her brat tight around her shoulders. Why were so many men gathered in the bailey? What task required torches? A search of some kind?

"Has someone gone missing?" she asked the guard.

Still no response.

The crowd in the bailey suddenly swarmed toward the gate, led by three figures. As they neared, Ana identified the three as the second guard, Mr. Hurley, and Friar Colban. The look on the friar's face turned her guts to jelly. He practically glowed with malicious triumph.

Dear Lord.

The mob in the bailey had something to do with *her*.

Barely able to breathe for the sudden wash of terror, she spun away—mindless of direction, just praying for safety. She did not get far. The gate guard anticipated her attempt to flee and dropped his spear in front of her, blocking her retreat. The wooden pole plowed into her belly, and bile rose into her mouth.

"Ana Bisset," called the constable.

She turned to face him, one hand on her stomach. He waved to a man above them on the wall, and the heavy groan of metal chain preceded the ascent of the gate. Hurley's expression was calm and reasonable. She allowed herself to hope.

"Mr. Hurley?"

"Serious charges have been leveled against you by Brother Colban and the handmaiden Bébinn. They are accusing you of witchcraft."

Ana's mouth went dry. "I am not a witch."

"So you say," Brother Colban said hotly, shaking the torch in his hands like a judgment staff, "and yet you've brought a demon to life in the baroness's belly."

"The bairn is no demon. It is a child, nothing more."

"It was dead, and now it is alive. What else could it be but a demon?"

"The babe was never dead," she protested.

"I felt the baroness's belly myself. There was no life in her womb."

"You were mistaken. The babe—"

"Cease," the friar roared, pointing a finger at her. "I know what I felt. Your lies will not sway us, witch."

The chill consumed her entire body. That one word—*witch*—brought back memories too horrific to contemplate. Desperate to calm her accusers, Ana appealed to the constable. "Mr. Hurley, please. The babe was not dead, just lying still for a time. Much like any of us might after a fall."

He shook his head. "I was not present. I cannot give evidence."

"Let me speak to the baron, then. He was there."

Hurley's expression hardened. "The baron is with his wife. Upon learning what had transpired, Lady Elayne became distraught. She tried to harm herself."

Madness. The entire situation was madness.

"But I did nothing wrong," she pleaded. "I simply

healed the Lady Elayne as I've healed many other people in the village." She gestured to the crowd. "As I've healed many of you."

"Nothing wrong?" snarled the friar. "You invited Satan into our homes, and into Lady Elayne's womb." Grabbing the wooden cross hanging at his belt, he stepped forward, shaking it at her. "Get thee gone. Back to hell, disciple of Satan. Back to hell."

Ana instinctively recoiled. And then wished she hadn't.

"See?" the friar crowed, smiling darkly. "It fears the sign of Christ."

He began to murmur words in Latin, and many of the men in the mob genuflected. Ana's head pounded. She madly sifted through her thoughts, hoping to find some argument that might calm the frenzy and return the villagers to sanity.

"Mr. Hurley," she appealed again. "You searched my bothy. Did you find *anything* to suggest I worship a god other than the Lord Almighty?"

"Nay."

"There," she said, satisfied. "You've heard from the constable himself."

"My word matters not," Hurley said quietly. "The baron has already ruled on the matter."

"But I'm innocent."

His gaze dropped. "The baron is the law."

"You cannot truly believe I am capable of bringing a dead bairn back to life."

"What I believe is irrelevant," the constable said. He waved to the guards. "Take her to the dungeon."

"Nay," protested the friar. He shoved aside the two men reaching for her arms. "Evil must be routed and routed swiftly, else it will taint every soul in the village. The witch must face the fire."

Ana closed her eyes. *Dear Lord, no.*

"The baron said nothing of slaying her," Hurley responded.

"The baron is dealing with his own troubles," Brother Colban said. "His wife has a demon in her belly. He cannot allow the devil's spawn to be born into this world."

Her eyes flew open. "What does he mean to do?"

The friar ignored her. He addressed the constable. "Take her to the market square. Have your men plant a stake."

Hurley's lips thinned. "I do not take my orders from you, Friar."

"Nor do I take mine from you," the holy man said. "When it comes to God's will, I am His interpreter, not the baron. The sanctity of all our souls is at risk. Our families are at risk. If I say she dies this night, then she dies."

Hurley stepped firmly between Ana and Brother Colban. "I cannot let you do that."

The friar turned to the mob behind him. "The witch must die for your families to be safe," he exhorted. "Let her live and your children will be forever haunted and bedeviled. Do what must be done."

The mob surged forward with an angry roar.

Mr. Hurley did his best to hold fast, but he was

swiftly overwhelmed. He fell beneath the thrashing, raging crowd. Ana's last sight of him before she was carried away was the sleeve of his red tunic and a fisted hand.

All was lost.

Chapter 17

They ambushed Isabail of Lochurkie's carriage in the dark of night in a narrow pass between two steep crags. Her guards numbered thirteen, which was ten more than Aiden's party was blessed with, but he had surprise and rocky terrain on his side.

A dropped boulder prevented the carriage from racing to safety through the pass, and the narrowness of the corridor prevented the carriage from turning around. Several strategically shot arrows cut the number of able opponents by half before they leapt into the gorge to do battle.

Aiden dove straight for Sir Robert. The knight was their most formidable foe, mounted on a sturdy destrier and covered head to thigh in ring mail. The fool was careless enough—or arrogant enough—to leave his shield tied to the back of his saddle, and Aiden took advantage. Ducking under the knight's swinging blade, he sliced through the leather thong holding the shield and spun out of reach.

Now protected by a solid steel barrier, he pressed in

close, absorbing blow upon blow from the knight's fiercely wielded short sword.

The man's horse was well trained. It held its ground despite the loudly clanging metal and showers of sparks. The splendid black-and-white beast was draped in a full set of cuir boille armor—a fact Aiden applauded when the tip of his sword went wide and struck the animal's neck. He took no pleasure from injuring a fine horse.

"You wretched sot," Sir Robert cried. "I knew you were a fiend the moment I cast eyes upon you. You've made a grievous error today. The lady is not yours to take."

"I mean no harm to the lady. Lay down your weapon."

Sir Robert snorted and struck the shield with a mighty blow that sent a tremor down Aiden's arm. "I think you mistake who has the advantage."

"Lay down your weapon and this can end without bloodshed."

"Nay! I'll see you into hell first."

Aiden allowed the big knight to pound on him, again and again, knowing every blow depleted the man's strength. When he saw the man's arm tremble slightly upon pulling back, he knew the time was right to make his move. Sir Robert's rage had not abated, but his swings were slower now and his underarm remained exposed a tad longer than it should have. Aiden dropped the shield and thrust his sword up and to the left. His aim was true. The blade went deep.

Sir Robert spat blood.

Aiden tugged his blade free, regret clawing at his

gut. This was no enemy in war—Sir Robert was a fellow Scotsman whose only fault was that he dared to protect a lady from harm. Aye, the man was a boor and a braggart, but he didn't deserve to die. Not this way.

"Harm one hair on her head," gurgled Sir Robert, "and I'll haunt you from the grave for eternity."

Aiden did not doubt him. Knowing his men were still outnumbered, he nodded respectfully to the knight, then picked up the shield and dove back into the fighting. He whacked a brawny young lad on the back of his helm with the shield. The lad dropped like a stone.

Duncan and Graeme were quick to wrap up their own conflicts once the tide turned. Minutes later, the surviving guards were kneeling on the ground in a tight circle, hands bound behind their backs.

Aiden yanked the carriage door open.

"Step out, my lady."

A woman emerged from the carriage and hastily descended the step, her skirts bunched in hand. A plump, older lady with a look of stark terror on her face. Not Lady Isabail. Her handmaiden.

"Now, my lady," Aiden said coldly. "Or I will carry you out without a care to how much of your sark and stockings are displayed to the world."

His ears caught the rustle of starched linens. The carriage wobbled and then a woman appeared in the doorway. Nay, not a woman. An angel in a pale blue gown. The color suited her, underscoring her silvery beauty, but Aiden wasn't about to tell her so.

This woman was threatening to take his beloved Dunstoras.

"Wise choice," he said. His hand itched to offer her aid as she descended to the ground, but he held tight to his sword instead. The punishment he'd endured at the hands of her brother was still too fresh in his mind. He pointed the tip of the blade toward Sir Robert's destrier. "Mount up."

She did not immediately obey. Instead, she took a moment to berate him in a quavering voice. "You will hang for this, orchard keeper. My cousin, the new earl, will avenge my honor with all due fury."

"I am not an orchard keeper. Nor am I interested in robbing you of your virtue." If he admitted he was the man she accused of murdering her brother, he suspected she would faint. Noblewomen were given to fainting spells. "Mount up."

She frowned. "That's a battle steed. You cannot expect me to ride such a powerful beast—especially with no gloves."

"You won't be holding the reins."

Her frown deepened. "Who will?"

"Me."

Confusion softened her face. "Am I to be led about like a child on a pony?"

"Up," he repeated, pointing to the huge horse again.

She crossed to the animal and reached for the cantle of the saddle, but failed to grab it. Her head barely topped the destrier's back. Graeme gave the lady a leg up and her handmaiden spread her shimmering blue skirts demurely across the horse's withers.

Aiden lit a loose pile of clothing on fire, then took the reins of the destrier, swept Isabail's skirts out of his way, and leapt upon the back of the horse. Without a word, he lifted the lady and settled her in front of him.

Isabail gave a short shriek, then held herself stiff.

Aiden wrapped an arm around her slender waist, cinching her securely to his chest, and turned the horse around to face the open end of Gildorm Pass. As he urged the big destrier past the bound men, Isabail found her voice again.

"Surely you don't mean to leave them like this."

"I do."

"But there are wildcats and wolves in these mountains." Which was why he'd lit the beacon—to alert guards from the castle below who would reach the pass within a few hours. But Aiden was not of a mind to explain that to Isabail. Not while he was struggling with the unexpected pleasure of holding her in his arms. The damned woman was soft in all the right places and smelled faintly of some flower he could not name.

She made his bloody head spin.

Determined to put as much distance between him and the ambush site as swiftly as possible, Aiden led his men out of the pass and headed west toward Dunstoras. They were headed home.

Niall made good time through the forest. He might have caught up with Ana had he not run across the remnants of a campfire just east of the ridge overlooking the road. The coals were dead but relatively fresh, and recalling Leod's claim to be serving another master, he sank into a crouch to take a closer look.

Animal bones, scorched by flame and chewed bare, were strewn about the ground. A poacher would know to bury such evidence to keep the constable's men off his back. Niall ran a finger over a deep cleft in a nearby log, clearly made by a long, narrow blade. Poachers did not carry swords, either.

He straightened.

Bent branches and half-melted footsteps in the snow told him the fellow had gone north, up past the clear water spring that pooled in the rocks.

Once Ana was safe, it might be wise to return to the woods and follow the trail. To tie up all the loose threads.

Niall jogged down the hill to the road, then picked up his pace.

When he reached the edge of the village, he slowed to a walk. In the distance, he could see torches lighting up the sky, which brought a frown to his brow. Duthes was a sleepy town and activities after dark were uncommon.

Ana's bothy was dark, so he continued up the lane toward the manor.

When he spied the crowd gathered at the gate, he ducked into the shadows of the village dye house. A mix of soldiers and gillies, half of them carrying torches, surrounded a smaller group under the archway. Niall recognized Hurley, the friar . . . and Ana. A strident voice carried on the night air, but the wind blurred the words beyond recognition—not that he had need to decipher their meaning. It was clear by his angry gestures that the friar was accusing Ana of something.

Niall eyed the half dozen bowmen on the wall. Their attention was locked on the mob.

The voices in the distance swelled and, in a flash, the constable was overrun and Ana grabbed. Led by the black-robed friar, the crowd dragged her down the lane toward the village square.

Niall instinctively stepped forward, his hand on the hilt of Leod's sword. It did not sit well to see Ana so roughly used.

But as the gate emptied and the open expanse of the manor courtyard beckoned, he halted. The archers on the wall were distracted by the mob. It would be a simple exercise to swing wide behind the shoemaker's hut and slip under the portcullis. With so many of the manor goodmen heading for the village square, he'd been granted an unexpected opportunity to retrieve the necklace. Deserted corridors and a dearth of watchmen would make the task near effortless. After four long months, redeeming his honor was within reach.

His gaze slid back to the men dragging Ana. As they marched past the dye house, he could see righteous anger and obvious loathing etched on their faces—a dangerous combination. Ana's beautiful face was pale and wrought with fear.

He sucked in a slow, deep breath.

No amount of redemption was worth that look.

He left the protection of the dye house and darted for the blacksmith's barn. At the corner, he paused and peered into the village square. The crowd was thick and blocked his view. Many of the men were chanting *witch, witch,* and those who carried torches shook them in the night air. He was just about to dash across the lane to the tavern, when someone whispered his name.

"Robbie."

Niall's gaze lifted to the upper window of the barn. A young man leaned out, waving. He did not recognize the fellow, but it was clear the fellow recognized him. "Gordie?"

"Aye. Come inside."

"Not the now—"

"You can see the square from here."

Niall tugged on the barn door and slid quickly inside. It took a moment for his eyes to adjust to the dimness. On the upper level, two young men—one draped in the tabard of a guard—stood by an open window. Niall mounted the ladder two rungs at a time and hastened to join them.

Gordie nodded to the guard. "My brother, Simon."

Niall acknowledged the other man with a nod, then peered out the window. In the center of the square two soldiers were digging a narrow hole in the frozen dirt. Two other men were shearing branches from a felled tree, creating a pole.

"They mean to burn her," Gordie said grimly. "They think her a witch."

Niall's stomach twisted.

Fear was a powerful weapon. Especially in the hands of a skilled orator like the friar. There was little chance he'd be able to reason with these men. Unfortunately, he was only one man against thirty—a frontal attack was out of the question. He'd have to snatch her away.

But how?

"We need to create a diversion," he told the two young men.

Gordie frowned. "What sort of diversion?"

"Something that will scatter the crowd."

"Whatever we do," said Simon solemnly, "we'd best be quick."

Niall looked down into the square. The stake had been planted and the men were now binding Ana to the pole, her arms tight behind her back.

"Fetch kindling," the friar shouted. "Only a truly scorching fire will banish her evil to hell."

Closing her eyes did nothing to calm the tumultuous heave of Ana's stomach. The horror of her situation still reached her a host of ways: the mob chanting, "Burn, witch, burn," the sharp scent of freshly cut wood, and the feel of the hemp rope biting into her wrists. Worst of all, the sounds and smells invoked the memories of another horror-filled day—a hot summer afternoon in June, ten years before.

The images of that day were still brutally vivid, and she could almost feel the press of her father's fingers on her shoulders. Half holding her back, half clenched with grief. She had cried herself hoarse that day, imploring the villagers to release her mother, and when that had no effect, begging her mother for forgiveness.

Her mother had smiled sadly in return.

How similar the events were—the wooden stake, the rope bindings, the piles of kindling—and yet how different. Her mother had burned in broad daylight, in the middle of a sweet green meadow, while she and her father watched in raw dismay. She would burn in darkness, with no family or loved one to witness her passing.

Perhaps that was for the best.

She remembered some of the more gruesome moments, including her mother's blood-chilling screams and the sickening smell.

"Please forgive me, Mother," she had whispered. "I did not mean to betray your secret. I did not know that when I told Aifric of your gift, the consequences would be so dire."

For years after her mother's death, Ana had refused to acknowledge her own burgeoning gift. Unable to understand why her mother had continued to heal ungrateful villagers in spite of great risk to herself, she vowed never to fall victim to the same curse. But faced with her father's broken and bleeding body in the streets of Aberdeen, she'd been unable to hold true to her vow. She'd dragged him to a narrow alley, summoned the healing heat, and cured him. Later, he'd given her his gold ring to acknowledge her passage into the role of healer. He'd been proud of her, just as he'd always been proud of her mother. Despite the risk inherent in her gift.

As men tossed bundle upon bundle of kindling at her feet, Ana felt hot tears roll down her cheeks and drip off her chin. This was it, then. The bitter end.

Friar Colban—a tall, thin specter in black robes—appeared out of the swarm of dark faces before her. Poisonous anger gave his features a bony, bleak cast, and she had no trouble imagining him as Death himself.

"Repent now," he shouted. "Repent your sins and God will save your soul."

Ana straightened against the pole and looked the friar boldly in the eye. She drew on strength she did not know she possessed. "I have nothing to repent. I am innocent."

"So be it," he cried.

Unable to look away, Ana watched the friar lower his torch toward the kindling.

Niall desperately glanced around the inside of the barn. His gaze caught on the ox cart, tipped upright in the corner. "Harness the oxen to the cart and fill it with hay. Hurry now."

As the lads slid down the ladder and grabbed the leather harnesses, he slipped his bow off his shoulder and drew an arrow from his quiver. A very different scenario from hunting in the woods, and failure would have far more dire consequences than an empty belly.

But he had faith in his abilities. In a single flowing movement, he nocked the arrow and let it fly.

The arrow struck true, knocking the torch out of the friar's hand and sending it tumbling.

The friar glared at the rolling torch and screamed, "Find the shooter!" Then he snatched a second torch from a burly soldier and without hesitation tossed it at the kindling.

Niall shot that torch, too. The arrow pierced the wad of tarred cloth at the top and drove the torch halfway across the square in a glorious arc of light.

"Stop him!" shrieked the friar, pointing at the barn.

A group of men turned and rushed the barn.

"Open the doors," Niall called to the two lads. Then he leapt from the window, breaking his fall on a charging villager. The fellow hit the ground with a solid thunk and was instantly rendered unconscious. Niall rolled to his feet, punched another villager who thought to tackle him, and snatched the fellow's torch. As the barn doors swung open, Niall tossed the torch to Gordie.

"Light the cart on fire," he said, turning to face a pair of oncoming soldiers.

Both men were armed, so Niall shouldered his bow and drew Leod's sword. He parried a vicious slice from one opponent and ducked under the blade of the other. Neither man was particularly adept, but both were strong and able. Luckily, the battle was short-lived—a few moments later, a pair of panicked oxen careened down the lane towing a burning cart. The two soldiers dove off to the side, one to the right and the other to the left. Niall loped after the cart. The wide-eyed oxen and their madly pitching fireball tore through the crowd. Wiser men leapt out of the way, but several fell victim to hoof or cart wheel.

Out of the corner of his eye, Niall saw the friar pick up a discarded torch and toss it on the kindling. With his bow shouldered, Niall had no chance to stop him. The wood took a moment to catch, and then it roared to life.

Niall's heart hammered in his chest.

Gods above. Ana was still bound to the stake. He had to cut her free.

Leaping over a groaning villager, he ran like the hounds of hell were at his feet.

Ana closed her eyes against the smoke and prayed for a miracle. But in her heart of hearts, she knew there wouldn't be one. And she was afraid. Afraid that she would suffer the same unbelievable agony as her mother had. The flames had consumed her in a furious rush, but not before her screams had filled the meadow for an endless, unbearable length of time.

Ana did not want to die that way.

A torrid wave of heat stirred her hair, and her stomach heaved. Any other death she could endure, but not this. *Please God.* Not this.

"Ana!"

Tears sprang to her eyes as Niall's voice cut through the chaos around her. Choking on smoke, she peered into the night, seeking a glimpse of him. One last look at his handsome face. Was that too much to ask?

Her gaze caught a flash of cream-colored lèine. There. Behind the pillory. Running toward her, raw determination etched on his face.

Niall.

But right behind him, swinging a mighty double-bladed battle-ax, was the big French soldier Ana remembered from the cellars. The one who'd called her *his small chicken.*

"Niall," she screamed hoarsely. "Behind you!"

Even before the words left Ana's mouth, Niall was ducking. The look on her face told him everything he needed to know. He dodged behind the pillory and heard the crunch of splintering wood only inches from his head.

Gripping his sword in both hands, Niall spun to face his opponent.

The Frenchman. *Of course.*

But Niall did not have time for a duel, especially with such a skilled foe. If he didn't free Ana in the next few minutes, she would die. And that would crush him in ways he could not yet imagine. He hadn't saved her that day in Lochurkie's dungeon just to lose her a few months later.

She'd fought so bloody hard to survive.

The Frenchman came at him with a roar, swinging his ax. Niall leapt back, narrowly avoiding a lost head. He actually felt the air at his neck stir. It went against his every instinct, but he dodged behind the pillory once more and sheathed his sword. Slipping his bow off his shoulder as he ducked another furious attack from his foe, he drew another arrow from his quiver.

By the gods, he hoped his skill with a bow was as good as he thought it was.

Because this shot could just as soon kill Ana as save her.

Pulling the bowstring taut, he took hasty aim and loosed the arrow.

Chapter 18

The leather on Ana's boots was curling from the intense heat, and a painful ache radiated up her legs. Her breaths came fast and shallow, despite the smoke, as panic set in. The flames were only inches away. Any moment now, her skirts would burst into flame. She strained to pull as far away from the singeing heat as she could, but her arms were bound tightly behind the pole.

She felt a sting on her arm, and for a moment assumed a spark had landed on her flesh. But when she jerked to shake off the burning ash, her hands came loose. It was only then that she realized she been freed. By an arrow.

Sobbing with amazement, she scrambled away from the stake.

As she leapt over the kindling, she noticed some of the fire came with her—the hem of her skirt was ablaze. Terrified that she might not have escaped after all, she dove to the ground and rolled in the dirt, praying that the cold earth would douse the flames. And to her immense relief, it did.

She lay there for a moment, listening to the sounds of chaos—the groans of injured men, the snap and crackle of burning wood, the mad braying of panicked oxen—and then she got to her feet. Her toes still hurt, but she was alive.

"So, you survived the flames," a soft voice said behind her.

She whirled around. Friar Colban stood a mere three paces away, his black robes smeared with gray soot, and a soldier's steel-tipped pike clutched in his hands.

"I am not a witch," she said. There was a twisted smile on his face that made her distinctly uneasy. Although he seemed calm, the pike he held was more than capable of skewering her.

"Witch or demon, it makes no difference. You are all Satan's minions."

"Nor am I a demon." With the burning stake to her right and the fishpond to her left, her only escape lay behind her. She slid a step back.

His eyes darkened. "Such protests will not save you."

Oh, but they might . . . if she could slip outside his reach without him noticing. Ana took another small step backward. "I am a simple healer, no more."

"No," he snarled, shaking his pike. "You are a snake in the garden waiting for your opportunity to strike."

His calm façade was cracking. It was only a matter of time before he lost all restraint and tried to run her through. Ana took a third step backward . . . and struck wood. Startled, she glanced over her shoulder. One of the permanent market stalls—a spare, three-sided wooden structure—blocked her egress. She was trapped.

Her gaze returned to the friar's face.

He smiled. "The best way to kill a snake is to cut off its head." And then he aimed the spearhead at her throat and charged.

Inexperienced in battle and unable to call upon even a single lesson in the martial arts, Ana allowed instinct to guide her actions. She dodged left. The spear shot past her and plunged deep into the back wall of the stall. Praying her opponent was as unseasoned as she, Ana grabbed the long ash pole and yanked on it. It came loose—of both the stall and the friar's hands. Colban made no attempt to regain the weapon—instead he rushed at her in a purple-faced rage, his hands reaching for her neck.

Ana tossed the heavy pike at him.

It was a weak and wobbly throw, but it was surprisingly effective. It struck him in the shin, and then got caught in his long robes. He tripped and went down on his knees.

Ana needed no further incentive—she skirted his outstretched arms and darted for freedom.

Only an instant after the arrow took flight, the Frenchman's ax split Niall's yew bow right in half. Niall flung the broken weapon aside and drew his sword. For the next minute, he gave every bit of his attention to parry-ing the mighty chops and swings of his opponent's blade. He wanted to check on Ana, but frankly, there was no opportunity.

The Frenchman was very strong and very skilled.

He was as good with an ax as any Norseman Niall had encountered in the northern isles. And that was saying a lot. His movements were spare and elegant, his swings a blur in the air. Few opportunities arose to break his guard, and any Niall took were swiftly parried.

Sweat rolled down his back, soaking his lèine.

The Frenchman wore a ring mail hauberk, which reached to his thighs. It made scoring a debilitating slice a difficult chore. As he stopped another powerful chop with the forte of his sword, Niall prayed that his large opponent was not as fit as he appeared to be. Against this sort of pummeling, the advantage of his easier movements would not last long.

Spinning to his right to avoid a calculated stroke, Niall shot a quick glance at the burning stake. Thankfully, it was empty. *Ana was free.* The knowledge lightened his heart and bolstered his will to succeed. He reached deep and summoned every last reserve of his strength. The Frenchman had to go down now.

His weakness was his legs.

Not only were they unprotected by mail, they lacked the smooth and graceful motions of the man's upper body. Awkward footwork could be a man's downfall, under the right circumstances. Niall pressed his attack, forcing the Frenchman back. The swineherd's hut stood just behind him, fronted by a fenced pig sty.

Mud was exactly the advantage he needed.

Ducking another humming ax swing, Niall slammed the flat of his sword against the Frenchman's ribs. The big man stumbled and hit the fence hard. Wood cracked, but did not break. Roaring with anger, the Frenchman chopped at Niall's head and missed. Niall aimed lower—he stomped on the man's instep and then kneed him in the groin.

Again the man stumbled back, and this time the fence snapped. The wallowing pigs leapt up as the Frenchman stepped into the mud.

Niall followed, hacking and slashing, buoyed by the pungent odor of success.

The Frenchman put up a good fight, but the mud did him in. As Niall directed a two-handed cut at the man's shoulder, he lifted his arm to parry, and lost his footing. He flailed briefly, then landed on his arse with a huge splat. Mud sprayed everywhere.

Niall could have finished him then. Instead, he bounded from the sty, leaving the man slipping and sliding and cursing his progeny for a thousand years. Finding Ana was more important.

He scanned the market square as he ran.

No females in skirts anywhere to be seen.

His eyes latched onto Gordie, who was waving his arms in the upper window of the blacksmith's barn. He darted for the open door, his sword at the ready.

But none of the men he encountered were interested in a fight—they all backed away as he approached.

Inside the barn, Simon stood waiting with two plow horses saddled and harnessed. Gordie slid down the ladder, then turned to help Ana descend.

"You're a damned fine swordsman, Robbie," Gordie said, grinning.

"No," Ana disputed crossly, "he's a damned fine fool." She glared at him. "Why didn't you simply run? He might have killed you."

Niall tossed Leod's sword into a hay pile, grabbed Ana by the elbows, and yanked her to his chest. Then he kissed her, hard and hot and long. He didn't stop kissing her until all the anxiety that had twisted his gut since he first heard her scream had eased from his body.

Gordie hooted.

When he finally pulled away, Ana's lips were swollen and her eyes were bright.

"You, wife, are a heaping midden of trouble."

She smiled tremulously. "Believe it or not, I merely wanted to help you get the necklace."

"Aye, well, next time—"

"Speaking of necklaces," Simon interrupted, thrusting the reins at Niall. "You'd best be on your way. The baron is calling for bloody murder."

"Oh?"

"Apparently, during all the excitement someone stole the ruby necklace he gifted to his wife," Simon said.

"Truly?"

The young guard nodded. "The constable is sporting a black eye and wounded pride. You know the first man he'll want to question is you."

Niall started to lift Ana into a saddle, but she dug her fingers into his arm, staying him. "Nay, I cannot leave. The friar suggested the baron might harm Lady Elayne."

"Fear not, Goodhealer," Simon said. "Whilst Brother Colban was attempting his witless form of justice, the Lady Elayne delivered her son with the help of her handmaiden, Bébinn. Word is, the lad's a bonny sort and he closely resembles his da. The baron has naught but praise for his wife at the moment."

"And the baroness? Is she well?"

"Weary but happily eating bread and honey, according to one of the weaver lasses."

Ana's fingers gentled on his arm. "That's good news indeed."

Niall helped her settle into the saddle. "We'll stop by the bothy to gather a few necessities. I trust you've no objection to leaving Duthes for good?"

She sighed heavily. "I never had a chance to grow a garden."

Niall mounted his own horse, then turned to look at her. "A garden can grow almost anywhere, with the proper attention."

"I used to believe that was true."

Niall was still convinced that it was. And if it wasn't, how important was a garden anyway? He waved his thanks to the two young men, prodded the big plow horse into a canter, and led Ana out of the barn and into the night.

They rode all night and most of the next morning without resting. A light drizzle started just after daybreak and it slowly but steadily soaked their clothing. Ana knew the constable would likely be on their trail, so she chewed on her dry bread without complaint. But her blistered toes still ached, her arse was getting chafed, and Niall had offered no information as to their destination.

As the horses picked their way down a rocky path into a small glen, she called to him.

"Can we stop a wee while?"

"Nay," he said, without turning.

"Why not?"

"We need to reach the bridge at Kildrummy before dark."

She studied his broad back as it swayed in the saddle. That was the first detail he had shared. "What's in Kildrummy?"

"Several of my men."

She bit off another piece of bread and chewed, considering that. "If they are your men, will they not wait for you if you are a wee bit late?"

"Nay."

"Why not?"

He sighed and reined in his thick-necked sorrel, waiting for her to catch up. Then he looked at her and said, "If I don't appear by dark, they'll consider me lost and move on."

She tilted her head and studied him. A droplet of rain plopped from her makeshift hood to her nose. "Would you be traveling faster if you were alone?"

He glanced away. "Aye."

"Then leave me behind."

A frown stormed onto his brow. "Don't be foolish."

"Why is that foolish?"

"I can't leave you out here in the wilds alone."

She held his gaze steady. "You did it once before."

Twin flags of color rose to his cheeks. "That was different. I barely knew you then."

"The only thing different is that this time we are ahorse."

"Nay," he said, glaring at her. "The last time I also had my brother to care for."

Ana blinked. "MacCurran is your brother?"

Niall's face tightened, and he prodded his horse forward. "Aye."

Well, that explained a lot . . . and yet nothing. It made sense of his willingness to risk his life breaking the man out of Lochurkie, but added to the confusion over his lineage. Hadn't he implied his mother was a whore?

"I'm perfectly able to fend for myself. You need not trouble yourself with my welfare."

He halted again, but did not turn around. "Is that what you think this is? A mere execution of chivalric duty?"

Ana frowned. "Isn't it?"

"Nay." He slid off his horse and strode over to Ana. Grabbing her by the waist with a pair of big, warm hands, he tugged her to the ground. "Let me make myself clear, as it appears that I have thus far failed. I do not risk life and limb to save women I don't give a damn about. I love you, you bloody frustrating woman."

Ana was charmed by his declaration. For a brief moment, she even envisioned throwing herself into his arms and vowing to love him forever in return.

But the memories of her grief-stricken father were haunting her again, clearer than ever. Her mother's death had ripped the heart from his chest, and even Ana's healing gift hadn't been able to soothe the wound. Niall didn't realize that the horror they had so recently escaped was a mere rehearsal for the troubles that lay ahead. As much as she loved him in return, how could she condemn him to that fate?

"I am flattered," she said slowly, the words thick as putty in her mouth. She willed the rain to temper her pink cheeks. "You've proven yourself a steady and courageous partner. I wish that I could say I returned your affections, but alas I cannot."

He stared at her, his handsome features still as stone.

After a long moment, he released her and stepped away. "If that's the way you wish to play the game, so be it. Mount your horse."

His voice was cold and hard. Much as it had been the day he'd first confronted her in the bothy. It took all of her courage to ask him, "Will we be parting ways?"

He pinned her gaze. "Nay."

Then he spun on his heel and marched to his horse.

Ana resigned herself to a very unpleasant journey. It was better that he hate her now, she reasoned. That way, she would never have to see his tearstained face across a village square. Not that she could imagine Niall weeping over anything.

She tried to put the toe of her boot in the stirrup, but the girth of the huge black plow horse made it impossible to reach. That failure, added to the pulsing pain in her toes, drew a very unladylike word from her lips.

"Shite."

Niall appeared at her side. He swept her charred skirts aside and peered at her curled boots. "What's wrong with your feet?"

"Nothing."

"I don't believe you. Take your boots off," he demanded.

"Nay."

A muscle in his jaw worked. "Take your damned boots off, or I'll cut them off with my dirk."

"I'm cold and wet," she protested with genuine misery. "I need my boots."

He glared at her. "Then it would be wise to ensure they remain in one piece. Take them off."

Ana limped over to a boulder and, leaning on it, untied her boots. Her toes throbbed as she loosened the ties, and it was with great care that she eased the first boot off.

"Bloody hell, Ana."

Her toes were bright red, swollen with blisters, and in some places peeling. Even the wind dancing lightly across them shot shards of pain up her legs, and she sucked in a sharp breath.

"I should have skewered the bastard," Niall said grimly. "Can you not heal them?"

"If I do, we'll arrive in Kildrummy too late to meet the others," she said.

He shrugged. "Then we'll join them later."

He said it as if it didn't matter, but Ana could see the shadows flicker in his eyes as he spoke. "Are you certain?"

"Aye. I'm certain." Then he set about making a camp for them, tenting his brat over several boulders and holding it in place with a few rocks. Hardly a sturdy shelter, but with the horses blocking the rain, some burlap on the ground, and Ana's thin woolen blanket around their shoulders, it was surprisingly cozy.

Ana removed her other boot and rubbed her hands together.

As the crimson vines swirled down her arms, she held her fingers over her toes and swallowed hard. Touching the burned flesh with her hot hands would hurt. A lot. She knew that because she'd healed burns on other people.

Niall pulled Ana back against his chest and hugged her tight.

"You can do it," he murmured into her hair. "I know you can. You're the bravest lass I know."

She shook her head. "I'm not brave."

"So speaks the woman who defied all odds and survived a chase through the woods when she was near starved to death."

"I had no choice."

"Oh, but you did," he said softly. "You could have given up a number of times along the way. But you never did. You kept moving. You kept running, even though it pained you. You showed me what real strength is that night, Ana."

Ana blinked back tears.

She didn't recall the night the same way at all, but the honesty of his words touched her deeply. Was she brave? Perhaps not. But strong enough to place her healing hands on her toes? She took a deep breath. Hopefully, yes.

She laid her hands on her feet.

And screamed.

Niall's arms tightened around her, and he murmured soft Gaelic endearments in her ear until the pain faded and her screams stopped. The fluid-filled blisters sank back into the skin, the angry red flesh became pink again, and the peeling skin became whole again.

Niall ran a finger over the tips of her toes.

"You are a miracle," he said.

Coming from his lips, it felt like a compliment. "Few people see it that way."

"Few people can accept what they cannot understand."

Ana relaxed against the hard planes of his chest and belly, relishing what would surely be a temporary truce. "But you do."

"I've borne witness to other inexplicable events," he said.

"Truly?" she asked curiously. "What sorts of events?"

He was silent for a long moment, and then he asked, "Are you familiar with the druids?"

She laughed. "You mean the priests of the ancient gods? Aye, I've heard the tales of magic and miracles."

"We had a druid living among us for many a year," he said. "He died three winters ago."

Ana grew still. Was he jesting? It didn't sound as if he was.

"He wore white robes, had a white beard that flowed to his knees, and carried a crooked willow staff."

Ana pulled away and stared at him, frowning. "But the druids are long gone. None have been sighted in a hundred years or more."

He returned her stare, calm and even. "You could say the same of the Picts, yet you have accepted that my kin are descended from them."

"Are you saying this druid was capable of miracles?"

Niall shrugged. "All I can speak to is that which I've seen with my own eyes. He cast a circle of fire around a small party beset by hungry wolves, and called forth a blinding mist during a battle."

Ana bit her lip. If such powerful beings had truly

existed, surely they would have resisted the press of Christianity? Stood like a heathen wall against the preachings of Saint Columba? It made no sense that they would disappear if they were as capable as Niall suggested. Could he not see that?

Niall smiled. "You think me a madman. I can see it on your face."

"Not a madman," she protested.

"A simpleton, then. But I assure you, I was not the only witness to the man's marvels. All of the Black Warriors were witnesses at one time or another."

Ana was tempted to give voice to her doubts, but his calm acceptance of her own strange gift curbed her tongue. Instead, she simply smiled and steered the conversation in another direction. "Another mention of the mysterious Black Warriors. Tell me, why does the group of men tasked with protecting your clan require such an ominous name?"

Niall noted the slight stiffening in Ana's body as she spoke. Telling her the truth about the Black Warriors— the whole truth—was a serious risk, but her insistence on parting ways worried him. She had lied when she told him she did not return his affections—he'd seen it in her cheeks. Why would she push him away when they had shared so much and were clearly well suited? Unless she was convinced that her gift would bring him grief, as it had surely brought grief to those who loved her in the past?

He wrapped his arms around Ana's shoulders, easing her back against his chest. "They are named thus because in days of old each warrior carried a black targe. Once, before this land was known as Alba, they were the personal guard of a mighty Pictish king. Now they only guard the ruins of his palace."

The blanket flapped wetly, allowing a glimpse of the gray drizzle of daylight.

"Why guard a ruin?" Ana asked.

He debated how much he should tell her, then decided there should be no secrets between them. Not if he wanted to make their relationship truly that of husband and wife. "The king's most prized possessions still lie within."

She tilted her head to look at him. "A treasure?"

"A small one, by any standard. His crown, his sword, and a number of decorative pieces, many engraved with the same detailed symbols that are carved into standing stones throughout Aberdeenshire."

"Why hide them?" she asked. "Why not proudly display them as your heritage?"

"Because we are sworn to keep them—and the symbols on the cavern walls around them—secret. According to legend, they have the power to change the history of Scotland."

"Is the necklace you seek part of the treasure?"

He shook his head. "The Dunstoras treasure is all silver. The gold and ruby necklace is a gift from the king to his new bride, Yolande de Dreux. My brother is accused of murdering the royal courier to claim it for himself."

"Oh."

"He is innocent," Niall said firmly. "I know him well. He would never put the clan in jeopardy for such a spurious cause as theft."

"Is he a Black Warrior as well?"

"Nay. He is the laird of our clan. The Black Warriors owe their fealty to him."

Her eyebrow lifted. "Even you? You seem a rather proud sort, not given to bending knee to another man."

"Aye, even me."

Smiling, she eased away from his side and reached for their pack of food. "I suppose a man blessed with as many natural talents as you has little need for a title."

He snorted. "If you wanted the last piece of bread, you had but to ask. Stooping to flattery is beneath you."

She laughed at that, the last of her reservations falling away. As it slowly died, she favored him with a thoughtful stare. "Are the Black Warriors skilled trackers?"

"Aye."

"Is that how you found me so swiftly?"

"To some measure. I also chanced upon Leod in the forest."

Her face wrinkled with a frown. "Was that his name? Leod?"

Niall nodded.

"Is he the one who shot you?"

Another nod.

"Did you kill him?"

He could tell by the way she stumbled over the word *kill* that the notion troubled her. "Aye, but only because he left me no choice. I'm not a man given to wasting lives."

His answer seemed to satisfy her. She scooted back alongside him and wrapped herself around his arm. "I rather like the idea that you can find me. If ever I'm lost, will you promise to come for me?"

Niall stared out of the tent at the growing dusk. He never wanted to relive another moment like the one he'd endured last night—witnessing Ana tied to a stake, the fagots at her feet alight, her red hair floating eerily on wafts of smoky air. But her gift came with a hefty price. She would always be in danger, always be at risk of some madman who thought her miracle was the hand of Satan. If it would ease her burden even a wee bit, he'd happily stand between her and the madmen of the world and protect her . . . no matter what the cost.

"Aye, I promise to come for you," he said softly into her hair. "Always."

Chapter 19

They made love until the rain stopped. It was a joyous lovemaking, the kind that can only come after an escape from near death. Or so Ana thought. Certainly, she'd never before been given to such loud screams or wild thrashings as she found her release. And when all was said and done, and they lay entwined body and soul, the glow of satisfaction took a delightfully endless time to wear off.

Beneath her cheek, the thud of Niall's heart slowly returned to a steady rhythm. It seemed as good a time to confess her feelings as any.

"I love you," she said.

"I know."

"How could you know the lay of my heart if I had not confessed it?" She tipped her head up to look at him, suddenly suspicious. "Did some druid magic tell you?"

"Nay, the blushes in your cheeks did."

Ana grimaced. "Damnable cheeks."

He planted a kiss on one cheek and then the other. "I rather like them."

"That's because they don't betray your every feeling, as they do mine," she said crustily.

"We should pack up," Niall said, pressing one last hard kiss on her lips. "Now that the rain has stopped, the constable will make better time."

"Do you think he's drawing near?"

He smiled. "I am, above all, a cautious man."

Ana sat up and began to dress. "How far are we from Kildrummy?"

"Another half day." Niall shrugged into his lèine, then lifted a saddle onto the back of the deep-chested sorrel, giving Ana a thoroughly enjoyable view of his rippling muscles. The man was beautiful. No other word did him justice.

He cinched the saddle tight on the black horse, then offered Ana a leg up.

"Wait," she said, hastily rolling the burlap floor of their tent and stuffing it in a pack. Then she grabbed a chunk of cheese and stepped into Niall's cradled hands. He tossed her atop the big animal like she was made of down.

Niall gathered up the rest of their belongings, pinned his brat around his shoulders, and mounted. "I aim to push us hard, lass, in hopes of catching up to my men on the other side of the bridge."

"Fair enough. I'll warn you now, though, I'm not much of a horsewoman. This is already longer than I've ever ridden a beast in my life."

"Just do what you can," he said. "There's one in my

party for whom my loss will be sorely felt. I would avoid that heartache, if I can."

He urged his huge horse into a canter and took off down the glen. Ana coaxed her mount into a rollicking gait with a few clicks of her tongue, and then gripped the horse's thick black mane and held on tight. While the speed of traveling by horseback couldn't be matched, she much preferred to make her way by foot.

The hills grew steadily steeper and rockier as they traveled north. The country was a frozen landscape, mostly rocks and snow and ice-crusted streams. Riding astride with her skirts hiked up, Ana's legs soon grew chilled, and she took to rubbing them on occasion, trying to keep warm. Seeing the grim lines of Niall's face, she dared not complain or beg for a rest.

The sun slipped toward the horizon, leaving long purple shadows on the snow. The air grew colder, and Ana pulled her brat and her blanket tighter around her shoulders. As was often the case on a winter's night, the day, when it faded, went swiftly into the dark.

They had been riding for a time with only the moon to guide them, when Niall suddenly halted. He twisted in his saddle and reached for Ana's bridle.

"Hold," he whispered. "There's someone in the rocks up ahead."

Once Ana's horse was tucked in close, he righted himself in the saddle and drew his sword. "If we're attacked, don't look back, lass. Ride hard and ride fast."

Ana couldn't imagine leaving Niall to face the brigands alone, but she knew she wouldn't be much help in keeping them at bay, either. She nodded.

A small slide of shale tumbled down the rock face and pooled on the white snow. Ana peered into the shadows, but saw nothing. Niall was as still as death, waiting for their attackers to show themselves.

"MacCurran, that bloody well best be you," boomed a deep voice that echoed off the cliff walls.

Niall relaxed and released the reins of Ana's horse. "Aye, it's me, you old goat. Show yourself before you give the lady a fright."

A huge bear of a man skidded down the rock face, landing at the bottom with a solid stance. The bearded man held a huge great-sword in one hand and a long-eared winter hare in the other. "About bloody time. We'd near given up on you."

"You were supposed to move on without me," Niall said.

"Aye," retorted the bear as he trudged across the snow toward them, "but the lad wouldn't hear of it."

When he reached them, Niall tossed Ana a smile. "This is Ivarr, one of the finest sword arms in all of Scotland."

Ivarr saluted her with a wave of the dead hare. "He's a liar, but I love him anyway."

"Ivarr, this is Ana." Ana waved in return, a little in awe of the giant standing before her.

"We made camp over yonder hill," said Ivarr, pointing ahead. "Cormac will be pleased to see you. He feared your odds were grave."

Niall slid to the ground, and Ana noticed with some surprise that he and Ivarr were of similar height. It was the thickness of their arms and middles that set them apart. Ivarr's arms were not just large; they were small trees.

Happy to see the last of her saddle for a while, Ana hopped down into the snow.

They waded through the ankle-deep snow to the other side of the hill, where a campfire flickered in the darkness and several figures huddled around its warmth. The people by the fire stood as they drew closer, and Ana's eyes were drawn to the shortest of them—a lad with a solemn face and dark eyes.

Eyes that lit up when Niall shoved his hood back and held his hands to the fire.

"I understand you insisted on waiting for me," Niall said quietly to the boy.

"Aye."

"See to my horse, then."

The lad nodded happily and ran off.

One of the others around the fire, a lean man with long brown hair, and an ashwood bow slung over his shoulder, clapped Niall on the arm. "You're a sight for troubled eyes."

"Did you get the necklace?"

The man's face brightened. "Aye. How did you know?"

Niall grinned. "The baron was loudly bemoaning its loss as we departed. I sincerely hoped it was you who had given him cause for grief."

"Luck was with me," Cormac said. "I found the

rosewood box in Lady Elayne's antechamber. Everyone was admiring the new addition to the baron's family, so no one witnessed me abscond with it. Does this mean we can reclaim Dunstoras?"

"Unfortunately, we've no evidence to tie the necklace to the thief," said Niall with a slow shake of his head. "Leod confessed his sins before he died, but would not name the wretch who drove him to betray us."

Ana sidled up to the fire, trying to warm her toes. "Perhaps it was the poacher."

Both men stared at her. She shrugged. "The constable has lamented the presence of someone helping himself to the baron's game for the past fortnight. If you can hide out in the woods, why not Leod's accomplice?"

Niall nodded. "I happened upon the leavings of a fire last night. Poacher or thief, I could not say, but there *was* someone in the woods."

She met his gaze. "Could you track him?"

"Perhaps. But returning to Duthes would be unwise at the moment, and I've a pressing need to rest my weary bones for a day or two."

The man with the bow grinned. "We're for Dunstoras, then?"

"Aye," said Niall, smiling slowly. "We're going home."

Ana was given a much finer horse to ride when they packed up the next morning—a gray dappled gelding with a gentle mouth and an easy gait. It was Cormac's horse, which he gave up easily, citing a preference for large black plow horses.

As her arse was still chafed, Ana did not complain.

They rode across the stone bridge at Kildrummy and west through the rolling hills for a day and a half. As they entered a deep wood, which extended as far as the eye could see, the men around her sat up straighter and laughed more easily. Even young Jamie lost the melancholy look in his eyes and leaned forward in his saddle. The horses pranced to the top of a wide ridge, their trappings ajingle.

Ana had been lazily following in Ivarr's tracks, playing a game of name-the-plant, when Niall called halt, and the party took a reprieve under the leafless canopy of the winter trees. She was squinting at a large evergreen bush in the distance, wondering if it were holly, when he rode back along the trail and stopped beside her.

"Dunstoras lies several leagues ahead, but you can glimpse it between the trees from the top of this cliff."

Ana frowned. "I'm not very fond of heights."

He leaned over, caught her about the waist, and lifted her onto his lap. "I'll keep you safe," he said, turning his mount—a sturdy Friesian with a flowing black fringe. "This is a sight not to be missed."

The horse displayed far more trust in its rider than Ana—it trotted out to the edge of the cliff and stopped on command. Ana clutched Niall's arms and pressed herself back against his chest. Unable to look down, she jammed her eyes shut.

"Look out, not down," Niall advised gently. "And have some faith in me, lass. I'll not let you fall."

Ana took a deep breath. Her faith in Niall was solid as bedrock. If he said he'd hold her fast, then he'd hold her fast. She opened her eyes and sought the horizon. The sun was setting over a distant mountain, and rays of golden light spilled over the trees in the valley. In the thick of the trees, a tall stone tower rose into the sky, its stones so pale a gray that they looked white. Leafless ivy climbed the tower in a swirling pattern not unlike the markings on her arms when she healed. There was something ancient and magical about the tower—almost as if it had stood in this very same spot for a thousand years.

"It's beautiful," she said breathlessly.

"Aye," said Niall. "Beautiful and strong. Just like you."

Ana smiled and snuggled into his arms. If Niall called this place home, then she'd make it hers, as well. As soon as the sun warmed and the earth thawed, she'd borrow a spade. It was long past time she planted that garden.

Continue reading for a preview of the next book in Rowan Keats's Claimed by a Highlander series,

WHEN A LAIRD TAKES A LADY

Coming from Signet Eclipse in May 2014!

The Eastern Highlands
Above Lochurkie Castle
January 1286

A top a huge black-and-white warhorse, Isabail's view of the destruction was unimpeded. Six of her guards, including the valiant Sir Robert, lay lifeless on the moonlit trail. The others had been forced to their knees and tightly bound like cattle. A pair of chests, packed with her belongings, had been rifled and the contents scattered. The reivers had gathered only a few items, mostly simple gowns and practical shoes. The more expensive items—those intended for her sojourn in the king's court—lay in careless heaps, trampled in the snow and mud.

Isabail had no sympathy to spare her fine clothes, however. Fear for what would next befall her and her maid, Muirne, had cinched her chest so tight, there was no room for anything else.

The fur-cloaked Highland raiders who had attacked

her party were small in number but large in size—a mouth-souring blur of fierce faces, broad shoulders, and brawny limbs. One of them, apparently the leader, wore a thunderous scowl so dark that her belly quailed each time she spied him.

To her amazement, the attackers numbered only three. How they had succeeded in defeating the dozen guards that accompanied her carriage, she could not fathom. But defeated them, they had. The raiders worked swiftly, their movements spare and deliberate. No pack was left unopened, no chest left unturned. They finished their looting in no time and were soon mounted and ready to depart.

Except for the leader.

He scooped a colorful selection of clothing into a pile, removed a flint from the pouch at his belt, and crouched with his back to the wind. With experienced ease, he soon had the pile in flames. Isabail had to bite her lip to stem a wail. As she watched, a sizable portion of her fine wool gowns, white linen sarks, and beaded slippers went up in a fiery pyre.

Under any other circumstance, Isabail would have burst into tears. But Muirne's pale plump face was turned to her, her eyes a silent plea for hope and guidance. Isabail could not give in to the waves of despair pummeling her body. Not now. Not when Muirne needed her to be strong.

The leader eyed the plume of gray smoke drifting its way into the sky, then grabbed the reins of Isabail's horse and, in a single fluid bound, leapt up behind her.

A steel band of an arm encircled her waist and hauled her into his lap. A short shriek escaped her lips before she could tame it. Instinct urged her to fight for release, to wriggle free and run, but fear held her fast. The man was huge. He could kill her with a solitary blow from one of those massive fists.

Better that she wait for rescue.

Surely their intent was to ransom her? If she but braved his inappropriate touch for a short while, Cousin Archibald would pay the ransom, and she would be freed. There was no need to risk life or limb to flee.

Her captor urged the horse forward, leading his small group toward the narrow opening at the end of the ravine. Isabail glanced at the fallen bodies and bound figures of her men, and the words spilled from her lips before she could stop them.

"Surely, you don't intend to leave them like this."

"I do." His terse response rumbled through his chest, vibrating against her back.

"But there are wildcats and wolves in these hills."

He said nothing, just urged his horse into a trot and then farther up the mountain slope. Higher and higher they climbed, the horse picking its way around boulders and thick patches of heather. As they traversed a steep ledge, she got a clear view of the moonlit glen and the mist-shrouded stone castle that was her home.

The folk in the fortress were no doubt going about their usual evening chores, oblivious to the tragedy that had struck her party. How long would it be before the remaining guards were found? Helpless as they were, would they not starve to death or be torn apart by wild animals?

Isabail chewed her lip.

One of the bearded outlaws riding alongside her caught her eye. "You fret for naught," he said. "The smoke will draw notice from the castle. Unless the earl's soldiers are asleep at their posts, your guards will be home by morn."

Her captor released a derisive snort.

Isabail breathed a sigh of relief, but did not relax. She was struggling to retain her dignity. The upward climb made it extremely difficult to hold herself aloof from the warrior at her back. She did her best to maintain a stiff ladylike poise, but every time the massive warhorse surged up a steep incline, she collided with her captor's very solid chest.

It was bad enough that their hips were so intimately connected. She refused to give up any more of her self-respect than was necessary. But as the air thinned and grew colder, the steady warmth he exuded held more and more appeal. Even with her lynx cloak wrapped tightly about her shoulders, the hours in the saddle and the frigid air began to take their toll. She slipped farther and farther back in the saddle. Several times, she stiffened abruptly when she realized her body had slumped wearily toward the wall of male flesh behind her.

Fortunately, her captor did not seem to notice her lapses. His attention was focused on carving a trail through the bleak wilderness that was the Highlands in January. Perhaps fearing pursuit, he kept their pace as hard and fast as the terrain would allow.

Isabail was just beginning to wonder how far he intended to take her from her home when he drew the massive destrier to a halt and barked out an order to his men. "Make camp here."

As he leapt down and icy air swirled around her in his absence, she took stock of his chosen campsite. She considered herself born of much hardier stock than her English cousins, but even to her seasoned Scot's eye, the spot looked anything but hospitable. Barren rock, blanketed by a thin layer of ice and snow. The only break to the north wind was a large boulder and, in the distance, a tall standing stone erected by the ancient Picts.

But the lack of obvious comfort did not dismay his men. They helped Isabail and Muirne dismount, then immediately set about making a fire. Once the peat bricks generated some heat, they tethered the horses and passed around meager portions of bread and cheese. The meal was too late to be supper and too early to be breakfast, but it tasted wonderful just the same.

Isabail and Muirne were left alone as the men went about their tasks. Muirne's thoughts had not eased on the long ride up the mountain. Her eyes were bright with unshed tears. "They mean to rape and kill us," she whispered.

"How can you know that?" asked Isabail. "They've not made any such threats."

"You only need to look at the dark look on that

one"—she pointed to the towering shape of the leader as he unsaddled the horses—"to know that we are doomed."

Isabail's stomach clenched. Muirne's assessment had merit. Everything about the man was terrifying, from the daunting width of his shoulders to the grim set of his chiseled jaw. And her maid was correct—the scowl on his face did not bode well. But to admit the bend of her thoughts to Muirne would not calm the maid's fears.

"The only reason for them to accost a noblewoman is to ransom her," she said quietly but firmly. "They will not harm us for fear of losing their reward."

"That may protect you, my lady, but it'll no protect me," muttered Muirne. "I'll no see my Fearghus again. I can feel it in my bones."

"You are seeing a badger where there is only a skunk," chided Isabail. "The possibility of rescue yet remains. We are still on Grant land."

Muirne frowned. "How can you be certain? We've journeyed several hours beyond sight of the castle."

Isabail nodded toward the standing stone in the distance. It was too dark to see the Pictish symbols engraved on its surface, but the shape was very familiar. "I recognize that stone. We are but a short distance from the bothy my brother used as a respite stop during lengthier hunts."

Her maid's face lit up. "Och! Then we are saved. We can escape there and await the earl's men."

"Nay," Isabail said sharply. "I will not risk the wrath

of these men by attempting an escape. Our best option is simply to wait. They will ransom us soon enough."

Her sharp tone drew the attention of one of the reivers. The heavyset fellow with the wiry dark beard stopped brushing the horses for a moment and stared at them. Neither woman dared to speak another word until he resumed his task.

"See?" hissed Isabail. "They watch us too closely. Escape is not possible."

Muirne nodded and sat silent for a time, chewing on her bread and cheese. Although morn was surely only an hour or two away, the reivers laid bedrolls near the fire and offered two of them to the women. Isabail claimed her spot with trepidation. She had never passed a night under the stars without a tent overhead. It hardly seemed possible that she would be able to rest here now. Especially with the fierce face of the leader staring at her across the campfire. The flickers of the firelight added harsh shadows to an already grim countenance and left her with the distinct impression that he resented her, though heaven only knew why. She'd seen him for the first time just two days ago in the orchard. At the time, unaware that he was a villain and a cad, she had silently admired his physical form. Few men of her acquaintance sported such a blatantly muscular body, and he possessed a rather handsome visage for a heathen brute—the sort of sharply masculine features a woman does not soon forget.

He stood suddenly, and Isabail's breath caught in her chest. By God, he was huge. Dark and powerful, a veritable thunderstorm of a man. He tossed back one side of his fur cloak, revealing a long, lethal sword strapped to his side. Beneath the cloak, he wore a leather jerkin atop a dark lèine and rough leather boots, which hugged his calves. His clothing was common enough, but there was something decidedly uncommon about the man.

Perhaps it was the intensity of his glacial blue stare—neither of the other two held her gaze for more than a glance. Or perhaps it was the way he held himself, shoulders loose but firm, like he was a direct descendant of Kenneth MacAlpin himself. Lord of all he surveyed.

He glared at her and drew his sword.

Muirne shrieked and Isabail's heart skipped a beat.

But the brute did not advance. With his gaze still locked on Isabail, he returned to his seat before the fire and began to clean his weapon.

It took long moments for Isabail's heart to resume its regular rhythm. Not one word had been exchanged, but she had felt the weight of his blame as surely as if he'd unleashed a furious diatribe. In his mind, it would seem, she was the cause of his troubles.

Perhaps Muirne was right. Perhaps he had no intention of ransoming her. If his intent was vengeance for some imagined slight, he would be far more interested in extracting his pound of flesh than in keeping her safe and whole. Perhaps escape was a wiser option after all.

Isabail dove beneath the blankets provided by his

men and lay on her side with her back to the fire. She could still feel the cold gaze of her captor, but she did her best to ignore it. The hunt camp was so very close. Yet how could they hope to reach it while under such intense scrutiny?

"The women are slowing us down," one of the men muttered. "At this pace, it'll take another full day to reach Dunstoras."

Isabail froze. *Dunstoras?*

"That assumes the earl's men don't catch us first," retorted another.

"You worry for naught," said their leader crisply. "The earl's men are a league behind us. They think we're headed south. We'll lose them when we turn west and descend into Strath Nethy."

Nausea rolled in Isabail's belly. Dunstoras was home to the MacCurrans—the clan whose chief had robbed the king and murdered her brother. The same chief who had escaped Lochurkie's dungeon and absconded to parts unknown. If the man seated across the fire was Aiden MacCurran, she was in far more dire straits than she thought. A murderous traitor to the Crown would hardly follow the unwritten rules of hostage taking.

She lay stiff and silent, unable to sleep.

MacCurran deserved to pay for his crimes. John had been a fine man and a good earl. Far more noble and worthy than her father had been. If only she could escape to the hunt bothy, she could ensure MacCurran was brought to justice. From the standing stone, she could find her way to the hut with ease—she and John had stopped there a dozen times over the years.

The challenge was getting away from MacCurran and his men. It might be possible for one of the women to sneak away, but two? Unlikely. Yet she could hardly leave Muirne behind. No, if an escape was to be made, it would be both of them or neither of them.

Available From
New York Times bestselling author

BERTRICE SMALL

The Silk Merchant's Daughter Novels

BIANCA

The shocking murder of Bianca's brutish husband proves more liberating. Unfortunately, Florentine society will never approve of the new man she's chosen: Prince Amir, grandson of Mehmet the Conqueror. How can two lovers from two cultures find happiness in a world determined to tear them apart?

FRANCESCA

Francesca's intended is a duke's heir—but she has no plans to marry him. Only when she flees the family does she find an unlikely lover. But the future holds many surprises for this runaway bride who is promised to another...

LUCIANNA

The Pietro d'Angelos cannot deny the attraction between their daughter, Lucianna, and Robert Minton, Earl of Lisle, so they scheme to send her to London. There, Lucianna pursues a love of which she never dreamed and rises in society...all the way to court of the new Tudor king.

Available wherever books are sold or at
penguin.com

facebook.com/LoveAlwaysBooks

S0437

AVAILABLE FROM
NEW YORK TIMES BESTSELLING AUTHOR

Tracy Anne Warren

HER HIGHNESS AND
THE HIGHLANDER
A Princess Brides Romance

While journeying home from Scotland, Princess Mercedes
of Alden's coach is set upon and her personal guard killed.
Barely escaping, she finds protection with the dispossessed
Laird Daniel MacKinnon, who is home after years
of warfare.

At first she only needs his sword, and he her open purse.
But Mercedes's life is still threatened, and as the dangers
increase, so does the desire she and Daniel feel for each
other, until the two of them must face the greatest danger
of all—falling in love.

"Tracy Anne Warren is brilliant."
—*New York Times* bestselling author
Cathy Maxwell

Available wherever books are sold or at
penguin.com

facebook.com/LoveAlwaysBooks

s0425

From *New York Times* bestselling author

JO BEVERLEY

The Secret Duke
A Novel Set in the Malloren World

When Arabella Barstowe is kidnapped, she believes her life and virtue are forfeit—until she's rescued by the notorious rogue Captain Rose. Bella never expects to see him again. But years later she learns the wicked truth behind her abduction, and she seeks out the only man who can help her take revenge.

What she doesn't know is that Captain Rose is just a disguise for the formidable Duke of Ithorne, who is intrigued to hear from the mysterious woman from his past. Their lives are soon entangled by danger and a growing forbidden passion.

Available wherever books are sold or at penguin.com

S0159

<u>Available from</u>

Allie Mackay

Must Love Kilts

Margo Menlove loves everything Scottish—especially the legendary warrior Magnus MacBride. But while exploring the Highlands, she picks up a magical stone on the shore and awakens to MacBride himself. And the reality may be much more dangerous—and passionate—than her dreams could ever be.

"Allie Mackay pens stories that sparkle."
—*New York Times* bestselling author Angela Knight

<u>ALSO AVAILABLE</u>
Highlander in Her Bed
Highlander in Her Dreams
Tall, Dark, and Kilted
Some Like It Kilted

Available wherever books are sold or at
penguin.com

S0320

31192020493688